AUS

Ruthless Seduction

Miranda Lee

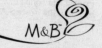

All the characters in this book have no existence outside the imagination
of the author, and have no relation whatsoever to anyone bearing the
same name or names. They are not even distantly inspired by any
individual known or unknown to the author, and all the incidents are
pure invention.

RUTHLESS SEDUCTION
© Harlequin Enterprises II B.V./S.à.r.l. 2010

The Ruthless Marriage Proposal and *Pleasured in the Billionaire's
Bed* have been previously published in the UK as separate, single
volumes as follows:

Pleasured in the Billionaire's Bed © Miranda Lee 2006
The Ruthless Marriage Proposal © Miranda Lee 2007

ISBN: 978 0 263 87474 7

024-0810

Harlequin Mills & Boon policy is to use papers that are
natural, renewable and recyclable products and made from
wood grown in sustainable forests. The logging and
manufacturing processes conform to the legal environmental
regulations of the country of origin.

Printed and bound in Spain
by Litografia Rosés S.A., Barcelona

Pleasured in the Billionaire's Bed

MIRANDA LEE

Miranda Lee is Australian, living near Sydney. Born and raised in the bush, she was boarding-school educated and briefly pursued a career in classical music, before moving to Sydney and embracing the world of computers. Happily married, with three daughters, she began writing when family commitments kept her at home. She likes to create stories that are believable, modern, fast-paced and sexy. Her interests include meaty sagas, doing word puzzles, gambling and going to the movies.

Miranda Lee's most recent novel, *A Night, a Secret...a Child*, was published by Mills & Boon in July in Modern™ romance.

CHAPTER ONE

LISA grimaced when the couple on the television screen started ripping each other's clothes off.

'As if people *really* act like that,' she muttered as she reached for the remote.

If there was one thing Lisa couldn't stand it was over-the-top love scenes in movies. As much as she appreciated she might not be a typical viewer, Lisa felt pretty sure sex was never the way it was portrayed in Hollywood.

She literally cringed when the man lifted the by now half-naked woman onto the kitchen counter and thrust into her. Or pretended to. The camera was on their faces. When the grunting and groaning started, Lisa pressed her finger firmly on the off button. She'd had enough of watching such ridiculous goings-on, thank you very much. Time to go upstairs and make sure Cory was asleep. It was after nine o'clock and tomorrow was a school day.

Lisa was halfway up the stairs when the phone rang.

Darn, she thought as she hurried on up the stairs and turned left, popping her head into Cory's bedroom on the way to her own bedroom.

Good, he was asleep.

Once in her bedroom, she closed the door behind her—so as not to risk waking her son—and picked up the cordless phone.

'Hello,' she said, fully expecting it to be her mother at this hour. All her girlfriends were married with children and were too busy each evening for gossipy chats.

'It's Gail, Lisa,' a woman's voice said down the line. 'Gail Robinson.'

Lisa decided she'd best sit down. When one of her employees rang her on her personal line on a week night, it usually meant there was some problem or other.

'Hi, Gail. What's up?'

'I've sprained my ankle,' Gail said dispiritedly. 'Slipped down that rotten steep driveway of ours. I've been sitting here with my foot in a bucket of iced water for ages but it's still up like a balloon. There's no way I can do Jack Cassidy's place tomorrow.'

Lisa frowned. Jack Cassidy was one of her newer clients. Sandra—her assistant-cum-bookkeeper—had signed him up whilst Lisa was away with Cory on a week's cruise of the South Pacific during the recent school holidays. A bachelor, Mr Cassidy owned a penthouse apartment in Terrigal which apparently had acres of tiled floors and took ages to clean. He also liked his sheets and towels changed and his weekly linen washed, dried and put away, not something her cleaners usually did. Their standard service lasted four hours and covered cleaning all floors, bathrooms and kitchens, not doing laundry or windows. Laundry could be very time-consuming and windows dangerous.

But he'd apparently talked Sandra into finding someone who would do the extra.

Gail took five hours to do everything, for which Clean-in-a-Day was paid one hundred and fifty dollars, with Gail's cut being one hundred and twenty. Their rates were very competitive.

'I'm really sorry to let you down at the last minute,' Gail said unhappily.

'That's all right. I'll get someone else.'

'On a Friday?'

Lisa knew why Gail sounded sceptical. Friday was the busiest day for housecleaning. Everyone wanted their homes to be clean for the weekend. Clean in a Day was fully booked on Fridays. Lisa had a couple of names she could ring if she was really desperate, but they were women who had not been through her rigorous training course and might not clean as thoroughly as she liked.

'Don't worry,' she said briskly. 'I'll do it myself. And Gail…'

'Yes?'

'Don't stress about the money. You'll still get paid.'

'Are you serious?'

'I'm well aware how tight things are for you at the moment.'

Gail's husband had been made redundant a few weeks earlier. She really needed her cleaning money.

'That's very good of you,' she choked out.

Lisa winced. Dear heaven, please don't let her start crying.

'Will you be up at the school tomorrow afternoon to pick up the kids?' she asked quickly.

'Yes.'

'I'll give you your money then.'

'Gosh, I don't know what to say.'

'Don't say a word. Especially not to the other girls. Can't have my sergeant-major reputation tarnished. They'll think I've become a soft touch and start taking advantage.'

Gail laughed. 'I can't see that happening. You have a very formidable air about you, you know.'

'So I'm told.'

'You always look so perfect as well. That's rather intimidating.'

'It's just the way I am,' she said defensively.

Lisa had heard such criticisms before. From girl-friends. From her mother. Even her husband. When he'd been alive...

Greg had complained incessantly about her compulsive need to have everything look right all the time. The house. The garden. Herself. The baby. Him.

'Why don't you lighten up a bit?' he'd thrown at her more than once. 'You're nothing like your mother. She's so easygoing. I thought daughters were supposed to be like their mothers!'

Lisa shuddered at the thought of being like her mother.

Despite Greg's nagging, she held on to the belief he hadn't *really* wanted her to be like her mother. He'd certainly liked inviting people back to their house, knowing she and it would always be neat and tidy.

'By the way, I don't have keys to Mr Cassidy's place,' Gail said, reefing Lisa's mind back to the problem at hand. 'He's always home on a Friday. I just press the button for the penthouse at the security entrance and he lets me in.'

Lisa's top lip curled. Pity. She hated having a client around when she cleaned.

'He's a writer of some sort,' Gail added. 'Works from home.'

'I see.'

'Don't worry. He won't bother you. He stays in his study most of the time. Only comes out to make coffee. Which reminds me. Don't attempt to clean his study. Or even to go in. He made that clear to me on my first day. His study is off limits.'

'That's fine by me. One less room to clean.'

'That's exactly what I thought.'

'Will I have a parking problem?' Lisa asked.

Terrigal was *the* place to live on the Central Coast. Only an hour and a half's drive north from Sydney, it had everything to attract tourists. The prettiest beach. Great shops and cafés. And a five-star hotel, right across from the water.

The only minus was demand for parking spaces.

'No worries,' Gail said. 'There are several guest bays at the back of the building. You have the address, don't you? It's on the main drag, halfway up the hill, just past the Crowne Plaza.'

'I'll find it. Well, I'd better get going, Gail. Have to have everything shipshape tonight if I'm to be out all day tomorrow.'

Which she would be. Terrigal Beach was a good fifteen-minute drive from where she lived at Tumbi Umbi. If she dropped Cory off at school at nine, she'd be cleaning by nine-thirty, finished by two-thirty, then back to pick up Cory at three.

'See you at the school around three. Bye.'

Lisa hung up and hurried back downstairs, making a mental list of jobs-to-do as she went. Load dishwasher. Hang out washing. Wipe over tiles. Iron Cory's uniform. Get both their lunches ready. Decide what to wear.

Loading the dishwasher wasn't exactly rocket science and Lisa found her thoughts drifting to tomorrow.

Penthouses in Terrigal were not cheap. So its owner was probably rich.

A writer, Gail had said. A successful writer, obviously.

No, not necessarily. Jack Cassidy could be a wealthy playboy who'd inherited his money and dabbled in writing as a hobby.

When Lisa started wondering if he was good-looking, she pulled herself up quite sharply. What did she care if he was good-looking or not?

She had no intention of dating, or ever getting married again. She had no reason to. And she had every reason not to.

For once you let a man into your life, sooner or later he would want sex.

The unfortunate truth was Lisa didn't like sex. Never had. Never would. No use pretending.

She found sex yucky. And no pleasure at all. Not quite repulsive, but close to.

She'd suspected this about herself from the moment her mother had told her the facts of life at the age of ten, a suspicion which had grown over her teenage years, then was confirmed, at the age of nineteen, when she'd finally given in and slept with Greg. Though only after they'd got engaged. And only because she'd known she'd lose him if she didn't.

He'd thought she would warm to lovemaking in time. But she never had. Sex during her marriage had been given grudgingly, and increasingly less often with the passing of time, especially after Cory was born. It was not surprising that she hadn't fallen pregnant again.

Lisa had been shattered by her husband's tragic death when she was twenty-five and poor Greg only twenty-eight. She had loved him in her own way. But she never wanted to go there again. Never wanted to feel guilty about something she had no control over.

Lisa knew she could never force herself to like physical intimacy. So the only sensible solution was to remain single and celibate, even if it meant she sometimes felt lonely.

Lately, she'd been feeling very lonely. Which was odd. She was busier than ever with the business. And her son was always on the go. Her leisure hours were filled with taking him to his various school and sporting activities.

It was at night, after Cory had gone to bed, that she felt the loneliest. She missed having someone there to talk to. Or to sit with whilst she watched television.

Her one solace was reading. She loved books, especially thrillers. Loved the way they could take her away from her day-to-day, rather humdrum existence into a world of excitement and suspense. Her current favourites were a series of action novels written by an Australian author, Nick Freeman.

Lisa had never read anything like them. They were simply unputdownable. During the last few months, she'd devoured all five of them.

Unfortunately, she'd finished the last one a few nights back, and passed it on to her mother, as she had the others in the series.

By comparison, the new book by another author that she'd brought home from the library yesterday seemed tame. And boring. Which meant she wasn't looking forward to going to bed tonight, as she had when she knew she was going to be swept away into Hal Hunter's rather wicked but fascinating world.

Whenever Lisa didn't have a good book to read at night, sleep would often elude her. She suspected that tonight would be one such night.

'Cleaning that penthouse tomorrow will do you good, Lisa, my girl,' she told herself as she closed the dishwasher door. 'Make you really tired.'

The thought occurred to her that she should ring Jack Cassidy and let him know of the change in his cleaning arrangements. It could prove awkward, explaining things on his doorstep in the morning.

Lisa turned on the dishwasher and trudged back upstairs, turning right this time and making her way down to the fourth bedroom, which she'd converted into a study soon after starting up her business. It was not a large room, but large enough to house her computer.

It only took her a few seconds to bring up Jack

Cassidy's file and to print out his address and phone number.

Lisa picked up her fax-phone, punched in the number, than sank back into her office chair as she waited for her client to answer.

Several rings went by before a deep, gruff voice snapped, 'Yep?'

'Mr Cassidy?' she said in her best business voice. 'Mr Jack Cassidy?'

'Yeah, that's me. And who might you be?'

'My name is Lisa, Mr Cassidy. Lisa Chapman. I'm from—'

'Stop right there, sweetheart. Look, I know you're probably only doing your job but I've had a gutful of telemarketers ringing me at all hours of the day and night. This is my private and personal number and I keep it for private and personal calls. If I want something, I go out and buy it. From a shop. I don't even buy over the internet. I also never answer stupid bloody surveys. Do I make myself clear?'

Clear as crystal, Lisa thought with a mixture of empathy and frustration. She too hated people trying to sell things to her over the phone and had recently started being less than polite when telemarketers called her in the evenings.

But he could have had the decency to wait till he found out if she *was* one of those.

Lisa opened her mouth to clarify her identity when she heard the unmistakable click of the call being terminated.

Her head jerked back to stare down at her handset. He'd hung up on her! The hide of him!

After slamming her own phone back down, Lisa sat there for a full minute with her hands clenched over the arm-rests of the chair and her teeth gritted together. Never in all her life had anyone hung up on her. Never ever!

Don't take it personally, her brain argued.

But it was difficult not to. Men were supposed to be polite to women, no matter what. And he'd been rude. *Very* rude.

What to do? No point in trying his number again. He'd probably hang up on her before she got two words out. And if he did that, she'd blow a gasket.

She glared at his printed-out file. It showed no email number. Clearly, he was a privacy freak. Or he just didn't like computers. Or the internet. Maybe he wrote in longhand.

He did have a fax number, she noted. She could send him a fax, explaining the situation. But something inside Lisa rebelled against giving Jack Cassidy that courtesy.

No, she would just show up on his doorstep in the morning and have great pleasure watching him cringe with embarrassment, once she explained who she was.

CHAPTER TWO

LISA'S stomach tightened as she drove across Terrigal Bridge and turned left at the small roundabout.

Maybe it hadn't been such a good idea not to fax Jack Cassidy last night. Embarrassing the man no longer held such appeal this morning. *She* was the one who was going to end up being embarrassed.

Lisa scooped in a deep, lung-filling breath as she drove up the hill, then let it out slowly, relaxing her stomach muscles and reassuring herself that there was nothing for *her* to be embarrassed about. Or to feel nervous about. She was being silly. This was just another cleaning job. One she'd never have to repeat, thank goodness.

Feeling marginally better, Lisa glanced around as she drove down the hill which led to Terrigal Beach. She hadn't been out this way for ages. When she took Cory to the beach these days, they usually went to Wamberal, or Shelly's Beach. Terrigal's cove-like shape meant it rarely had a big surf, which was great for tourists and families, but not relished by nine-year-old thrill-seekers.

But my, it was beautiful, especially when the sun

was shining. Although it was still only springtime, the beach had a fair share of people in the water, and even more stretched out on the golden sand.

Lisa could see why wealthy Sydneysiders bought beach-houses here. And penthouse apartments. Especially ones whose balconies faced north, with an unimpeded view of the sparkling blue sea and the long stretch of coastline.

Jack Cassidy's place would have all that, Lisa realised by the time she turned into the driveway of the pale blue, cement-rendered apartment block. Despite the building only being three storeys high, its position was second to none.

Lisa's nervous tension had returned with a vengeance by the time she walked round to the front entrance and pressed the button marked 'Penthouse' on the security panel.

'Come on up, Gail,' Jack Cassidy's deep male voice growled through the intercom.

Lisa opened her mouth to explain once again who she was when the intercom clicked off and the front door began to buzz.

Giving vent to a groan of sheer frustration, Lisa pushed her way in, the door automatically closing and locking behind her.

She just stood there for a long moment, trying to calm her thudding heart. What was it about this man which rattled her so? She was normally very cool when it came to dealing with difficult clients and situations. Cool and composed.

Time for some coolness and composure right now,

Lisa, she lectured herself as she practised some more deep breathing, taking in her surroundings at the same time.

The foyer was cool and spacious, with a marble-tiled floor and lots of windows. Despite the amount of glass, you couldn't hear the traffic or the sea from inside, which meant the windows had to be double-glazed. A no-expense-spared building, Lisa conceded as she bypassed the lift at the back of the foyer to take the stairs, walking briskly up the grey-carpeted steps to the top floor.

No large foyer up there. Possibly the architect hadn't wanted to waste valuable floor space, although the landing was large enough to have a hall stand and wall mirror set beside the one and only door, perhaps put there for people to check their appearance before knocking.

Before she could do little more than give her face a cursory glance, the door was wrenched open by a very tall, very tanned, very fit-looking man in dark blue jeans and a chest-hugging white T-shirt.

Jack Cassidy, Lisa presumed, her neck craning a little as she looked up into his face.

He wasn't handsome. Not the way Greg had been handsome. But he *was* attractive, despite the three-day growth on his chin and the hard, almost cold grey eyes which swept over her from head to toe.

'You're not Gail,' were his first words, delivered with his now familiar lack of charm.

Lisa bristled inside, but maintained what she hoped was a professional expression.

'You're absolutely correct,' came her crisp reply. 'I'm Lisa Chapman from Clean-in-a-Day. Gail sprained her ankle yesterday and won't be able to do your place today. I did try to explain this to you last night on the phone, but you hung up on me.'

He didn't look embarrassed at all. He just shrugged. 'Sorry. You should have said who you were up front.'

If apologies had been an Olympic event, his would not have even qualified for a semi-final.

'You didn't exactly give me much opportunity,' she said with a tight little smile. 'But not to worry. I'm here now and I'll be doing your place today.'

'You have to be kidding me.'

Lisa gritted her teeth. 'Not at all.'

His eyes flicked over her again, this time with a coolly sceptical expression. 'You're going to clean in that get-up?'

'I don't see why not,' came Lisa's tart reply.

She had never subscribed to the theory that a cleaner had to look like a chimney sweep. Today she was wearing white stretch Capri pants, white trainers and a chocolate-brown singlet top which showed off her nicely toned arms and honey-coloured skin. Her platinum-blonde hair was up in a white scrunchie, the way she always wore it when cleaning. Her jewellery was a simple gold chain around her neck, a narrow gold watch on her wrist and small gold hoops in her ears. Her make-up was subtle and so was her perfume. In her roomy straw hold-all—currently slung over her shoulder—was a navy, chef-size apron and two pairs of cleaning gloves, along with her calorie-friendly packed lunch and a bottle of chilled mineral water.

'I assure you I will leave here with your place

spotless and without a mark on my clothes,' she informed him, a tad haughtily.

'You know what, sweetheart? I believe you.'

Lisa gritted her teeth. She was within a hair's breadth of telling him she was not his sweetheart, but the owner of Clean-in-a-Day, when he stepped back and waved her inside.

The uninterrupted sight of the spectacular living area compelled Lisa to forget her irritation, her love of all things beautiful drawing her forward till she was standing in the middle of the spacious room, surrounded by the sort of place she dreamt about owning one day. She almost sighed over the huge tinted windows, the amazing view, the acres of cream marble tiles and the wonderfully clean lines of the furniture. Nothing fussy. Everything classy and expensive. Cool leathers, in cream and a muted gold colour. The coffee- and side-tables were made of a pale wood. The rugs blended in. Nothing bright or gaudy.

Ever since she'd been a child, Lisa had hated bright colours, both in décor and clothes. She could not bear the recent fashion of putting loud, clashing colours together, oranges with pinks, and electric blues with lime greens. She literally shuddered whenever she saw red anywhere near purple.

'I do realise that there are a lot of tiles to clean,' he said abruptly from just behind her. 'But Gail never had a problem.'

Lisa swung round to face him, grateful that he hadn't thought she'd been envying him his house.

'They won't be any problem to me, either,' she said swiftly. 'I've been cleaning houses for years.'

'You continue to amaze me. You look like you've never had a chipped fingernail in your life.'

'Looks can be deceiving, Mr Cassidy.'

'For pity's sake, call me Jack. Now, a few instructions before I get back to work. Do you know about the extras I like done?'

'You wish your sheets and towels to be changed, washed, dried and put away.'

His eyebrows lifted, then fell, his expression betraying a slight disappointment that he hadn't caught her out in some way.

'You'll find everything you need in the laundry,' he told her. 'My bedroom is the last door on the left down that hallway,' he said, pointing to his right. 'My study is the first door. Did Gail warn you I don't like to be disturbed when I work?'

'She did mention it. She said you were a writer of some sort.'

Lisa almost asked him what kind of books he wrote, but pulled herself up in time. She'd always instructed her cleaners during their training never to become too familiar with male clients, especially ones who were in the house whilst they cleaned.

The corner of his mouth lifted in a wry fashion. 'Yeah. A writer of some sort just about describes me at the moment.'

The sound of a telephone ringing somewhere in the penthouse brought a scowl to his face. 'Damn! I should have switched on the answering machine. Still, I doubt it's telemarketers at this hour in the morning. I'd better answer the darned thing,' he grumbled before turning and marching off down the hallway to his right. 'You might not see me later,' he called back over his shoulder. 'I'm on a deadly deadline. Your money's on the kitchen counter. If I don't surface, just leave when you're finished.'

When he disappeared into his study and shut the door after him Lisa was flooded by a weird wave of disappointment.

The realisation that she'd actually been enjoying their conversation shocked her. What was there to like about it? Or about him?

Absolutely nothing, she decided emphatically as she whirled and went in search of the laundry.

CHAPTER THREE

JACK plonked himself down in front of his computer before snatching up the nearby phone.

'Jack Cassidy,' he answered, leaning back into his large and very comfy office chair.

'Jack, it's Helene.'

'I had a feeling it might be you,' he said drily. Helene hadn't become a top literary agent by letting her clients fall down on the job. This was her fourth call this week.

'Have you finished the book yet?'

'I'm on the last chapter.'

'Your publisher in London has been on to me again. He said if you don't deliver that manuscript by the end of this week, he might not be able to get it on the shelves for the British and North American summers. And you know what that means. Lower sales.'

'It'll be there, Helene. Tonight.'

'Is that a promise?'

'Have I ever let you down before?'

'No. But that's because I hound you to death. Which brings me to the other reason for this call. The annual literary-awards dinner is tomorrow night. You're the hot favourite for the Golden Gun award again, so you will show up, won't you?'

'Wild horses won't keep me away, Helene.'

Although he wasn't overly fond of award nights, Jack was actually looking forward to going out tomorrow night. It had been weeks since he'd socialised in any way, shape or form. Weeks, too, since he'd slept with a woman, a fact brought home to him this morning when he'd answered the door and found a drop-dead gorgeous blonde standing there, instead of plump, homely Gail.

Despite her hoity-toity, touch-me-not manner, Lisa Chapman had certainly reminded him that there was more to life than work.

Too bad she was married. Jack's observant eyes had noted the rings on her left hand within seconds of her introducing herself.

'Jack! Are you there?'

'Yeah, yeah, I'm here, Helene. Just wool-gathering.'

'Thinking about that last chapter, I hope.'

'All the time.'

Jack hated last chapters. He had a tendency to want to end his stories with a happily-ever-after scene. But that would be so wrong for a Hal Hunter book, especially at this stage in the series. Jack needed to come up with something seriously anti-heroish for his hero to do this time to finish up on. Couldn't have his readers start thinking Hal was some kind of saint, just because he went around making sure the baddies got their comeuppances.

Jack knew that it was Hal's political incorrectness which appealed to his fans. They enjoyed Hal doing what they would never dare do themselves. They thrilled to his ruthlessness, plus his uncompromising sense of justice and vengeance.

'I'd better get back to work, Helene.'

'Fine. But one last thing about tomorrow night. Do try to bring a girl who's read a book this time, will you?'

Jack laughed. The blonde he'd taken to the awards dinner last year had been none too bright, something he hadn't realised when he'd first met her on Bondi Beach and asked her to come with him. He'd been distracted at the time by how well she'd filled out her bikini.

By the end of the evening, any desire he'd originally felt for her had well and truly disappeared. He'd taken her straight home, much to her obvious disappointment.

'Look, I'll probably come alone.'

'I find that hard to believe. Jack Cassidy, without a gorgeous blonde on his arm?'

'I don't just take out blondes,' he protested.

'Yes, you do. The same way Hal does.'

Jack's eyebrows rose. He hadn't realised.

Still, there was no gorgeous blonde in his life at the moment, except for the very beautiful girl who was currently cleaning his penthouse.

If only she wasn't married…

Some people tagged Jack as a womaniser. But he wasn't. Married women were off limits in his view, no matter how attractive they were.

On the other hand, Hal *was* a womaniser. The so-called hero in Jack's books wouldn't have cared less if Lisa Chapman was married. Not one iota.

This last thought flashed a light on in Jack's head.

'Get off the phone, Helene. I've just had a brilliant idea for my last chapter.'

'Can I take any credit?'

'None whatsoever. I'll see you tomorrow night.'

Jack hung up and set to work with renewed gusto, plunging into the final chapter, smiling wickedly to himself as Hal blotted his hero status with the beautiful blonde housemaid who'd come to change the linen in his hotel room. She was married, of course. But she forgot about that once Hal went into seduction mode. The girl knew that he was just using her. But the fiery passion in his kisses proved irresistible. She felt powerless to say no, powerless to stop him.

Hal made love to her several times, making her do things she'd never done before. But she thrilled to her own unexpected wantonness.

The last page saw her dressing afterwards, then bending over the bed to kiss the tattoo on Hal's bare shoulder.

He didn't stir. He seemed to be asleep. He didn't want her any more and she knew it. She sighed as she left the room. Only then did Hal roll over and reach for a cigarette. He lit up and dragged in deeply. His eyes were blank and cold.

'Done!' Jack muttered as he punched in 'THE END', then copied everything onto two flash discs, putting one in his top-drawer and the other into the lead-lined safe he'd had built into the bottom drawer. Jack believed in solid security. He would read the last chapter through again later this afternoon before emailing the manuscript to London, but he felt sure he'd got it right.

Of course, there would be a hue and cry from his editor. She'd complain that his hero was getting too dark. But he'd weather the storm and have his way. And his readers would love it.

Jack chuckled when he thought of Hollywood's reaction. But they'd just have to like it or lump it as well. Helene had done a fabulous job, not only selling options for all the Hal Hunter books—including those not written yet—to a top movie studio for an absolute fortune, but also in forcing them to sign a rock-solid contract. They had to bring his books to the screen as he'd written them. No changes in titles, plot-lines, settings or characters. Definitely no changes to endings.

Jack wondered who they'd cast for the blonde in this last scene. Not anyone obvious or voluptuous, he hoped. Someone slender and classy-looking. Someone like Mrs Hoity-Toity out there.

Damn, but she'd stirred his hormones. A lot.

For a split-second, Jack toyed with the temptation of making her an indecent proposition. But he quickly got over it.

He was not Hal. He did not seduce married women.

Neither did he right the dreadful wrongs in this world.

That only happened in fiction. In the real world, the baddies didn't get their comeuppances. They lived on with their millions and their mistresses. They destroyed countries and slaughtered innocent people, but rarely faced punishment.

Jack grimaced. Not that bandwagon again, he

lectured himself. There was nothing you could do back then. Nothing you could *ever* do. None of it was your fault.

Jack's brain knew that. But his heart didn't always feel the same, that unexpectedly sensitive heart which had been stripped bare by his experiences in the army.

Despite not having worn a soldier's uniform for six years, the memories of all Jack had witnessed still haunted him. He would never forget. Or forgive.

But at least now, with the success of his books, he'd rediscovered some pleasure in living.

Which brought him right back to one pleasure he'd been doing without lately.

'What you need is to get laid,' he muttered to himself as he rose from his chair and left his study.

Lisa was bending over, about to take the towels out of the front-loading washing machine, when she sensed someone standing behind her.

Even before she straightened and spun around, she knew it was Jack Cassidy.

He was standing in the laundry doorway, watching her with those steely grey eyes of his.

'Can I help you?' she snapped, annoyed with the way her heart had started pounding.

'I didn't mean to startle you,' he returned. 'You can put my study on your cleaning list as well now. I've finished my book.'

'You want me to clean your study on top of everything else?' she asked, her voice still sharp.

'I'll pay you extra.'

'It's not a matter of money, Mr Cassidy, but time. I have to be gone from here by two-thirty to pick up my son from school.'

'I see. You can't get anyone else to pick him up?'

'No. I can't.'

'Could you come back tomorrow perhaps? My study hasn't been cleaned for a few weeks, and frankly, it's a mess.'

'I'm sorry, I can't do it tomorrow, either.' Lisa was beginning to regret not telling him she was the owner of Clean-in-a-Day, not just a contract cleaner. But it was too late now. He'd think she was weird for not mentioning it sooner.

'Why not?' he persisted. 'Will your husband object, is that it?'

'What? No. No, I don't have a husband,' she confessed.

'But you're wearing a wedding ring,' he said, confusion in his face and voice.

'I'm a widow.'

CHAPTER FOUR

JACK hoped he didn't look as gobsmacked by this news as he felt. Or as excited.

A widow no less. Now, that was a different ball game entirely.

'But you're so young,' he remarked whilst his brain started making plans which his body definitely approved of.

'I'm thirty,' she retorted.

'You don't look it.'

'I've always looked young for my age.'

'What happened to your husband?'

'He died in an accident, five years ago.'

'A car accident?'

'No. He fell off the roof of our house.'

'Good lord. That must have been dreadful for you.'

'It was,' she replied stiffly.

'Do you have any other children?'

'No. Just the one,' she told him. 'Cory. He's nine.'

Nine! She must have married very young. Either that, or she'd fallen pregnant *before* the wedding.

No. Jack didn't think that would have happened.

Mrs Lisa Chapman wasn't the sort of girl who had un-planned pregnancies.

'Is your son the problem, then?' he asked. 'Can't you get someone to look after him tomorrow morning?'

'No, I can't.'

Mmm. No live-in boyfriend, then.

He was tempted to suggest she bring the boy with her, but decided that was going a bit fast. Jack was smart enough to realise that was not the way to go with this particular lady. She was what he and his mates in the army had used to call an ice princess. Back then, they'd all steered well clear of ice princesses, none of them having the money or the time it took to melt them.

If he wanted to know his cleaner better—and his body kept screaming at him that he did—Jack would have to be super-patient. And super-subtle.

'OK,' he said with a nonchalant shrug. 'Tell me what else you've got left to do. It can't be the kitchen. I've just been through there and it positively gleamed at me.'

His compliment surprised Lisa. As did his change in manner. Where had the grumpy guy gone who'd answered the phone last night? *And* who'd let her in this morning?

Finishing his book had certainly changed his person-ality.

But Lisa could understand that. When she finished a job, she often experienced a rush of warmth and well-being.

Cleaning the kitchen in this penthouse had brought considerable satisfaction. But then, what a magnificent kitchen it was! Lisa had never seen anything like it before. The bench tops were made of cream marble.

The cupboards, a light warm wood. The appliances, stainless steel.

It had been such a pleasure to clean. As had the rest of the penthouse. But she hadn't finished yet.

'I have to iron these towels and put them away,' she said. 'And I haven't washed any of the tiles yet.'

'Aah yes, the dreaded tiles. What say you leave them and tackle my study instead?'

Lisa stared down at the tiles around her. They really needed doing. She would not feel right leaving them undone. Neither did she want to come back tomorrow morning. There was something about Jack Cassidy which still perturbed her. She wasn't sure what.

'If I hurry, I should be able to do everything,' she said. 'It's only ten past one.'

Jack could not believe it when she set to work at a speed which made his head spin. This girl was a cleaner to beat all cleaners. Focused, and very fast. By ten to two, all the tiled floors were shining and she bustled off in the direction of his study, vacuum cleaner and feather duster in hand.

There hadn't been a single opportunity to chat her up in any way. It was work, work and more work. His chances of asking her to come to the dinner with him tomorrow night were fast running out. On top of that, Jack wasn't sure she'd say yes, anyway. Not once today had she looked at him with any interest, which was highly unusual. Most women found him attractive.

Maybe she had a boyfriend. Or maybe he just wasn't her type.

This last thought rankled. But there wasn't much he could do about it. If she didn't fancy him, she didn't fancy him.

Shaking his head, Jack brewed himself some coffee and was about to take it out onto the terrace when she materialised in the kitchen doorway, a strange look on her face.

'Yes?' he said.

'Are you Nick Freeman?'

'That's the name I write under. Yes.'

'Oh, my!'

Jack wasn't sure if that was a sign she was a fan. Or not.

Either way, he'd finally snared her interest.

'You've read some of my books?' he asked.

'All of them.'

'And what did you think?'

'I loved them.'

Even better. Clearly, Nick Freeman was her type. Or maybe it was wicked old Hal which brought that excited sparkle into her lovely blue eyes.

'Now, that's music to a writer's ears. Come and have coffee with me and tell me more.'

'But I haven't finished your study yet. In fact, I've hardly started. When I saw your books on the shelves, I...I—'

'Forget the study,' he interrupted, pleased as punch with this development. 'I'd much rather have my ego stroked. How do you like your coffee?'

'What? Oh—er—black, with no sugar.'

'A true coffee-lover. Like me,' he added with a smile.

'Now, don't give me any more objections, Lisa. I'm the boss here.'

She didn't like taking orders, he could see. Or not finishing her job. But he insisted and she grudgingly complied, sitting opposite him at the table on the terrace, primly sipping her cup of coffee whilst he attempted to draw her out some more.

Jack was careful not to stray from the subject of books. He'd noted that the moment he'd smiled at her, a frosty wariness had crept into her face.

She was widely read, he soon realised. And very intelligent. Clearly, she was wasted as a cleaner.

When she started glancing at her wrist-watch, however, Jack decided he could not wait much longer before making his move. If he let her leave, she might never come back. Next Friday, it would be homely Gail showing up to clean his penthouse and that would be that.

'I have to go to the annual literary-awards dinner tomorrow night in Sydney,' he said. 'One of my books is a finalist in the Golden Gun award for best thriller of the year.'

She put down her cup. 'Which one?'

'The Kiss Of Death.'

'Oh, you'll win. That was a great book.'

'Thank you. You're very kind. Actually, I was wondering if you'd like to come with me.'

Jack had had various reactions from women to his asking them out. But not once had a female stared at him the way Lisa Chapman was currently staring at him. As if he'd asked her to climb Mount Everest. In her bare feet.

'You mean…as your date?' she choked out.

'Yes, of course.'

She blinked, then shook her head.

'I'm sorry. I don't date.'

Jack could not have been more stunned. Didn't *date*? What kind of crazy lifestyle was that for a beautiful young woman whose husband had been dead for five years?

'What do you mean, you don't date?' Jack shot back at her.

Her eyes flashed resentment at him for questioning her. 'I mean, I don't date,' she repeated firmly.

'Why on earth not?'

She stood up abruptly, her shoulders straightening, her expression turning haughty. 'I think that's my private business, don't you?'

Jack stood up also, his face just as uncompromising. 'You can't blame me for being curious. And for being disappointed. I was enjoying your company just now. I thought you were enjoying mine.'

She looked a little flummoxed by this last statement. 'Well, yes, I was,' she said, almost as though the concept surprised her.

'Then come to the dinner with me.'

She hesitated, but then shook her head again, quite vigorously. 'I'm sorry. I…I can't.'

Can't, she'd said. Not *won't*.

Can't suggested there was some other reason why she was saying no. Other than her ridiculous claim that she didn't date.

The penny suddenly dropped. Maybe she had no

one to mind her son. And not enough money to pay for a sitter. Cleaners who only worked during school hours couldn't earn all that much. Maybe she didn't have any suitable clothes, either. Despite her very smart appearance today, Jack knew evening wear cost a lot.

'I'll pay for a sitter,' he offered. 'And buy you a suitable dress, if you don't have one.'

Her mouth dropped open again, her eyes glittering this time with more anger than shock. 'I have more than enough money to do both,' she snapped. 'For your information, Mr Cassidy, I am not an employee of Clean-in-a-Day. I own the company!'

For the second time that day, Jack was totally gobsmacked. Then pretty angry himself. 'Well, why didn't you say so? Why pretend you were a lowly cleaner?'

'*Lowly*? What's lowly about being a cleaner? It's honest work, with honest pay.'

'Yes, you're right. I shouldn't have said that.'

'No, you shouldn't. And you shouldn't have tried to buy me just now. Maybe that's what men do in your world, but they don't in mine.'

'I wasn't trying to buy you.'

'Yes, you were,' she said, crossing her arms and giving him a killer look. 'Don't try to weasel your way out of it.'

Jack could feel his level of frustration rising as it hadn't risen in years. 'Why don't you get off your high horse for a moment and stop overreacting! I wasn't trying to buy you. I was trying to overcome any obstacles which I thought might be in your path. Because I can't believe that a beautiful young woman like yourself would *choose* not to date. I presumed it had to be because of some other reason.'

'Then you'd be wrong. I *did* choose not to date after my husband died.'

'But that doesn't make sense, Lisa. Most young widows marry again. How do you expect to meet anyone if you lock yourself in your house and never go out?'

'I don't lock myself in my house. And I have no intention of *ever* getting married again.'

Jack noted the emphasis on the *ever*, plus the emotional timbre of her voice. Clearly, this was a subject which touched a nerve.

An old friend of Jack's—an army widow—had once told him that there were two reasons women decided not to marry again. They either had been so happy and so in love with their husbands they believed no other man would ever compare. Or they had been so miserable, they didn't want to risk putting their lives into the hands of a rotter a second time.

Jack didn't know enough about Lisa yet to decide which was her reason.

'Fair enough,' he said. 'I don't want to get married, either, even *once*. But don't you get bored? And lonely?'

A frustrated-sounding sigh escaped her lips as she uncrossed her arms. 'Boredom and loneliness are not the worst things in this world.'

'They come pretty high on my list.' Jack had a very low boredom threshold. He liked to keep active when he wasn't writing. During the winter he skied and went snow-boarding. In the summer he surfed and water-

skied. When he was forced indoors by the weather, he
worked out. Obsessively.

'Give me one good reason why you don't date and
we'll leave it at that.'

She pursed her lips at him, her chin lifting. 'One
good reason,' she repeated tartly. 'No trouble. When a
single mother goes out with a man these days, he
expects more than a goodnight kiss at the door. He
wants to come inside and stay the night. No way would
I have my son wake up in the morning to some strange
man at the breakfast table. If I'm a little lonely sometimes, then that's the price I have to pay for giving my
boy the example of good moral standards.'

Jack was impressed, but not entirely convinced. He
feared she protested too much. There was something
else here, something she wasn't admitting to. But he
could see she wasn't about to confide in him at this
early stage. If he could somehow persuade her to come
out with him tomorrow night, he might eventually
uncover some of the mystery behind this intriguing ice
princess.

'I promise I won't expect more than a goodnight kiss
at the door,' he said.

Now she looked seriously rattled. And tempted. Oh,
yes, she was tempted. He could see it in her eyes.

'I'm sorry,' she said again after a more lengthy hes-
itation. 'My answer's still no. Now I really must go. I'm
running late.'

Jack didn't try to stop her from leaving. He even
reminded her about the money on the counter, which
she almost forgot. But he took comfort from her

obvious fluster. She'd definitely wanted to say yes to him. Or, if he was strictly honest with himself, she'd wanted to say yes to Nick Freeman.

It didn't really matter. They were one and the same, as she would find out, when she went to the dinner with him tomorrow night.

Jack had her phone number somewhere. At least, he had the phone number for Clean-in-a-Day. He would ring later this evening, after her boy had gone to bed. By then, Jack would have all his arguments ready to get her to change her mind.

And he would *not* take no for an answer!

CHAPTER FIVE

'MUM!' Cory exclaimed from the passenger seat. 'Where are you going?'

'What?'

'You drove straight past our street.'

Lisa sighed. It didn't surprise her. Since she'd left Jack Cassidy's place, it had been a struggle to keep her mind on what she was doing. She'd only just remembered to give Gail her money at the school.

Thank heavens Gail hadn't had time to chat. No way did Lisa want to talk about her day. She still hadn't come to terms with Jack Cassidy turning out to be Nick Freeman. *Or* with his asking her out to that awards dinner tomorrow night. *Or* her actually being tempted to say yes.

As Lisa negotiated the roundabout which would bring her back the way she'd come, she reiterated to herself that she'd done the right thing, saying no to his invitation.

She wasn't a complete fool. She could read between the lines. Jack Cassidy—alias Nick Freeman—was a ladies' man. Just like his character, Hal Hunter. Jack's

penthouse had 'playboy pad' written all over it, from
the indoor pool and spa to the private gym, the home
theatre and the simply huge master bedroom, which had
every seductive mod con built in. A huge plasma screen
dominated the wall opposite the bed. There were
dimmer switches on the lights. And a corner spa in the
en suite bathroom definitely built for two. Or even
three.

Aside from that, she'd noted his off-the-cuff remark
that he didn't want to ever get married, even once. Yet
he had to be in his mid-to-late thirties, past the age most
men thought about settling down and having a family.

Clearly, his lifestyle of choice was that of swinging
bachelor.

Mr Playboy would definitely not settle for a platonic
peck at the door. He'd just been saying that to get her
to go out with him. No doubt he thought she was an
easy target, once he'd found out she was a widow.

Jack wasn't the first man to ask her out. But he was
the first she'd been tempted to say yes to.

Why *was* that? Lisa asked herself as she drove
slowly down her street.

His being her favourite author had to be the main
factor. But she suspected it was also because a glamorous night out in Sydney was an exciting prospect for a
suburban single mother who hadn't been anywhere
glamorous in years. Up here on the coast, everything
was very casual. You never got seriously dressed up for
anything. Not even at Christmas.

Lisa loved getting dressed up. Or she had, when
Greg had been alive.

Her wanting to say yes to Jack Cassidy's invitation had nothing to do with her finding him physically attractive, she told herself firmly. She liked slim, elegant-looking men with nice manners and soft blue eyes, not big, macho devils with faces carved out of granite and the coldest grey eyes she'd ever seen.

Lisa supposed Jack's surprise at her declaration that she didn't date was understandable. But she thought she'd handled the situation quite well. Of course, she hadn't been able to tell him the *real* reason she didn't date. That would have been embarrassing in the extreme.

Still, the reason she'd given was also true. She hated the way some single mothers went from man to man, most of whom didn't give a damn about their children. Yet they let these men into their children's lives; let the poor little mites get attached.

How many single mothers and divorcees actually found a decent fellow to marry? Not many. Once the man got bored with the sex, he moved on. She'd seen it happen amongst her women friends too many times to count, leaving behind broken hearts and sad, mixed-up children.

'Yes, I definitely did the right thing,' she muttered under her breath.

Her house came into view, a two-storeyed blond brick building which Lisa was very proud of, but which she'd struggled to keep after Greg died. His insurance payout had not covered the mortgage. But she'd been determined not to lose her home. And she hadn't, working very hard to make herself and her son financially secure. Even if she'd *wanted* to date, she hadn't had the time back then.

Lisa turned into her driveway, Cory jumping out of the car before she'd switched off the engine, bolting along the front path and dropping his school bag on the porch.

'Can I go and play up at Finn's place?' he called out as she climbed out of the car.

'Not until you've changed out of your uniform,' she told him sternly once she joined him on the porch. 'And done your homework.'

'But it's the weekend,' he protested. 'I can do my homework tomorrow.'

'No, you can't. You're going to your grandma's tomorrow while I go shopping. We both know there won't be any homework done there, don't we?' she added drily as she pulled the house keys from her bag.

'I'm glad I'm going to Grandma's,' Cory said, a belligerent look on his face. 'She lets me have fun. Not like you.'

'Don't you dare speak to me in that tone, young man,' Lisa snapped, jamming the key into the deadlock and thinking how thankless a job being a mother was. 'Now, get yourself inside and do as you're told.'

Five hours later, she was still brooding over Cory's cheekiness. And simmering with jealousy over his affection for his grandmother.

He didn't seem to care that his grandmother was the messiest woman on the planet. Always had been. Not only was Jill Chapman allergic to cleaning, but she couldn't cook to save her soul either. Lisa had grown up eating baked beans on toast for dinner most nights. Her mother's only talent was as a potter, and even then she didn't make much money at her craft.

'Mum,' Cory said in a wheedling tone, 'can I stay up and watch a movie with you tonight?'

Lisa glanced up from where she was stacking the dishwasher. Cory was a few feet away in the family room, watching TV.

'I don't think so, Cory. You've had a long week at school and I don't want you all tired and grumpy tomorrow. Off to bed now. It's eight-thirty.'

'Oh, Mum, *please.*'

'Not this time,' she said firmly.

'You never let me do anything,' he grumbled.

'You can stay up extra late tomorrow night. We'll go to the video shop after I finish my shopping and get you whatever movie you like. Provided it's not too violent.'

His blue eyes lit up. 'You promise?'

'I promise.'

'Cool!'

Lisa smiled at her son's obvious delight. And his obeying her orders to go to bed without any further fuss. When she went upstairs five minutes later, his handsome little face was still beaming with happiness.

'Goodnight and God bless,' she murmured as she ruffled his soft blond hair, then bent to kiss him. 'Love you.'

'Love you, too, Mum,' he said, making her heart squeeze tight.

Lisa supposed there were some rewards in being a mother. But it was hard, not having a partner to help with the parenting.

Not that Greg had been a firm father. He'd been way too soft with Cory. Way too soft with her as well. He'd let her run the show. And whilst Lisa liked being the boss of the household, there had been times when she'd wished Greg had taken the reins. In hindsight, he'd been a nice, but weak man. He should not have put up with her denying him sex...

When those old feelings of guilt threatened, Lisa pulled herself up sharply. The past was the past. No point in becoming maudlin over it.

As she always did when she started worrying about things, Lisa worked, mopping the kitchen floor and hanging out the washing which she'd put in the machine earlier. After that she went upstairs to the third bedroom, where she kept her iron and ironing board.

A lot of women hated ironing. But Lisa found it quite therapeutic. She ironed everything, enjoying seeing the neat piles of freshly pressed things set out on the spare bed. She was tackling Cory's school shirts when the phone rang in her office, just across the hall. Knowing that the answering machine would pick up, she kept on ironing, keeping one ear open to see who it was. The office door was ajar and she could hear quite clearly. Her recorded voice came on first, asking the caller to leave a message after the beep.

When she heard Jack's deep male voice come on to the line, she almost dropped the iron.

'Jack Cassidy here, Lisa. Unfortunately, it seems I only have your business number. Hopefully, you're home and check your messages on a regular basis. If so, please call me back some time tonight. You have my number. If I don't hear from you by morning, I'll have to ring Gail and find out your home or mobile number.

I'm sure she'll have it. If you don't want me to do this—and I suspect you might not—then ring me. ASAP.'

After Jack had hung up, Lisa remained standing right where she was for several seconds, still gripping the iron mid-air. Her head had gone into a total whirl with his message, her heart racing like mad.

Eventually, she lowered the iron back onto its cradle, then sat down on the side of the bed whilst she assembled her scattered thoughts.

Somehow, she didn't think Jack wanted her to call him to organise another cleaner to do his study. If he had, he would have simply said so.

He was going to ask her out again. She was sure of it!

Lisa could not understand why. A man like him could have his pick of women. Why pursue her?

'Because you said no to him,' she muttered out loud.

Lisa could think of no other reason.

Under any other circumstances, she would have ignored his call. Lisa didn't like bully boys. But his threat to ring Gail in the morning was a worry. He was right. She wouldn't like that. Gail would jump to all the wrong conclusions and start gossiping about her and Jack.

She had no alternative but to ring the infernal man. But she intended to put him in his place. And tell him in no uncertain terms that she didn't appreciate being harassed, or threatened.

The thought of having a confrontation with him made her stomach churn. But it had to be done. And the sooner the better.

Steeling herself, Lisa stood up and marched across the hallway into her office. The piece of paper with Jack's number on it was still in the top drawer of her desk, Lisa's hand trembling slightly as she snatched up the phone.

He answered on the second ring, suggesting that he had been waiting for her call.

'I'm so glad you rang,' he said straight away in such a pleased voice that she felt some of her resentment drain away.

But her voice was still sharp.

'What is it that you want, Jack?'

You, Jack was tempted to reply. But didn't.

'I wanted to give you the chance to change your mind about tomorrow night,' came his diplomatic but still truthful reply.

He heard her sigh down the line. Unfortunately, it didn't sound like a sigh of pleasure. Or surrender. 'I won't change my mind, Jack.'

'Wait till you hear what I have to say.'

'Very well.'

'How long has it been since you've been taken out to dinner?'

Another exasperated sigh. 'I told you. I don't date.'

'How long, Lisa?'

'Over five years, I guess.'

'And how long since you've had a night out in Sydney?'

'About the same.'

Just as he had thought. She had to be one of the

loneliest girls in the world. And ripe and ready for some male attention.

'What if we don't call tomorrow night a date? Would that help? What if you think of it as a favour to a business client?'

'A favour?'

'A big favour. You've no idea what it's like going to these dos alone, Lisa. Which is what I'll have to do if you don't come with me.'

'Why would you have to go alone? There must be scads of women of your acquaintance who'd be only too happy to go with you.'

'Believe it or not, I'm not that social a guy. Or I haven't been, since buying this place a couple months back. I've had my nose to the grindstone for weeks, finishing that damned book. Hardly been outside the door, except for the occasional surf, or shop. Trust me when I say there's no one I could ask.'

'I find it hard to believe you don't have a little black book with loads of phone numbers in it.'

He did, actually. But he didn't want to ring any of them. All of the women in that book paled in comparison to the very lovely, very intriguing and very challenging Mrs Chapman.

'I think you're mixing me up with Hal,' Jack said. 'He's the one with the little black book.'

'Oh.'

'People do that a lot. Confuse me with Hal. Which is another reason why I want you to come with me tomorrow night. I get besieged by female fans at these awards dinners. He's a very popular guy, old Hal. Now, if I have a beautiful blonde on my arm, I just might survive the night in one piece. They'll take one look at you and know they don't have a hope in Hades of getting my personal attention.'

'I don't know, Jack…'

A rush of adrenalin charged through his blood. She was wavering.

'I promise I'll be a perfect gentleman all evening. You won't have to fight me off at the door.'

No answer.

'Think of the five-star food,' he went on seductively. 'And the five-star wine. Not to mention the five-star surroundings. This restaurant is top drawer, and right on the harbour, overlooking the bridge and the opera house.'

Her sigh this time sounded much closer to a sigh of surrender.

'You do know how to tempt a girl…'

'You'd be crazy not to come. I'll pick you up and deliver you home to your door. Minus the grope-fest.'

She actually laughed.

'It'll be a truly fun evening. How long is it, Lisa, since you've had fun?'

'Too long, my mother would say.'

'Your mother sounds like a wise woman. You should listen to her.'

'My mother wants me to get married again,' Lisa said drily.

'Mothers are like that.'

'Does your mother get on your back to get married, Jack?'

'My mother's dead,' came his rather curt reply.

'Oh. I'm sorry. I didn't think. I mean…you're not that old.'

'Both my parents were killed in a car accident when I was fifteen.'

'Oh, how tragic.'

'It was. The truck driver who killed them was unlicenced, driving an unsafe, unregistered vehicle. He got a miserable twelve months for murder.'

'Jack, that's appalling! You wonder what these judges are thinking of, giving light sentences like that.'

'Yeah, but it doesn't really hit home till it happens to you. Injustice is just a word till you experience it for yourself.'

'I suppose so,' Lisa murmured, thinking how dreadful to lose both one's parents like that. Her parents had been divorced, but it had been an amicable enough parting. Her perfectionist father hadn't been able to stand her mother's sloppy ways, and had bolted as soon as he found someone more to his liking.

He'd never come back.

Lisa might have resented his defection more if she'd been able to remember him. Or if she hadn't understood full well why he'd left. She'd left home, too, as soon as she could.

'I think we're getting too serious here,' Jack said. 'Back to tomorrow night. I presume you don't want to tell your mother you're going out with me.'

'If she found out I was going out anywhere with any man, she'd nag me to death. If she finds out I'm going to a fancy awards dinner with the famous Nick Freeman, I'd never hear the end of it.'

'She's a fan of Nick Freeman's?'

'Unfortunately. I introduced you to her a couple of months back.'

'Then don't tell her. It's not as though this dinner is going to be on TV, or anything like that. The only media coverage it'll get is in the *Australian Writers Monthly*. And who reads that, except the literati? I certainly don't.'

'You're very persuasive.'

'Is that a yes?'

'Yes. But…'

'No buts, Lisa. You're coming and that's that.'

'I was just going to say that I'll have to tell my mother I'm going somewhere with someone. She's the one who'll be minding Cory. I won't leave him with anyone else.'

'You're a woman. You'll think of something.'

'I don't have your imagination.'

Jack didn't think he had that great an imagination. Lots of things which happened in his books were things which had really happened. But he wasn't about to tell her that.

'Always stick as close to the truth as possible when you're being sneaky,' Jack suggested, thinking to himself that he had been doing just that. 'Why not say that a girlfriend of yours has been given two free tickets to the awards dinner and wants you to go with her? That way you can talk freely about your night out and not have to make anything up.'

'That's brilliant, Jack!'

'I *am* brilliant.'

'And so modest.'

'That, too.'

'But are you a man of your word?'

'Do you doubt it?'

'Hal's not always a man of his word.'

'I'm not Hal.'

'I'm not so sure. Your books are told in the first person.'

'That's just a tool to create immediate empathy with the reader. And a more intense emotional involvement with Hal's character.'

'You succeeded very well.'

'Thanks. Now, let's get off Hal for a moment. At the risk of offending you again, are you set, clothes-wise, for tomorrow night? It's black tie.'

'Do I have to wear a long evening dress?'

'Not necessarily. A cocktail or party dress will do fine.'

'I'll buy something tomorrow. I was going Christmas shopping, anyway.'

'Christmas shopping! But it's only October.'

'I don't like to leave present-shopping till the last minute,' came her prim reply. 'The pre-summer sales are on at Tuggerah tomorrow.'

'Where the hell is Tuggerah?'

'You don't know the coast too well, do you?'

'I know the Erina shopping centre. Why don't you go there? I could meet you and we could have coffee. Or lunch?'

'I don't think so, Jack. Don't forget, I'm only going with you tomorrow night as a favour. It is not a real date. It's a one-off. There won't be any encores. Or prequels. Take it or leave it, Jack.'

'I'll take it,' he said, and smiled to himself.

You can pretend to yourself all you like, sweetheart. But tomorrow night is not going to be any one-off. You like me. I can tell. Tomorrow night is just the beginning.

'I'll pick you up at six,' he added. 'That will give us plenty of time to get down to Sydney. Now, where do you live? Give me your address and some directions so that I don't get lost. And your mobile number, in case I need to contact you tomorrow and you're not home.'

'Why would you need to contact me?'

'The world's an unpredictable place, Lisa. I like to be prepared.'

'That's what Hal always says.'

'Does he? Well, I suppose I do have some things in common with my main man.'

Like his womanising ways, Lisa thought, suddenly concerned over her decision to go out with Jack.

What on earth had she been thinking when she let him change her mind?

She'd rung him up to put him in his place and ended up agreeing to be his pretend girlfriend for the night, letting him persuade her with the promise of adult company, great food and the fantasy of actually having some fun.

But what fun would it be if she was on tenterhooks all night, worried about fighting him off at the front door?

'You're not having second thoughts, are you?'

Lisa rolled her eyes. What was he, a mind-reader?

'Not at all,' she replied crisply. If he did try something when he brought her home, she'd be ready for him. He wouldn't get so much as a *toe* in her front door.

'How about your address and phone number, then? I have pen and paper at the ready.'

She gave him both, plus good directions. It was perfectly clear, however, that he hadn't been far afield from Terrigal, since he'd never heard of Tumbi Umbi Road.

'There's a Central Coast map in the local phone directory,' she said. 'Study it up.'

'I'll do that. And thanks, Lisa. I really appreciate your coming with me. You're a good sport.'

A good sport. Was that what playboys called foolish females these days?

'Bye for now,' he said breezily. 'See you tomorrow night.'

Tomorrow night...

Just the thought made her feel sick.

Oh, Lisa, Lisa, what have you done?

CHAPTER SIX

LISA's chest tightened as it always did when she pulled into the driveway of her mother's place. Not so much these days because the ramshackle farmhouse would be a mess. But because her mother always seemed to say something to get her hackles up.

Lisa could hear implied criticism in even the most innocent of her mother's comments. As soon as she pulled up on the weed-filled patch of lawn which masqueraded as a front garden, Cory was out of the car like a shot, running up onto the veranda and giving his emerging grandma a big hug before dashing off to play on the tyre which swung from a nearby tree.

'Thanks for looking after Cory for me, Mum,' Lisa called out through the driver's window, trying not to really look at her mother. But it was impossible. Her hair was as red as the red in the multicoloured kaftan she was wearing. 'Not sure what time I'll be back. Probably not till after lunch.'

Lisa had decided on the way here not to tell her mother about going out tonight till she returned from shopping. She'd say she'd run into this mythical girlfriend at Tuggerah and been asked out when another girlfriend couldn't go with her.

'What's the hurry?' Jill Chapman called back as she walked down the rickety front steps. 'Can't you come in for a cup of coffee?'

'I'll do that when I come back. I don't want to be late. You know what the parking's like when the sales are on.'

'You look very nice today,' her mother said, drawing closer to the driver's window. 'There again, you always look nice. I wouldn't have thought you needed any new clothes.'

Lisa struggled to find a smile. 'Actually, I'm looking for Christmas presents today. But I think it's always good to buy a few new things at the start of each season,' she said through clenched teeth. 'Otherwise, your wardrobe ends up getting very dated.'

'Like mine, you mean,' her mother said with a hearty laugh.

'I didn't say that.'

'You didn't have to. I know I look like an escapee from the sixties most of the time. But that's what I am.'

Who would have guessed? Lisa thought wearily.

'I have to go, Mum,' she said. 'Keep an eye on Cory, would you? Don't let him wander off.' Her mother lived on a small acreage in the Yarramalong Valley, where there was a lot of bush. And snakes.

'He'll be fine.'

Lisa sighed under her breath as she waved goodbye and drove off. That was what her mother always said. And what she thought. Everything and everyone was always fine. Except her daughter, of course. Her daughter was a fussy, frigid fool who had no idea how to relax, or really enjoy herself.

Maybe she was right, Lisa conceded unexpectedly for the first time in her life. Here she was, going out to a slap-up dinner in Sydney tonight with her favourite author and was she happy? No! She was already worrying herself sick over how to act and what might or might not happen when Jack brought her home.

At least her mother was always happy. She'd been happy even after her husband left her.

I should be happy, Lisa lectured herself as she drove towards Tuggerah. I have a lovely home. A wonderful son. A flourishing business. And a good, if irritating, mother.

I also shouldn't be worrying about tonight. I am an adult woman, in control over what happens to me and what does not. If Jack makes a pass, I can handle it. There's no reason why I can't relax and enjoy myself.

The trouble was she always had difficulty relaxing. She seemed condemned to feel slightly uptight about everything, as if nothing was ever quite right, or good enough, or clean enough.

Lisa pulled a face. She was sick of this. Sick of herself.

Thank goodness it wasn't far from her mother's house to the shopping centre, the sight of Tuggerah ahead soothing her anxiety somewhat. Clothes shopping was one thing she *did* truly enjoy. She had a good sense of fashion and knew what suited her. When she'd attended the company Christmas parties with Greg he'd always been very proud of her.

Hopefully, Jack would feel just as proud when he came to pick her up tonight.

* * *

'You don't mind, Mum?' Lisa said, glancing up from where she was sitting at her mother's messy kitchen table, sipping coffee. The clock on the wall showed ten to one. Finding that special dress had taken Lisa longer than she'd anticipated.

'Mind? Why should I mind? I love having Cory over.'

'Where is he, by the way?'

'Down at the creek, looking for tadpoles.'

'He's OK by himself down there?'

'He can swim, can't he? Of course he's all right. You fuss over him too much, Lisa. Boys needs some space. And some freedom.'

'Maybe. But it's a dangerous world out there, Mum.'

'The world is whatever you believe it to be. I believe it to be good. And I believe people to be good. Until it's proven otherwise.'

Lisa sighed. Her mother was naïve, in her opinion. And out of touch. At the same time, she could see that Cory grew whenever he spent time with her. Not physically. But in maturity and experience. Her mother did allow him to do things she never would.

'It's good that you're going out,' her mother went on. 'Even if it is just with a girlfriend. So you're off to Sydney, are you? To a posh dinner in a posh restaurant. That's great. But watch yourself.'

Lisa blinked. 'What do you mean?'

'Sydney on a Saturday night can be a wild place. Don't go walking around the streets by yourself.'

'We're going to a restaurant, Mum. It's a literary-awards dinner with speeches and things. We won't be walking around the streets.'

'What are you going to wear?'

Lisa had decided not to show her mother the dress she'd bought. She wasn't in the mood for being criticised.

'I have plenty of party dresses in my wardrobe.'

'You know, you might see our favourite author there.'

'And who would that be?' Lisa said, trying to keep a straight face.

'Nick Freeman, of course. His books always win awards. It says so on the inside flaps. You'll have to tell me what he looks like. There's never a picture on the back cover. And not much of a biography. I think he writes under an assumed name.'

'He might be a woman,' came Lisa's oddly mischievous comment.

'Oh, no,' her mother said with a rather knowing smile. 'The creator of Hal is no woman. My guess is he's ex-military. He knows much too much about weapons not to have personal experience.'

'Maybe he just does a lot of research,' Lisa said, whilst thinking to herself that her mother was probably right.

'No. It's all too real. I sure hope he's going to write some more Hal Hunter books. I'm addicted to them already. Yet strangely enough, I think I like the first one the best. *The Scales of Justice*. That's where you really get to know Hal. You understand why he is the way he is after the way his parents get killed.'

Lisa frowned, only then making the connection

between Jack's parents being tragically killed and the way Hal's parents were killed. Not in a car accident. In a terrorist bombing.

Was that why Jack had become a loner, like Hal? Why he didn't want to marry and have a family of his own?

The answers to those questions possibly lay in that first book.

'You know, Mum, I think I'd like to read that one again. You haven't lent it to any of your friends, have you?'

'Nope. It's in my bedroom, under the bed. I'll go get it for you.'

Her mother had just left when the back screen door was yanked open and Cory charged into the kitchen, holding an old coffee jar full of muddy water.

The nicely washed and ironed clothes which she'd put on him that morning were also muddy. So was his face. It always pained Lisa to see her good-looking boy looking like a ruffian. But she held her tongue for once.

'Hi there, Mum! Where's Grandma?'

'Right here, sweetie,' Lisa's mother replied as she bustled back into the kitchen, handing Lisa the book before going straight over to Cory. 'Show me what you've got. Heavens! You've done well. We'll put them in the pond later. Hopefully, some of them might turn into frogs. By the way, you're staying the night,' she continued before Lisa could tell Cory herself. 'Your mum's going out to some fancy dinner in Sydney tonight.'

'Wow! Cool.'

Lisa wasn't sure if he meant it was cool she was going to Sydney, or cool that he was staying the night.

'Don't let him stay up too late,' she said.

Grandmother and grandson exchanged a conspiratorial glance. They were as thick as thieves, those two.

'It's Saturday night,' her mother said. 'Cory doesn't have to go to school tomorrow. He can sleep in in the morning. You're not going to be here to pick him up till lunch-time, I'll bet. It'll be *you* having the late night.'

Lisa didn't plan on being *that* late. But she didn't want to argue the point, for fear of making a slip-up with her story.

'Oh, all right,' she agreed. 'But not *too* late,' Lisa added as she picked up Jack's book and got to her feet. 'Don't go taking advantage of your grandmother, young man. And don't eat too much ice cream. You know what it does to your stomach.' Cory was lactose intolerant.

Cory's blue eyes went blank, exactly like his father's had when she used to nag him over something.

'Go give your mother a hug,' his grandmother said, giving Cory a nudge in the ribs.

'Be a good boy,' Lisa whispered as she held him to her for a little longer than she usually did.

His weary-sounding sigh made her feel guilty.

'Love you,' she added.

'Love you too, Mum,' Cory returned. But there wasn't a great deal of warmth in his words.

Suddenly, Lisa wanted to cry. And to keep holding him. Close.

But she knew he would hate that.

'See you tomorrow,' she choked out, struggling to keep back the tears as she let him go and hurried towards the door.

Her mother followed her out whilst Cory dashed off towards the pond with his jar of tadpoles.

'You all right, love?' her mother said.

Lisa tossed Jack's book onto the passenger seat as she climbed in behind the wheel. 'Yes, of course. Why shouldn't I be?'

'You seem a little more uptight than usual.'

'I'm not uptight at all,' Lisa suddenly snapped before banging the door shut and glaring at her mother through the open window. 'Why do you always criticise me, Mum? I've been a good daughter, haven't I? And I'm a good mother to Cory. I support myself and always try to do the right thing. So get off my back, will you?'

Regret at her sharp words consumed Lisa when her mother reeled back on her heels, shock in her eyes.

'I…I didn't realise,' her mother said, obviously shaken by Lisa having a go at her. 'I only ever want the best for you, love. But I can see I might have been a bit critical on occasions. Sorry. I'll try to keep my big mouth shut in future.'

Lisa was torn between feeling vindicated at having stood up for herself, and guilty over hurting her mother's feelings.

'I'm sorry, too, Mum,' she said. 'I know I'm touchy. I…I haven't been sleeping very well lately.'

'Then it will do you good to get out,' her mother said, all smiles again. Nothing ever got Jill Chapman down for long. 'Who knows? You might meet a man.'

'Mum…'Lisa warned.

'What's wrong with a mother wanting her beautiful daughter to meet a man?'

'You know I don't want to get married again.'

'So? I don't, either. But that's never stopped me having a boyfriend.'

'Or two,' Lisa muttered under her breath as she started the engine. 'Bye, Mum,' she said as she let go of the handbrake and moved off. 'See you in the morning.'

'No need to rush,' her mother shouted after her. 'Sleep in, if you want to.'

Lisa found herself shaking her head as she drove off. In a weird way, she wished she'd told her mother the total truth about tonight. She would have liked to see the look on her face.

But the consequences were not worth that small moment of satisfaction. Her mother would have asked her all sorts of awkward questions, and jumped to all the wrong conclusions.

No, it was much better this way.

Once out onto the road, Lisa glanced across at the copy of *The Scales of Justice* lying on the passenger seat. She could not wait to get home and read it. Not the whole book, unfortunately. She wouldn't have time for that. Not if she was to be perfectly groomed when Jack picked her up at six.

But she could surely manage a few chapters whilst she was soaking in the bath.

Lisa was anxious to find out just how much Hal was like Jack. He'd said on the phone last night how he liked to be prepared. Well, Lisa was going to be prepared too.

For him.

CHAPTER SEVEN

As Jack drove up Tumbi Umbi Road, he started thinking it had been a long time since he'd looked forward to a date as much as he was looking forward to tonight.

Though tonight was not quite like any date he'd ever been on before. He had no expectation of ending up in bed with Lisa Chapman. In fact, he would put his money on that *not* happening.

His goal this evening was simply to get her to go out with him again. To make her see that she could have a social life without endangering her son's moral standards. That she didn't have to live like a nun, just because her husband had passed away and she didn't want to marry again.

Jack still had no idea whether Lisa had loved the man, or loathed him. But he aimed to find that out tonight as well.

A tricky mission, however, he appreciated. Because Lisa was not the sort of woman who confided easily. She kept her own counsel. Look how she hadn't told him she owned Clean-in-a-Day. That had been very secretive of her.

Still, a few glasses of wine might loosen her tongue.

There was always a lot of toasting at these award dinners. Surely she wouldn't say no to a glass or two of champagne.

The large roundabout came up that Lisa had told him about, then the street on the left she'd said to take. Shortly he'd be there, at her house.

A quick glance at his Rolex showed Jack it was one minute to six. Punctuality was one habit from the army which he'd never shaken. As was wearing his hair cut very short.

He did manage to go a few days without shaving occasionally. But that was as sloppy as he could manage. He'd been sporting quite a bit of stubble yesterday, however, something which he'd thought afterwards might not have found favour with the very particular Mrs Chapman.

But his chin was as smooth as silk tonight. So was his very expensive tuxedo, which he'd had made to measure a couple of years back.

Jack hoped his more sophisticated look would spark some sexual interest this evening. Most women liked men in dinner suits.

Unfortunately, Lisa was not most women. She was different. *Very* different.

Challenging, that was what she was.

Jack smiled as he turned down her street. There was nothing that excited him more than a challenge.

* * *

At five to six, Lisa had been close to panic. Nothing had gone as she'd planned this afternoon. Everything had taken simply ages!

Longest had been the applying of some false tan, necessary because the dress she'd bought was a one-shouldered style which showed a white strap mark. A tedious task in itself. But first, she'd had to bathe and shave her legs and exfoliate properly.

Absolutely no time for lying back and reading.

By the time all that was done to her satisfaction, it was after three. After a hurried snack, she tackled her hair, a time-consuming job as well. Again, probably because of nerves, the style she'd chosen to suit her very feminine dress just didn't work out. In the end she shampooed her hair a second time and started from scratch again, this time putting it up into a French pleat, which she could have done in her sleep. But she was disappointed and frustrated that she couldn't manage the softer, curlier look she'd wanted.

By this stage it was ten past five, leaving her less than an hour to do her nails and make-up and get dressed. The nails she managed without smudging, but it took twenty minutes. Transforming her naturally pretty face into something much more glamorous and sophisticated took another fifteen.

Foundation first, then blusher, then powder, then eye-shadow; smoky grey colours which deepened her corn-flower-blue eyes. Her hand had started shaking as she applied her eye-liner, Lisa muttering some uncharacteristic swearwords when she poked herself in the eye.

Her mouth came last, with Lisa waffling over which

lipstick to use. And what colour. Her full lips didn't really need to be made to look bigger. Lisa hated that bee-stung look. In the end, she just rubbed in some lip-gloss with her fingertips.

Deciding what earrings to wear wasted another five minutes, her more severe hair-do crying out for something glamorous, not the simple pearl drops she'd been planning on wearing.

Unfortunately, glamorous hadn't been on Lisa's shopping list for some years. In desperation she dragged out some long, dangling gold ones Greg had bought for her one Christmas, also changing her cream high heels for open-toed gold sandals which hadn't seen the light of day for yonks either.

Just as well they weren't a style which dated.

By then it was ten to six. Time to get into her dress.

Stripping off her bathrobe, Lisa carefully slipped the dress over her head, sliding her left arm through the one armhole whilst protecting her hair with her free hand. The dress slithered down her body, the shoulder strap halting its progress. Lisa did up the cleverly hidden side-zip, slipped her feet into her sandals then walked over to inspect the final product in the full-length mirror which hung on the back of her bedroom door.

This was where the panic set in. Instead of looking ultra-sophisticated and coolly glamorous, she looked... well...she looked sexy!

Lisa could not believe it. The dress in itself wasn't sexy. Just a chiffon sheath which skimmed her slender figure, the material graduating from cream at the top to a coffee colour down at the handkerchief hemline.

Unfortunately, the one-shouldered style meant she either had to wear a strapless bra or no bra. Given that the dress was fully lined and Lisa didn't have large breasts, she'd decided on the no-bra option. She'd always hated strapless bras, which had a tendency to slip.

She hadn't realised till this moment that her nipples would be so obvious. Or that she might look as if she had not a stitch on underneath.

Of course, she *was* wearing panties. But they were the sleek, stretchy kind which didn't show a line underneath your clothes.

Lisa was about to rummage through her underwear drawer in search of a strapless bra when she heard the sound of a car coming down the street.

Too late, she realised when it throttled down outside her house.

Grabbing her cream clutch bag, she dashed over to her bedroom window, which overlooked the street below. The sight of a sleek black sports car parked next to her post-box made her groan. The neighbours were going to have a field-day if they saw her getting into that!

She was about to run downstairs and make a quick exit when the driver's door opened and Jack climbed out.

At least, Lisa presumed it was Jack. The male who'd emerged and was currently striding up to her front door *was* remotely similar to the man she'd met the previous day. He did have the same nicely shaped head. And the same short, dark hair.

But that was where the similarity ended.

'Oh, my,' Lisa said in a soft, uncharacteristically breathy voice.

By the time he disappeared under the front porch, Lisa was shaking her head. Who would have believed that a change of clothes—and a shave—could make that much of a difference? Jack now looked just like his car. Sleek and powerful and sexy.

Sexy?

Lisa was taken aback. Since when did she start thinking any man was sexy?

Whirling away from the window, she marched off in the direction of downstairs, reminding herself the whole way down that being superficially attracted to a man was just that. Superficial.

She'd been attracted to Greg, who'd been a very handsome man. But she still hadn't liked sex with him.

Nothing has changed, she warned herself, *so don't start hoping that it has.*

The front doorbell rang on the way downstairs, Lisa's wayward thoughts back in check by the time she reached for the door knob. There were still some butterflies in her stomach over the evening ahead, but she had every confidence she could hide those. She'd been hiding her anxious nature for years.

Jack appreciated, the instant she opened the door, why he hadn't been able to get Lisa out of his mind all day.

He'd dated a lot of blondes in his time, as Helene had pointed out. But none had ever exuded what this one did.

She reminded Jack of an Alfred Hitchcock heroine. Lovely to look at. Sexy, in an understated way. But so icily self-contained that you wanted to reach out and pull her into your arms. Wanted to break her down. Wanted to make her lose her much prided self-control.

Her smile was polite. But her eyes remained annoyingly unreadable as they swept over him. 'My, don't you look simply splendid? Like James Bond on his way to a casino.'

It was a type of compliment, he supposed.

'And you look like Grace Kelly, in *To Catch a Thief*,' he countered.

Only with less underwear, he suddenly noticed.

Actually, if Jack hadn't known better, he might have thought she was totally naked underneath her dress. She certainly wasn't wearing a bra.

What he wouldn't give to reach out right now and slip that thin strap off her shoulder. In his mind's eye the dress was already slithering down her delicious body onto the doorstep, leaving her standing there wearing not much more but those sexy gold shoes.

When his own body began to respond to his mental fantasy, Jack forced himself to get a grip, clearing his throat and adopting what he hoped was a gentlemanly expression before reefing his eyes back up to her extremely beautiful face.

Her sudden blush startled him.

Because ice princesses didn't blush. They accepted compliments with cool little smiles. Their cheeks didn't go a bright red. Their composure was rarely rattled.

But Lisa was definitely rattled at that moment.

How interesting.

'Thank you,' she returned, confusion in her eyes, as

though she was well aware she was not acting like her normal self.

Even more interesting.

'Are you ready?' he asked, quite pleased at how the evening was going so far. Who knew? He might not have to be super-patient after all. If he wasn't mistaken, his little ice princess was already on the thaw.

Ready?

No, Lisa suddenly wanted to scream at him. No, I'm not ready. Not ready at all! I need a few minutes to find myself again. To find control. And composure. And to work out what happened when you looked me up and down just now.

Lisa was no stranger to men staring at her. She was used to hot, desire-filled glances. Even lecherous ogling.

Jack's gaze, however, had not been at all lecherous. His eyes had betrayed nothing but a natural interest in her appearance. In truth, Lisa would have been piqued if he hadn't complimented her.

What had upset her was her own reaction when he'd looked her up and down. Her skin had burned under the silky lining of her dress, her nipples tightening in a most disgraceful fashion.

She'd felt naked before him. Naked, and excited.

Yes, excited. That was what she'd felt.

No wonder she'd blushed.

'Have you got your house keys with you?' Jack prodded when she made no sign of moving.

'What? Oh. Yes. Yes, I think so.' She opened the gold clasp on her bag and made a pretext of inspecting its contents. 'Yes. They're here.'

'Lock up, then, and let's get going. I don't like being late.'

Lisa used the few seconds it took to lock up to calm herself. But any headway she'd made was obliterated when Jack took her arm and started steering her down the front path towards his car.

Such a simple gesture. A gentlemanly gesture, really. But the moment his large palm cupped around her elbow, electric currents went charging up and down her arm, making Lisa stiffen all over.

She smothered a sigh of relief when he let her arm go to open the passenger door of his car, grateful when he allowed her to settle herself into the seat, unaided. But she could feel his eyes on her bare legs as she swung them inside, once again making her hotly aware of her semi-naked body underneath her clothes.

She clutched her bag in her lap as he swung the door shut after her, keeping her eyes steadfastly ahead, resisting the temptation to glance up at him, for fear of what he might see in her face. But when he came into view through the front windscreen, striding round the low front of his car, Lisa surrendered to the temptation to gaze openly at him, her thoughts reflecting her ongoing shock at how he was affecting her tonight.

Just before he opened the door and climbed in behind the wheel Lisa wrenched her eyes away, hopeful he hadn't noticed her staring at him.

But what if he had?

Embarrassment curled her stomach. Please don't let him have noticed. Please let me get through this evening without making a fool of myself.

Because that was what Lisa was suddenly feeling like. A fool. Not a frigid fool any longer. Just a fool.

CHAPTER EIGHT

JACK frowned as he gunned the engine. Talk about one step forward and three steps backwards.

For a split-second, when she'd blushed, he'd thought she was warming to him.

But just when Jack had started counting his chickens, the hatching had ground to a halt. She'd acted like a marble statue when he'd taken her arm. And now she was staring out of the passenger window and clutching that bag in her lap as if she was scared stiff he was about to pounce.

Clearly, he hadn't hidden his desire for her as well as he thought he had.

Time to calm her fears with some distracting conversation, or this evening was going to be a total disaster.

'Very nice place you've got there, Lisa,' he said as he executed a U-turn and accelerated away. 'It's a credit to you.'

Her head turned and there was no mistaking the relief in her eyes. Obviously, she didn't mind his complimenting her house.

'I do like keeping it nice,' she said. 'But my mother says I'm too house-proud.'

'Nothing wrong with being house-proud. Have you always lived here?'

'Ever since my marriage. Though it looked like I'd lose the house for a while after Greg died. His insurance payout didn't cover the mortgage.'

'So what did you do?'

'I couldn't go out to work. I had a child and I hadn't booked him into childcare. So I took in ironing and cleaned houses whilst people were at work. Anywhere where I was allowed to take Cory with me. I worked seven days a week. By the time I started my business, I was close to paying off the mortgage. I'm now free and clear of debt.'

'Wow. That's impressive, Lisa.'

She shrugged those slender shoulders of hers. 'I did what I had to do. But what about you? Where did you live before you bought up here?'

'In Sydney's eastern suburbs. I still have an apartment in Double Bay. But I was finding it hard to write there. I bought the place in Terrigal as a kind of writer's retreat.'

'You must be very wealthy.'

'I've been lucky.'

'I don't believe that. People make their own luck. I'll bet writing is hard work.'

'It's becoming more so with time. When I first left the army, the words seemed to just flow.'

'Oh, so you *were* in the army. My mother said you must have been. She said you knew too much about weapons not to have handled them yourself. Once I thought about it, I agreed with her.'

'I was in the army for twelve years. Joined when I was eighteen. Left when I was thirty. I'd had enough.'

'How long ago was that?'

'Six years. Do I look thirty-six?' he asked, slanting her a quick smile. 'Or older?'

She stared back at him for a few seconds. 'Thirty-six looks about right,' she said at last. 'Though I wouldn't have been surprised if you'd been older. You do have years of experience in your eyes.'

Jack nodded. 'Some days I feel a hundred. I saw lots of things I'd rather not have seen in the army, I can tell you.'

'Hal is you, Jack, isn't he?' she suddenly said, her eyes still on him.

'He's only part me. I'm not a one-man instrument of justice and vengeance. I certainly don't go round killing people.'

'But you'd like to.'

Jack laughed. 'How perceptive of you.'

'Hal's rather ruthless.'

'He is,' Jack agreed as he negotiated the first of a series of roundabouts which would lead them past the Tuggerah shopping centre where she'd been this morning, then onto the motorway to Sydney.

'Do you think you'll win the award tonight?' Lisa asked him once they were on the motorway.

'Probably.'

'You don't sound like you really care.'

'The novelty of winning awards wears off pretty quickly.'

'That sounded cynical.'

'I *am* cynical. But awards sometimes translate into more money. And money I like. So does my agent.'

'Do you have to have an agent to become successful as a writer?'

'You do if you want to make it overseas. And especially if you want your books to be made into movies.'

'Your books are going to be made into movies?'

No doubt, that surprised her.

'They already have been. The first one premières in Los Angeles in April next year. I've been invited to attend as a special guest.'

'Wow! That's fabulous, Jack. Who's playing the part of Hal?'

'An unknown actor. The studio didn't want a big name. They wanted the person who played the part to really become Hal in people's minds. His name is Chad Furness. I hear he's very good. And very handsome.'

'Well, Hal's very handsome, isn't he? Oh, you must be so proud.'

Proud.

Jack thought about that word for a long moment.

Proud.

No. That wasn't what he felt.

Satisfied, perhaps. But not proud.

'It's certainly made me a very rich man,' came his considered reply. 'I bought this car and my penthouse at Terrigal with some of the money Hollywood paid me. Plus I hired myself a cleaner from the top cleaning establishment on the coast,' he added with a wry grin.

She laughed, the sound reassuring Jack. He would

hate to think she felt tense in his company. And she had been, earlier on.

Suddenly, the thought of never seeing her again after this evening was unbearable.

'I suppose I can't talk you into cleaning my study this Monday, could I?' he said, doing his best to sound very casual. 'Gail's ankle wouldn't have recovered yet and my study's crying out for a thorough cleaning.'

When she didn't answer, he glanced over at her.

'At the risk of being accused of trying to buy you, I'll pay you double,' he said. *And a million dollars if you'll sleep with me*, came the added Hal-like thought.

Her head turned, her eyes betraying the most intriguing dilemma. She wanted to do as he asked. He could see it. But she was hesitant. Which meant what? She did like him, but was afraid of him for some reason? Clearly, she was still worried that he was going to pounce, sexually.

'I…I can't, Jack. I have other work to do on Monday.'

'Tuesday, then.' He had no intention of letting her off the hook that easily.

'I'll send someone else.'

'No,' he snapped. 'I don't want anyone else. I want you.'

Jack could have bitten his tongue out. He'd done it now. Showed his hand. He could feel her eyes on him. Feel her tension welling up again.

'You're the best cleaner I've ever had,' he went on, hoping it wasn't too late to salvage the situation. 'You leave Gail for dead. It's difficult to go back to second rate when you've experienced perfection.'

'You're being persuasive again,' she said.

'Is it my fault if you're perfect?'

'Don't flatter me, Jack.'

'The truth is not flattery.'

'You have a way with words.'

'You have a way with floors.'

Her laugh delighted him. And made him want to roar in relief.

'All right,' she said. 'I'll clean your study. Once. On Tuesday. But after that, you're back to Gail.'

'Oh, cruel woman.'

'Stop it, Jack,' she said, but smilingly.

After that she seemed much more relaxed, and they chatted away about all sorts of things. Music. Movies. Their families. Or lack of them. Lisa's parents were divorced, and, like himself, she had no siblings. All their grandparents had passed away, too.

In a way, they were both loners. Both self-sufficient.

Occasionally, she brought the topic of conversation back to his writing. But Jack managed to steer her away from further discussion of his books, or his so-called hero.

Jack didn't want to think about Hal too much tonight. Hal could sometimes be bad for him. He appealed to his dark side. It was difficult enough ignoring the sexual thoughts and feelings Lisa could so easily evoke without Hal getting into his head, tempting him with truly wicked ideas.

Would *two* million tempt her to sleep with him? *Five?* Ten?

Jack clenched his jaw-line, then concentrated on keeping their casual conversation going, forcing himself not to fall broodingly silent as he could do on occasion when his thoughts turned dark. Which they were on the verge of doing every time he glanced over at Lisa.

Damn, but he wanted her!

His body was rock-hard with desire, his resolve to have her threatening to turn more ruthless with each passing minute.

'Not far to go now,' he said with some relief as they approached the harbour bridge. Best get out of this confining car and into somewhere public.

The traffic was a bit heavy across the bridge, but moving along steadily. Jack knew where he was going, taking the correct lanes and exit to whiz them down to the harbourside restaurant where the awards dinner was being held. Thankfully the restaurant had a private car park, reserved for patrons, an attendant swiftly directing them to a spot just metres from the entrance.

'I'd better warn you about Helene before you meet her,' he said as he extracted his car keys.

'Helene? Who's Helene?' Lisa asked.

'My agent. She's a darling woman underneath her tough-bird exterior. But she does have a big mouth. Puts her foot into it occasionally. She's also going through a gypsy-cum-gothic stage in her wardrobe, which can be a bit startling. If she'd dressed me tonight I'd have been wearing black leather trousers, with a full-sleeved white silk shirt, topped off with a scarlet cummerbund. I'd have looked like a camp pirate from the Caribbean.'

Lisa laughed, her lovely blue eyes sparkling with amusement. 'If there's one thing you could never look,

Jack, it's camp. But I'm glad this Helene didn't dress you tonight. What you're wearing is superb. That suit must have cost a small fortune.'

'It did. And I would think that little number you have on didn't come cheap. I wish you'd let me pay for it, Lisa. You shouldn't be out of pocket because you did me the favour of being my pretend girlfriend for the night.'

CHAPTER NINE

Lisa found herself piqued by that word, *pretend*.

Yet she should have been reassured.

So why wasn't she?

Female vanity, she supposed. Or was it something else, that faint hope she'd been harbouring that at last she was becoming a normal woman, sexually?

During the drive down, that startling incident with her nipples had stayed at the back of her mind, as had the heat which Jack had generated in her when he'd taken her arm. Despite finally relaxing in his company and enjoying their conversation very much, she'd begun secretly hoping that he *would* make a pass when he brought her home, just to see how she would react.

The word 'pretend' indicated that Jack wasn't about to try anything. His insistence that she come and clean his study had not been a sign of personal interest. He just wanted his study cleaned. He didn't fancy her one bit.

Lisa wished now she'd accepted his offer to pay her double.

Paying for her dress, however, was still out of the question.

'Don't start that again, Jack,' she said with a cool glance his way.

The trouble with practised womanisers, she decided, was that women fell easily for their superficial charms.

When Jack came round to open the passenger door and reach his hand down towards her, Lisa smothered a groan of dismay.

There really was no option but to accept his help. Still, Lisa delayed as long as possible, swinging her feet out of the car first, her bag clutched tightly in her left hand. Finally, she put her clammy right hand into his outstretched palm, plastering a plastic smile on her face as she glanced up into his.

'Thank you,' she said with stiff politeness whilst her heart hammered away behind her ribs.

'My pleasure,' he returned, his fingers closing tightly around hers as he pulled her up onto her feet.

Lisa had a few seconds of respite when he dropped her hand and attended to locking up the car. But no sooner had she managed to calm her pulse rate a little than he slid his arm around her waist.

Naturally, she froze.

'Don't panic,' he murmured. 'Just window-dressing.'

Just window-dressing, Lisa thought almost bitterly as he propelled her towards the restaurant door. What an apt phrase to describe her! For years she'd acted like a mannequin, designed and dressed to look attractive, but not a flesh and blood woman.

No wonder Jack didn't fancy her.

'Jack! Jack!'

The owner of the voice came rushing over to them, a tall, skinny, black-haired woman dressed in the weirdest black clothes. There were lots of layers and beads, and her make-up was extremely pale and heavy, except for her bright red lipstick. Once closer, Lisa could see she was at least in her fifties.

'Helene,' Jack muttered under his breath. 'Have patience.'

'So!' The agent's beady black eyes glittered as she looked Lisa up and down. 'I knew you wouldn't come alone. Not Jack Cassidy.'

'I decided it wasn't wise to go into the lion's den without a shield by my side,' he said drily.

Helene cackled. 'It's a bit like that with you at these dos, isn't it? You're a brave woman, love,' she directed at Lisa. 'Our Jack here gets swamped by fans wanting his autograph. And a lot more of him if they can get it,' she added with a wicked wink.

'I can imagine,' Lisa replied somewhat ruefully.

Helene laughed. 'Jack, do introduce me to this delightful creature.'

'This delightful creature is Lisa, Helene. Lisa, this is Helene, my brilliant agent.'

'Heavens to Betsy! A compliment as well as a classy girlfriend! My cup runneth over! Hello, my love,' she directed at Lisa. 'You're going to wow them in the States. You are taking her with you next year, Jack. Don't tell me you're not or I'll have a pink fit right here and now.'

'I'd love to take her with me,' Jack said, pulling Lisa even closer to his side. 'But Lisa has a company to run and a son to raise. I don't think she can get away for a trip to the States, can you, darling?'

Lisa knew it was just pretend. Just window-dressing. Especially the darling bit.

But from the moment Jack's side pressed hard against hers, everything inside her began to go to mush.

'I'll have to see,' she heard herself say whilst she struggled to stop the amazing meltdown which was currently threatening her entire body.

'Make her go with you, Jack,' Helene insisted.

'I'm afraid I can't make Lisa do anything she doesn't want to do,' he said with a wry laugh. 'She's very strong-willed.'

Lisa almost laughed as well. Rather hysterically.

'Do what Hal did in your second book, Jack,' Helene advised. 'Kidnap the girl and keep her your prisoner till she says yes to everything you want.'

'I just might do that. But first, shall we go inside? Helene, look after Lisa for me for a couple of minutes, will you?'

'Will do,' the agent replied. 'Come along, lovely Lisa. We'll go in and find our table. I did ask for one of the smaller ones, knowing Jack's distaste for making idle conversation with people he cares nothing for. Hopefully, we're not stuck in some ghastly corner.'

They weren't stuck in some ghastly corner. There were no real corners, the main body of the restaurant being semicircular, with huge windows overlooking the harbour. They had, probably, *the* best table in the house, very close to a window, with a great view of the bridge *and* the opera house. The table itself was round,

covered in a crisp white tablecloth with matching ser-
viettes, extremely expensive crystal glasses and a most
spectacular, candlelit centre-piece. The carpet under-
foot was a deep blue, and the overhead lighting very
subdued.

'Golly,' Lisa said in impressed tones after the *maître
d'* had departed. 'This is a fabulous place.'

'It's OK. At least they took notice of what I asked
for. Jack's going to be pleased that it's only us.'

'But the table is set for four,' Lisa pointed out.

Helene grinned. 'I told them I had a partner.'

'And you don't?'

'Lord, no! Who'd have me? I'm a selfish, opinion-
ated, ambitious bitch. On top of that, I'm skinny and
downright ugly. Always have been.'

'You are *not* ugly,' Lisa protested. 'You're very
striking-looking.'

Helene was still preening when Jack pulled out a
chair and sat down.

'I like your Lisa, Jack. Where did you meet her?'

Lisa held her breath, hoping he didn't say she was
his cleaner.

'When I bought the penthouse at Terrigal, I
employed a cleaner. Gail. Lisa owns the cleaning
company Gail works for.'

'Oh, so you've been going out for quite a while. My,
but you're a dark horse, Jack. You never mentioned
her.'

'Didn't I?'

'You know you didn't.'

'Lisa's a very private girl, aren't you, darling?' And

he leant over and gave her a light peck on her bare shoulder.

Lisa tried not to wince. Or to cry out loud. But as window-dressing went, this was a little too close to the bone, those same bones which had almost gone to jelly the last time he'd touched her and called her darling.

Her head turned and caught his eye just as his head lifted. She meant to flash him an icy warning. Instead, she just stared at him with dazed eyes.

He stared back for a long moment, then smiled, a slow, wickedly sexy smile.

Lisa swallowed, then somehow found a smile of her own.

'Jack likes to tease me,' she said through clenched teeth. 'He knows how I hate displays of affection in public.'

'Not true,' Jack said. 'She secretly loves it.' And he kissed her shoulder again.

This time, Lisa's skin broke out into goose-pimples.

'Jack, *please*,' she choked out.

His head lifted and their eyes met once more. His were unreadable, whereas she knew hers had to be full of blind panic.

'I…I have to go to the ladies',' she said with a strained smile as she got to her feet. 'If you have to order anything whilst I'm gone, you do it for me, Jack, will you?'

Jack watched her go. Watched the other men in the place watch her go, too.

'She's very beautiful, Jack,' Helene remarked. 'Divorced?'

'No, widowed.'

'Really? So young! Still, it explains quite a bit. You know, Jack, nice girls like that don't come along too often.'

'No,' Jack agreed.

'Be good to her.'

Jack would have liked to be good to her, if she'd let him. But she wouldn't. She made that clear at every turn. Yet he knew that she *was* attracted to him, despite all her contrary body language. He'd seen the truth in her eyes just now. *Felt* it in her tensely held shoulder when he kissed it.

For whatever reason, she refused to surrender to that attraction. She was afraid.

Of *him*? Jack wondered. Or of involvement of any kind?

'Don't let her get away,' Helene added wryly.

He could, of course. Let her get away.

But Jack knew he wasn't going to do that. He'd been spot-on when he'd said she secretly liked his kissing her shoulder. She had. And it had been his total undoing.

Next time, it wouldn't be her shoulder he'd kiss. And next time, she'd wouldn't find it so easy to escape.

'Have you ordered any drinks yet?' he asked Helene abruptly.

'No, I was waiting for you.'

'I think the occasion calls for champagne, don't you?' He snapped his fingers, a waiter materialising by his side in moments. 'A magnum of your best champagne.'

'Certainly, sir.'

'A magnum!' Helen exclaimed. 'Thank heavens I came in a taxi!'

And thank heavens Lisa hadn't, Jack thought with ruthless resolve. She'd come with him.

And she'd be going home with him.

He would not break his word tonight. But he would claim a kiss goodnight at her door.

A lot could be achieved with the right kind of kiss. Jack didn't aim to stop till her eventual surrender was assured. By the time she returned to him on Tuesday on the pretext of cleaning his study, it would just be a matter of time.

Yes, indeed, he vowed darkly as he watched her weave her way through the tables back towards him, that floaty dress clinging to her body in several tantalising places. She was going to be his.

And soon.

CHAPTER TEN

LISA had given herself a solid lecture in the ladies' room, reminding herself sternly that *she'd* made the decision to come here this evening as Jack's pretend girlfriend. It wasn't *his* fault that her hormones had suddenly come to life.

OK, so it had been a shock after all these years, to want a man the way she did Jack. And somewhat disappointing that he didn't want her back. But that was life, wasn't it? She was here now. The restaurant was lovely, the food and wine were sure to be excellent and so was the company. All she had to do was relax and enjoy herself.

An hour later, Lisa was doing just that. Amazing what a few glasses of champagne could achieve! She felt not one iota of tension. She'd become a totally different woman, tucking into her meal with gusto, not worrying over calories as she usually did. Not worrying over anything.

Conversation flowed easily from her lips whilst the champagne continued to flow past them. She even dared to flirt with Jack a little. And he flirted right back. Quite outrageously, really.

Lisa knew it was just an act. But she no longer cared. It was fun. He was fun. The evening was fun.

Whenever female fans sought him out—and after Jack won the Golden Gun award, there were quite a few of those—Jack made a big show of introducing her as his girlfriend, often giving her another of those provocative kisses, either on her shoulder or on her cheek. By then she'd long stopped freezing up, behaving in an almost cavalier way in her response to his attentions.

That she was seriously intoxicated did not cross Lisa's mind. Nothing serious crossed her mind. She felt happy for once. Genuinely happy.

Or so she deluded herself.

Coffee arrived, as did some more female fans. Three of them, all carrying copies of Jack's prize-winning book, all gushing over him as he signed them. Helene was, at that moment, away at another table, talking business to people she knew in the publishing world.

Jack went through his usual spiel of introducing Lisa as his girlfriend, this time picking up her hand and lifting it towards his mouth.

'Isn't she lovely?' he said just before his lips made contact.

If his fans said anything in reply, Lisa didn't hear it. Her focus was entirely on what Jack was doing to her hand. He wasn't just kissing it. He was making love to it, his index finger stroking the soft skin of her palm whilst his mouth moved sensually over the back of her hand, his tongue-tip leaving a wet trail as it worked its way down her middle finger.

By the time he reached the fingertip, her skin had broken out into goose-pimples. When she went to pull her hand away, his hand tightened around hers, making it impossible for her to free herself without struggling. His lips parted over the tip, sucking it slightly into his mouth.

'Jack, *really*,' she reprimanded, throwing a desperate smile at the goggle-eyed fans.

But all they did was swoon.

His head immediately lifted.

'Yes, my darling?' he enquired in a low, thickish voice.

He'd been calling her darling all evening. Up till this point, Lisa had accepted his endearment as part of the game. Part of the pretence. Suddenly, nothing felt like pretence. His eyes, usually so hard and so cool, had darkened to a smoky grey, his eyelids heavy with what looked like desire. If she wasn't badly mistaken, he wanted to make love to her for real. And not just to her hand.

'We're...we're not alone,' she pointed out, her voice shaking.

His eyes cleared abruptly as he smiled over at his by now blushing female fans.

'Forgive me,' he said, and nonchalantly dropped her hand. 'But it's not really my fault. She does dreadful things to me.'

They forgave him, of course. But could she, for acting that well? For a moment there...

'Could you take me home, please, Jack,' she said once they were gone.

'Are you serious?'

'I'm tired.' Tired of you kissing me and calling me darling. Tired of being your pretend girlfriend.

'Very well,' he said sharply, standing up and sweeping up his award in one motion.

She picked up her bag and stood up too, swaying till Jack clamped a firm hand around her elbow for support. She hadn't realised till that moment just how much champagne she'd consumed. She'd have a colossal hangover in the morning, her first in years.

Thinking about her alcohol consumption brought his to her mind.

'Are you fit to drive?' she asked.

'I'm always fit to drive.'

'You know what I mean.'

'You and Helene drank most of the champagne, Lisa. Not me.'

'Oh. I didn't notice. Shouldn't we go and say goodbye to Helene?' she said shakily when Jack urged her forward.

'She'll know where we've gone.'

He steered her from the restaurant with impolite speed, brushing off people who tried to congratulate him.

Lisa cringed with embarrassment.

'Do you know you can be very rude?' she informed him heatedly once they reached his car.

'Yes,' he threw back at her as he wrenched open the passenger door. 'It's one of my many flaws. As is arrogance and presumption. Get in, please.'

She scrambled into the passenger seat, and was still sitting there, wide-eyed with confusion, when he climbed in behind the wheel and tossed his award over into the back.

'Don't look at me like that,' he commanded after yanking his door shut and stabbing his car key into the ignition.

'Like what?'

'Like a hurt animal. If I've offended you tonight, then I'm sorry. I genuinely thought you might enjoy a night out, along with some male company. Clearly, I was wrong.'

'You weren't wrong. I did enjoy myself.'

He shook his head frustratedly at her. 'More mixed messages, Lisa? Is that a game you like to play with men? Turn them on, then turn on them?'

'I have no idea what you're talking about. You were the one kissing my shoulder and sucking on my finger. I didn't do a thing!'

'You were *liking* it,' he muttered, leaning over and putting his face so close to hers she could feel his hot breath on her skin.

'Don't,' she cried when he snaked a hand around her throat, his thumb pad tipping her chin up so that her mouth was breathtakingly close to his.

'Don't what? Don't call your bluff?'

'No, I—'

His kiss cut off any further protest, blanking her mind to everything but the feel of his mouth on hers.

It had been some years since Lisa had been kissed. She vaguely recalled liking Greg's kisses at first, till she knew where they invariably led. After that, she hadn't enjoyed them at all, her lips always remaining still and unresponsive under her husband's mouth.

Not so under Jack's.

Her lips moved restlessly against his, then parted, inviting him in. She moaned when he accepted that invitation, his tongue sliding between her teeth. She moaned again when his tongue-tip touched hers. Moaned a third time when his mouth abruptly abandoned her.

'Is this what you're afraid of?' he growled as he stared down at her flushed face. 'And why you don't date? Because you might lose some of that precious control you seem to value above everything?'

'You don't understand,' she cried.

'Don't understand what?'

'Anything.'

'Then explain it to me. Tell me what it is I don't understand.'

'I don't like sex,' she blurted out. 'That's why I don't date. Because men always want sex and I…I hate it.'

His eyebrows shot up. '*Hate* it. That wasn't hate, honey, which I felt and heard just now. You didn't want me to stop. I could have you tonight, if I wanted to.'

'You could *not*!' she exploded, pushing him back into his own seat. 'You certainly are an arrogant and presumptuous man, Jack Cassidy. Now take me home. And don't you dare touch me again, do you hear?'

'I hear you, but I don't believe you. Think about your attitude on the drive home, Lisa, and we'll talk when we get there. Because for a girl who doesn't like sex, you sure as hell liked me kissing you just now.'

'Kissing is just kissing,' she pronounced self-righteously. 'Intercourse is something else.'

* * *

Intercourse?

Jack stared over at Lisa. Was this girl for real? Did she live in the twenty-first century?

There were lots of words used to describe the sex act these days. But intercourse was rarely one of them. It was as outdated as beautiful young blondes not liking sex.

'How many men have you been to bed with?' he demanded to know before he drove anywhere.

'I don't have to tell you that.'

'You were a virgin when you got married, weren't you?'

'No,' she replied defensively. 'I was not.'

'So how many cretin lovers have you had?'

'None. One. I mean…Greg was *not* a cretin!'

'You've only ever been with your husband? I thought you said you weren't a virgin when you got married.'

'We slept with each other before we were married.'

'I see. And you never enjoyed sleeping with him?'

'No.'

'Then why in heaven's name did you marry him?'

'You don't understand! I…I needed to get married. To have my own home. My own family. Greg was a good man. And I loved him.'

'But you weren't *in* love with him. If you were, you'd have liked anything he did to you. Even if you didn't come, you'd have liked the lovemaking. And the intimacy.'

Lisa's old nemesis, guilt, consumed her again. She should not have married Greg. She could see that now.

But this man—this playboy!—had no right to judge her.

Jack sighed. 'What on earth am I going to do with you?'

'You're going to take me home,' she snapped, fighting back tears.

'I don't think so. You're coming home with me.'

'I am not!'

'*Think*, Lisa,' he said, his eyes turning strangely tender. 'You're thirty years old, and you've never enjoyed sex. If you keep going the way you've been going, you'll go to your death never knowing what you've missed. I'm a good lover. A skilled lover. I know what a woman likes. Let me show you what you've been missing.'

She just stared at him, not knowing what to say. Or what to do.

She was tempted. Of course she was tempted.

But she was also terrified.

'Don't be afraid,' he whispered, leaning over to kiss her again. Very lightly this time, sipping at her lips till they fell wantonly apart once more.

His head slowly lifted, his eyes locking with hers as his hands gently cupped her cheeks.

'You need to come home with me, Lisa. You're not a coward. You have great courage. More courage than any woman I've ever known. Take this leap of faith and trust me. I won't hurt you, I promise. I'll be good to you.'

'But you don't really fancy me!' she blurted out.

His laughter was soft and wry. 'Not fancy you? Oh, Lisa, how little you comprehend the true nature of men.

Of course I fancy you. I've fancied you since the first moment I set eyes on you.'

'But you…you…'

'Yes,' he said, nodding, 'I let you think otherwise. I confess. I'm a ruthless bastard when I want something. And I wanted you, my lovely. Now lean back and fasten your seat belt.'

'I didn't agree to come home with you!'

'Yes, you did. The last time I kissed you. Of course, you do have the right to change your mind at any stage. And to say no. Are you saying no now?'

She shook her head in the negative, her whole being suddenly consumed by a breathless excitement.

'Good,' Jack said as he gunned the engine. 'Now close your eyes and rest. You could be in for a rather long night.'

CHAPTER ELEVEN

SHE didn't close her eyes, Jack noted as he drove. She sat there with her hands clasped nervously around that infernal bag, her body language betraying an increasingly uptight state.

He put on some music in an attempt to relax her but to no avail. All she did was grip that bag tighter and stare out of the passenger window.

On Jack's part, he found his initial sense of triumph at her agreeing to come home with him soon fading to frustration. He half expected her to tell him to take her straight home as he drove down the hill from Kariong. His own knuckles were white on the steering wheel by the time he made it through West Gosford.

It took all of his will-power not to sigh with relief once he was safely on the road which led out to the beaches, and Terrigal.

But he sensed she was still worried. Or afraid. Or both.

An understandable state of mind, he supposed, given her sexual history.

She must have had a miserable marriage, poor darling.

Jack hoped she would let him show her that she didn't have to shun men and sex forever just because she'd been incompatible with one partner.

People were not machines, especially women. The chemistry had to be right on both sides for a sensitive female like Lisa to find satisfaction. She needed to desire as well as be desired.

Jack knew the chemistry between them was right. But she had to give him the chance to show her that.

By the time Jack reefed the Porsche into his driveway and shot down the side-ramp which led to the underground car-park, he had resolved to be patient, but persistent. He would not let her change her mind. Or give in to her doubts and fears.

'I can see your main problem,' he remarked as he released his seat belt. 'You think too much. What star sign are you?'

'Virgo,' she said, and he nodded.

'How come I'm not surprised? The sign of the worrier. So what have you been worrying about during the drive here?'

She turned to him, still clutching that bag as if it were a lifeline. 'I've been thinking it could have been the champagne, Jack,' she said, her tone anxious. 'That's why I liked you kissing me.'

'What are you saying exactly? You only liked me kissing you because you were drunk?'

'Yes. That's what I'm saying.'

'Do you feel drunk now?'

'No,' she said with surprise in her voice. 'Actually, my head feels quite clear.'

'I can believe that,' he pointed out drily. 'Because you're back to being all uptight again.'

Her lovely face screwed up in an expression of sheer frustration. 'I know I am. I hate it when I get like this. I really do.'

'In that case, I have a bottle of excellent white wine chilling in the fridge door. Let's go open it and get you right back to being nicely relaxed again.'

Her blue eyes widened. 'You want to get me drunk again?'

'I want you not thinking. Or worrying. If that means you have to be on the tipsy side, then yes, I do.'

Again, he could see temptation in her eyes. And that irritating fear as well.

'Come on, beautiful,' he said softly. 'I dare you to do something out of your comfort zone for once. Put the ice princess away for tonight and let me bring out the woman you've always wanted to be.'

Lisa winced at the term 'ice princess'. Was that how he saw her?

It made her angry. Because it was true. That was how lots of people saw her. Her employees. Her mother. And now Jack.

She supposed she couldn't blame them. She was the girl who turned off movies once the sex scenes started. And skipped the really raunchy parts in books.

Though never in Jack's books, Lisa suddenly realised. She always read the pages where Hal made love to a woman.

No, not made love. Hal never made love. He had sex with women. All kinds of sex.

Lisa swallowed. She hoped Jack wouldn't be expecting the sort of foreplay Hal always demanded. She would die rather than do that.

Thinking about it made her feel sick.

'I'm sorry, Jack,' she choked out, her eyes dropping to her lap. 'I can't do this.'

'Yes, you can. Look at me, Lisa!' he commanded.

She looked up at him.

'You're not drunk now, are you?'

'No.'

'Good.'

He leant over and kissed her again, a hot, hungry kiss which was as demanding as it was irresistible. She moaned softly when his tongue dipped deep into her mouth, her nipples tightening once more, her heart pounding within her chest. Soon, she wanted more than his mouth on her. She wanted his hands as well.

'No,' she cried out in confusion when his head lifted.

'I don't want to hear that word again tonight,' he replied thickly. 'It's going to be yes. To everything. Come on. Time I got you upstairs.'

She's like a virgin, Jack reminded himself as he helped her out of the car. Just look at her eyes. So wide. And innocent.

He would have to be gentle, and patient. Have to contain his own desire and think of nothing the first time but giving *her* pleasure.

He'd never done that before. Not really. Yes, he was

an accomplished lover. And yes, he knew how to satisfy a woman. But his intentions in doing so in the past had always been totally selfish. A well-satisfied woman always came back for more.

Lisa, however, inspired him to be less selfish and more gallant. Yes, of course he still wanted her to come back for more. But that wasn't as important, suddenly, as seeing the rapture in her eyes when she came for the first time.

'Now, don't start thinking,' he whispered, holding her close as he steered her over to the lift well.

'It's hard not to.'

'Every time I see you thinking I'm going to kiss you,' he promised.

And he did. In the lift. At his front door. In the middle of the living room. Even whilst he carried her down to his bedroom.

By the time he lowered her down onto her feet by his bed, her breathing was quick and her eyes dilated, two sure signs that she was seriously turned on.

His job now was to undress her, *without* turning her off again.

Earrings first, Jack decided, blowing softly into her ear after he unhooked each one and dropped it on the nearest bedside table. Her shivers were reassuring. But he still kissed her again after the second earring had been disposed of.

By the time his head lifted, her breathing was very fast.

'Now, how do I get you out of this dress?' he asked softly.

Her hands were visibly shaking when they reached

up to slide down the zip which was hidden in the side-seam.

'Aah,' he said, and slowly pushed the strap off her shoulder and down her arm. The dress went too, as it had in his mental fantasy, slithering down her body before pooling on the floor at her feet.

The sudden sight of her near-naked body jolted his resolve to stay cool. Lord, but she was beautiful. Beautiful shape, beautiful skin, beautiful breasts. They were small, but quite exquisite.

She was exquisite.

No one would have believed she'd had a child. Only her nipples gave her away. They were comparatively large, and dusky coloured. And very erect, calling out to him to touch them...

'Jack,' she choked out, snapping his eyes back up to her face.

The fear was back, he saw, widening her eyes again and stiffening her shoulders.

Damn you, Jack, get your act together!

He had no option but to kiss her again. But the feel of her bare breasts pressed against his chest threatened to unravel him. When she wound her arms up around his neck and melted against him, his battle for control looked in danger of being lost.

He wrenched his mouth away, his own breathing very ragged. He had to get her away from him for a while.

He sat her down on the side of the bed, keeping his eyes averted from her breasts—and the rest of her delicious body—whilst he removed her shoes. As a distancing ploy, it failed miserably. His hands would not obey him, sliding up her calves, caressing her knees then moving on to her by then quivering thighs.

A desire such as he'd never known gripped him, compelling him to tip her back onto the bed and remove her panties.

How he managed to ease them down her legs slowly instead of ripping them off her, he had no idea.

Just in time, he reefed his mind back from the brink, steeling himself to ignore his own increasingly desperate need and take his time with her.

But it was going to be difficult. More difficult than he'd ever imagined. She affected him, this girl, in ways he had yet to understand. If he didn't know better, he might think he was falling in love with her.

The thought startled him. Jack didn't fall in love. He *never* fell in love. He was like Hal. Dead inside. And hard.

But not with this girl. She brought out the softness in him.

She stared up at him as he rose to his feet, her eyes wide yet trusting. She was waiting for him to make love to her. *Make love*, Jack. Not have sex.

Make love to her, then, man. And do it well.

Because she deserves it.

CHAPTER TWELVE

Lisa swallowed as she watched his hands go to his bow-tie, flicking it undone whilst he kicked his shoes off. His jacket followed next. Then his socks.

He was going to take everything off, she realised dazedly. Going to get naked. As naked as she was.

Why wasn't she embarrassed, lying there in front of Jack without any clothes on? Why wasn't she trying to cover herself up? Why wasn't she searching her mind for any excuse to cut and run?

She certainly had been earlier.

But that was before he'd kissed her a zillion times. And before she'd been consumed with the craving for more.

His kisses were no longer enough.

So she lay there, with a huge lump in her throat and the desperate hope that he was right and she was about to become the woman she'd always secretly wanted to be.

His shirt went the same way as his jacket and bow-tie, revealing the magnificent upper body Lisa already suspected he had. His skin was deeply tanned, a V of dark curls covering the area between his broad chest muscles, arrowing down past his washboard stomach into the waistband of his trousers...that waist band which he'd just snapped open.

Lisa found herself holding her breath as he reefed the zip down and pushed the trousers off his slim hips.

His legs were as muscular as his arms, his black briefs straining to contain his erection.

Lisa's mouth dried when they hit the floor as well.

'Let's get that quilt off,' he said with a warm smile as he walked towards the bed. 'And you up onto the pillows.'

He scooped her up as if she were a feather, holding her against him with one arm whilst he flung back the black velvet quilt with the other.

Lisa could not help thinking how she'd made this very bed yesterday, never imagining that tonight she would be sleeping in it.

Yet here she was, being lowered into the crisp white sheets, naked as the day she was born.

She shivered when Jack stretched out beside her.

'Not cold, are you?' he enquired.

'No,' she choked out. Just shockingly nervous.

'Methinks she needs some more kissing.'

His lips took a passionate possession of hers, his right hand cupping her chin and keeping her mouth captive beneath his.

Not that it needed to be kept captive. She was already addicted to Jack's kisses, loving the way he dominated her with his mouth, and his tongue.

But this was the first time he'd kissed her lying down. And the first time they'd been naked together.

The feel of his bare body pressed up against hers was

electrifying. She yearned for more contact, wanting his hands on other, more intimate places.

As though he sensed her need, his hand slid down from her chin to her breast, caressing the rock-like tip till she shuddered uncontrollably. He immediately stopped kissing her and bent down to put his mouth where his hand had been.

Lisa almost jackknifed from the bed when he sucked on her breast, the tugging sensation sending wild *frissons* of pleasure rippling down her spine. He pressed her back down with his large hand splayed wide over her stomach, and kept on sucking her nipple.

Oh, yes, she thought. Yes!

When his hand moved lower and slid between her legs, her pleasure doubled. No, *tripled!*

Jack seemed to know just where to touch to make her squirm with delight. And all the while his mouth remained on her breast, sometimes sucking, sometimes licking, sometimes taking her sensitised nipple between his teeth and tugging it ever so gently.

Soon, she wanted still more. Not his fingers. Him. She wanted *him*. How amazing! She'd never wanted a man like this before. Never wanted sex like this before. Never wanted to feel a man plunging deep into her.

Yet she wanted Jack. And she wanted him now.

'Jack,' she cried out in a voice she did not recognise.

His head lifted and their eyes met.

'Please,' she begged him. 'Please…'

'I have to get a condom, Lisa.'

'No, no, don't leave me. It's safe. I promise you it's safe.' She hadn't long finished her period. 'I can't possibly get pregnant.'

Jack would have loved to just keep going. But he hadn't exercised an iron will over his own control to lose his head now.

The fact she was so turned on pleased him no end. Hell, he couldn't have felt more thrilled. But she would hate herself afterwards if he did what she thought she wanted. She would worry about other things. She was a Virgo, after all.

Still, he could understand her desperation. There were times, especially with women, when any delay could be disastrous. She needed a climax and she needed it now.

'Close your eyes and don't think,' he ordered her brusquely.

Lisa gasped with shock when Jack slid even further down her body, once again putting his mouth where his hands had been.

Never had she allowed Greg such an intimacy with her. Never ever!

For a split-second her mind revolted, but then his lips and tongue found the right spot and she was lost to sensations which could only be described as deliciously decadent. Her body wallowed in the most primal pleasure whilst her prudish mind tried to get around all that he was doing to her down there. One part of her wanted to push him away. But the overriding part refused to obey. His mouth kept her in thrall whilst his fingers entered her, filling her, stretching her. *Tormenting* her.

Her head threshed from side to side, her mouth gaping wide as the cruellest tension gripped her body. Her chest felt like a vice around her heart, her belly tightening in a way she had never felt before. Her inner muscles followed suit, gripping Jack's fingers.

'Oh!' she cried out when the first spasm hit. Then, 'Ooooh,' as more spasms followed, exquisitely pleasurable contractions which released her from wanting anything but that they go on forever.

Unfortunately, they didn't, slowly declining in intensity till they stopped altogether.

'Oooooh,' she moaned, then went all limp and languid.

Lisa was lying there with heavy eyes and much slower breathing when Jack's face materialised above hers, his hard grey eyes quite smug.

'Good?' he said.

For a moment, embarrassment threatened to raise its spoiling head. He'd just been down there, after all, seeing and invading her with stunning intimacy.

But she refused to go back to being the woman she'd been before meeting Jack. That frigid failure of a female was about to be banished. Forever.

At the same time, Lisa could not seem to stop a hot blush from invading her cheeks.

'Now, none of that, madam,' Jack chided. 'You've done nothing to feel ashamed of. You're a normal, healthy woman who deserves a normal, healthy sex life. You've wasted too many years thinking you don't like making love. You do. You just needed the right lover. Now, don't go away, beautiful. And don't start worrying. I'll be back in a moment.'

Lisa barely had time to think before he came back. And this time, he was wearing a condom.

That Jack hadn't yet been sexually satisfied had slipped Lisa's mind. Which just showed how inexperienced she was when it came to matters in the bedroom.

'So what did you think of your first orgasm?' he asked after he'd rejoined her on the bed, startling her when he immediately began caressing her body, his fingertips running up and down her sides with long, feathery strokes.

'What? Oh…yes. It was…incredible.'

'The next one will be better.'

'The next one?'

'I did say you were in for a long night.'

'But…'

He rolled over and braced himself on his elbows above her, his erection resting high on her stomach.

'Lift your knees,' he ordered her.

She didn't even think about disobeying him. He was that sort of man.

'This should feel better than my fingers,' he said as he reached down and directed himself slowly into her.

Lisa swallowed. He was right. It felt much better than his fingers.

'Now, wrap your legs around my waist. No, higher. You know, you're amazingly tight for a woman who's had a child.'

Lisa frowned at this last statement, which showed an intimate and expert knowledge of the female body.

You're having sex with a playboy, she reminded herself, a man who's been with a lot of women in his life. Don't forget that he doesn't fall in love with them, or keep them. You're just a plaything, his latest penthouse pet. Don't ever imagine you'll be anything else.

But she still did as she was told, and he slid in even deeper, making her gasp.

'I'm not hurting you, am I?'

'No no, it's…lovely.' An understatement. It was…amazing.

He smiled. 'That's my girl.'

No, I'm not, she thought with a jolt to her potentially vulnerable heart. I'm just someone you fancy. For the moment. I'm disposable. And replaceable.

Always remember that, Lisa. Don't let him con you. Or use you.

Jack's a charming and very sexy man. But he's a practised womaniser.

The thought distressed her to a degree.

Till she got hold of her silly self again.

'Jack…'

'What?'

'Why do I like this with you? Why didn't I like it with my husband? He really wasn't that bad a lover.'

He shrugged his broad shoulders. 'Who knows? Maybe you were too young. Some women mature late, sexually. And like I said, you weren't in love with him.'

'But I'm not in love with you, either.'

'Thanks a bunch.'

'You know what I mean. I don't even know you. We only met yesterday.'

'Falling in love has nothing to do with knowing each other, Lisa. It's a physical thing, a chemistry. That's where the saying *love at first sight* comes from. Still, maybe it should be called falling in lust, not love.'

'I see. And did you fall in lust with me at first sight?' she asked, intrigued by the concept.

'Undoubtedly. Now, why don't you shut up and let me show you how much.'

His moving inside her very definitely shut her up. She wrapped her arms and ankles around his back. Soon, she felt compelled to move with him, her hips lifting. Her hands dropped back down to grab his buttocks, her nails digging in as she pulled him even deeper into her.

'If there's anything I hate,' Jack said with a raw groan, 'it's a quick learner.'

'I'm going to come, Jack,' she blurted out.

'The heavens be praised!'

If she'd thought her first climax was fabulous, this one was beyond that. It wasn't a shattering apart so much as a coming together. They cried out together, shuddered together, then found peace together, wrapped in each other's arms.

This was what making love should always be like, Lisa thought rapturously.

Her yawn came out of the blue.

'Time for a little nap, perhaps,' Jack said softly, easing himself out of her and pulling a sheet up over her shoulders.

'But I don't want to sleep,' she protested, even as she yawned again.

'Don't worry. I won't let you sleep for long.'

CHAPTER THIRTEEN

JACK watched her go to sleep, waiting till her eyelids stopped fluttering and her breathing was deep before he left her to go to the bathroom.

He just stood there, staring in the mirror, having a silent conversation with himself.

She's a very special girl, Jack. Don't you hurt her.

Of course I won't. I'll be good to her. And for her. She needed liberating from the prison of her imagined frigidity. She needs a man who can make her relax and have some fun for a change. But most of all, she needs a lot of great sex!

Jack's next mission was to show her that making love did not always have to take place in the bedroom.

But first, he'd let her sleep for a while. He might even have a reviving nap himself. Make sure he was on top of his game for the next round.

Lisa stirred to the lightest touch on her shoulder.

For a split-second, she thought it was Cory, waking her after having a bad dream. But it wasn't her son leaning over her. It was Jack.

He was sitting on the side of the bed and smiling down at her.

'Feeling refreshed?' he asked.

'What…what time is it?'

'Two-ish. You've been asleep for a couple of hours.'

'Oh,' Lisa said weakly as a whole rush of memories and emotions bombarded her.

There was still amazement over what had happened. But more than a dampening suspicion that her champagne consumption during dinner *had* played a role in making her more receptive to Jack's lovemaking. A dull thudding in her temples indicated a hangover. Even worse was the shame that she'd been so easy to seduce, after all she'd said to him.

Her only solace was that she was at his place, and not her own.

At least Cory wasn't around to witness his mother's downfall.

'Oh, no,' Jack said, wagging his finger at her. 'There'll be none of that.'

'None of what?'

'Regrets and recriminations.'

'But I *was* drunk, Jack,' she insisted, clutching the sheet up over her breasts. 'I have a splitting headache to prove it.' It was an exaggeration, she knew. But she had to find some excuse for her behaviour.

'You were not drunk. Not by the time we arrived here.'

'Then why have I got a hangover?'

'Sex can sometimes give people headaches. It's the rise in blood pressure, then the sudden relaxing. I have some painkillers in the bathroom. Stay where you are. I'll get you some.'

It wasn't till he rose from the bed and began striding over to the bathroom that she realised he was still as naked as she was.

She stared at his bare bottom, shocked by the red scratch marks on his untanned buttocks.

Did I do that?

I must have.

It was a startling realisation, evidence of a wild passion which was already becoming a hazy memory. So were her climaxes. Had they really been so mind-blowing?

Jack wasn't gone more than thirty seconds, returning with a glass of water and two tablets in his hand.

Not that she overly noticed either till he practically shoved them in her face. She'd been staring at his naked front this time. Didn't he get embarrassed, walking around like that?

'Here,' he said.

Taking the glass and tablets from him forced Lisa to drop the sheet which she'd been holding over her breasts. Their sudden exposure—along with Jack's staring down at them—made her squirm inside.

'I...I need to go to the bathroom,' she said after gulping down the tablets.

He shrugged. 'Be my guest.'

'I...I haven't got a robe.'

'You don't need one. The bathroom's just over there.'

There was a note of challenge in his voice. A kind of dare in his eyes.

Steeling herself, Lisa threw back the sheet and

swung her feet over the side of the bed. Really, it was ridiculous for her to feel so embarrassed. He'd seen more of her, after all.

But this was different somehow. Yet still strangely exciting, she had to admit. To have him watch her walk, naked, across the room. To feel his eyes following her every move.

And her knowing all the while how much he wanted her.

Was that what was making her skin flush and her heart race like mad? Her awareness of *his* desire?

Or was it her own?

Lisa shook her head as she washed her hands afterwards. What to do? Demand that he take her home? Or let him do whatever he wanted to do to her?

When she glanced up into the vanity mirror, her brilliant blue eyes showed her that there really wasn't any contest. She could not leave just yet. She had to know what more there was.

Returning to the bedroom took more courage than leaving it.

Finding it empty came as a shock. Where had Jack gone to?

When he didn't come back after a couple of minutes, Lisa had no option but to go in search of him. But not in the nude, she decided. She wasn't that brave. Or that bold.

Her clothes, however, were not on the floor where he'd dropped them before. And there was no sign of a robe anywhere. Clearly, Jack didn't wear one.

In the end she wrapped a bath-sheet around herself and padded in her bare feet down the hallway, popping her head into his study on the way. Not there. But brother, he was right. That room was seriously messy.

He wasn't in the living room, either. She found him in the kitchen, brewing coffee and making toasted sandwiches.

His having donned some black satin boxer shorts was a huge relief.

'Feeling better?' he asked with a quick smile her way.

'A bit. What happened to my dress and underwear?'

'Your dress is hanging up in my walk-in closet and your panties are currently in the washing machine. I'll pop them in the dryer shortly.'

'Oh. Thank you, but you didn't have to.'

'I thought you might enjoy someone looking after you for a change.'

Lisa didn't know what to say to that. No one had ever looked after her. She'd pretty well looked after herself when she was growing up. Plus all the time during her marriage to Greg. She'd worn the trousers in the family, right from the start. Which was the way she'd liked it. But she'd worked hard for the privilege of being the boss, doing all of the housework, controlling the money, paying all the bills.

Then, after Greg died, and she'd really been on her own, she'd had to do absolutely everything herself, even the garden. Nowadays, she paid a man to mow her lawns, but she hadn't been able to afford that at first. She'd bogged in and done it all herself, even learning how to change light bulbs and washers, jobs she'd used to delegate to Greg.

Jack smiled over at her again. 'Why don't you let your hair down?'

'What?'

'Your hair. It's come loose at the back. Here, let me do it for you.'

His moving behind her was unnerving, so were his hands in her hair. She held herself stiffly whilst he removed the hidden pins then stroked her hair down to her shoulders.

When he bent to kiss her on the shoulder, she froze some more.

'Relax,' he murmured. 'I won't bite.'

'Then stop acting like the big bad wolf,' she shot back at him.

He laughed, but moved back to what he'd been doing at the kitchen counter, leaving her annoyed with herself for being silly. She'd decided to stay, hadn't she? Why start snapping at him?

'I'm sorry, Jack,' she said, climbing up onto one of the leather-topped stools which faced the huge breakfast bar. 'That was uncalled-for.'

'No, no,' he said, grinning over at her. 'You were quite right. I *was* acting like the big bad wolf. In truth, I'd like to gobble you up right here and now. But I can wait. Hope you like melted cheese on your toast.'

'I'm not fussy,' she said, and he laughed.

'Now, that's a big fib, Miss Prissy. But I'll forgive you if you take that towel off while we eat.'

Lisa gaped at him. 'You want me to sit and eat in the nude?'

'I'm game if you're game,' he said and, pushing the

black boxer shorts down to the floor, he stepped out of them and kicked them away.

Lisa's mouth dropped further open before snapping shut. 'Why do I suspect you've done things like this before?'

'Never! Not here, anyway. I haven't brought a single woman back to this place since I bought it. I've been celibate for weeks and weeks, finishing that infernal book.'

Lisa thrilled to the thought he hadn't slept with any other woman recently. Though perhaps that was why he was pursuing her so avidly. He was seriously frustrated.

'Well?' Jack prompted, walking over to the breakfast bar with two plates of toasted sandwiches in his hands. 'I'm waiting.'

'I can't, Jack.'

'Don't be ridiculous. I won't even be able to see all of you from here. Just your top half. You're not shy about showing off your very pretty breasts, are you?'

She was suddenly shy about showing anything!

Yet she wanted to. That was the weirdest thing with Jack. He could make her want to do things that she found embarrassing.

'But you'll *know* I'm totally naked,' she protested.

'That's the point, Lisa. My *knowing*. It's a turn-on.'

'But you don't need turning on.'

'I wasn't talking about me, beautiful.'

'Oh…'

'Just do it,' he said. 'And see for yourself.'

Her heart started hammering behind her ribs even

before her hand moved to do his bidding. By the time she'd removed the towel and draped it over the stool next to her, Lisa was feeling light-headed. And hot. When Jack placed her plate and mug in front of her, she just stared blankly down at them, then up at him.

'I...I don't think I'm hungry,' she said quietly.

'You should eat something. And drink the coffee. I don't want you fainting on me.'

'I never faint.'

'There's a first time for everything.'

Yes, Lisa thought shakily. And tonight she'd experienced a lot of firsts.

If only her mother could see her now...

Thinking of her mother brought Lisa up with a jolt.

Jill Chapman had had quite a few lovers after her husband had left her, Lisa hating the times she'd come home from school to find the evidence of her mother's affairs. The extra-wet towel in the bathroom. The smell of sex in the house. Her mother's smudged lipstick and lack of underwear.

Lisa had always prided herself on being nothing like her mother in that regard.

Yet here she was, sitting naked in Jack Cassidy's kitchen, totally breathless and shockingly aroused.

The whole scenario seemed unbelievable.

'You're doing it again,' Jack growled, moving his coffee away from his lips.

'Doing what?'

'Thinking.'

'There's nothing wrong with thinking.'

'There is when *you* do it.'

'I think I should go home,' she suddenly blurted out.

His eyes darkened as he slowly lowered his coffee back down to the marble counter. 'Is that what you really want to do?'

'Yes… No… I don't know! And I don't *like* not knowing, Jack,' she cried in dismay. 'I don't like being out of control.'

He grimaced, then shook his head. 'Maybe I've gone too fast. Maybe we should leave things as they are till another day.'

Lisa blinked. 'Another day?'

His eyes were as uncompromising as the set of his mouth. 'You don't honestly think tonight is the end of us, do you?'

'Well, I…I know I promised to clean your study on Tuesday.'

'That's not what I mean and you know it.'

'But you're not into relationships,' she argued. 'I mean…you said as much up front.'

'I said I didn't want to get married. But that doesn't stop me having a girlfriend. I want you to be my girlfriend, Lisa. I want to take you places. Buy you things. Spoil you rotten.'

She just stared at him. Oh, but he was wicked.

'I *can't* be your girlfriend,' she threw at him. 'I mean…I don't *want* to be your girlfriend.'

His head jerked back as if she'd slapped him in the face. 'Might I ask why not?'

'Because I don't have the time!'

'That's bulldust. You have lots of time. You're your own boss. Tell me the truth.'

'All right. It will complicate things.'

'In what way?'

'Cory is my first priority in life. I refuse to do anything which will jeopardise his happiness.'

'How will your being my girlfriend jeopardise your son's happiness? I won't interfere in his upbringing and I'll be good to him. I'll take him places too, and buy him things. Things all boys like.'

Now he was being even more wicked. Trying to seduce her through her son. But he'd made a mistake, thinking his materialistic offer would sway her.

'That's exactly what I'm talking about. Cory will start thinking how wonderful you are. You're his kind of man, Jack. Then one day, you'll say, *Sorry, Lisa, but I'm getting bored playing father*. And that will be that. And Cory will be broken-hearted all over again. It was tough enough for him losing his dad. And he wasn't all that old then. He's nine now. He can be really hurt this time.'

'In that case, we'll keep Cory out of our relationship.'

Lisa shook her head. 'How? I have no intention of leaving Cory alone, or shipping him round to neighbours to mind. I'd have to tell my mother about us and…'

'And what's wrong with that?' Jack broke in, his face becoming more frustrated with each second.

'You don't understand!' she cried.

'No, I don't.' His hands lifted to rake agitatedly through his hair. 'We're having our first fight and we're not even going together yet. Look, why don't we just stop this and go back to bed? We get along in bed. Very nicely.'

She just stared at him, her head whirling. He wasn't going to let her say no to him again. She could see that.

'If that doesn't appeal,' he went on with a very sexy smile, 'we could go skinny-dipping in the pool and make leisurely love in the water.'

Lisa swallowed at this last thought. She'd never made love in water. Or anywhere other than in a bed.

The idea was both tantalising and tempting, exactly as Jack knew it would be. He was the devil in disguise, she decided. An accomplished seducer of women, especially silly, inexperienced women like herself.

'You choose,' Jack said, any talk of taking her home apparently overridden and forgotten.

The pool room, Lisa knew from having cleaned it, was like a decadent Roman bath-house. The walls of the room were covered in black marble tiles, the surrounds of the pool and spa in white, and the pool itself in a deep blue.

When she didn't say anything, he strode round and scooped her up off the stool.

'Don't you ever know what's good for you?' he growled as he carried her, not back to the bedroom but in the direction of the pool.

Yes, she thought with despairing insight. And it's not you, Jack Cassidy. You're a dangerous man to be with. A ruthless, charming, cold-blooded womaniser. I know you. I've read all your books. You're not the devil in disguise. You're Hal Hunter in disguise.

That man eats women for breakfast and spits them out.

But at the same time, you're the first man to make me feel like this. I can't turn my back on what you have to offer. I just can't.

But I'm going to do my level best to keep my head.
I am *not* going to fall in love with you, Jack Cassidy.
Absolutely and positively not!

CHAPTER FOURTEEN

'I NEVER thought I'd see you without make-up,' was her mother's first comment when Lisa arrived at her place the following day. 'Or without blow-drying your hair.'

Lisa's hands lifted to run through her hair, still damp from the second shower she'd had after Jack drove her home, and after she'd made a hurried call to her mother, saying she'd be right out. Lisa hadn't had the time—or the inclination—for hair and make-up. Her head was too full of other things.

'I was too tired to bother,' she said distractedly. 'I guess I look a mess.'

'Not at all. You look lovely. Still, you must have had a really good time to stay out so late. Come on, come inside. I want to hear every single detail.'

Lisa rolled her eyes as she followed her mother into the house. She had no intention of telling her mother any such thing.

Not because her mother would be scandalised. But because she would ask Lisa awkward questions which she had no answers for.

Never had Lisa felt so confused, or so rattled. Her life had suddenly spun out of control—as had she—and she didn't know where it would all end.

The only surety in her mind was that her affair with Jack was a long way from being over. Overnight, she'd turned into a sex maniac, totally obsessed by the man and what she felt when she was with him.

It had taken every bit of will-power she had not to agree to race over to Jack's place after dropping Cory off at school tomorrow morning. He'd certainly pressed her to do just that when he drove her home today.

She'd sounded surprisingly cool and matter-of-fact as she'd pointed out that she had a business to run and Monday was her busiest day in her office.

At the time, Lisa had felt quite proud of her resolve not to be at Jack's total beck and call. Because she knew she could have made time to meet him on the Monday afternoon. But the moment he drove away, she'd been consumed with instant regret, plus an awful, empty feeling.

It swamped her again, bringing a sigh to her lips.

Her mother threw her a questioning glance over her shoulder. 'You sound like you could do with a strong cup of coffee.'

'I'd love one,' Lisa replied with a grateful smile. She'd refused Jack's offer of brunch this morning, anxious to get home after sleeping in terribly late.

When she pulled out a chair to sit down at her mother's large kitchen table, Lisa's mind suddenly shot back to when she'd sat at Jack's breakfast bar last night, in the nude.

She'd never felt so shamed—yet so excited—in her life.

Her mother turned from where she was making the coffee at the nearby bench. 'By the way, Cory's over at the neighbours' place, if you were wondering. They have their grandkids up for the weekend. One of them's a boy of twelve and very responsible, so you don't have to worry.'

Guilt consumed Lisa when she realised she hadn't been wondering. Or worrying. Cory seemed to have taken a back-seat in her thoughts all of a sudden. Now, that was truly shameful! And not to be tolerated. Her son was the most important person in her life. She would not let a playboy like Jack Cassidy supplant him in either her thoughts, or her heart.

'Has he been a good boy?' she asked, trying desperately to revert to the caring, over-protective mother she usually was.

'He's been a typical boy, Lisa. Boys are rarely good all the time. But who would want that? Nothing worse than a goody-two-shoes boy. They grow up into wimpy, wishy-washy men. By the way, he says he wants to be a soldier when he grows up.'

'A soldier! I thought he wanted to become a doctor!'

'Not since he saw a movie on TV last night about commandos.'

'Mum, you haven't been letting him watch violence, have you?'

Her mother looked sheepish. 'Only the bad guys got killed.'

'You know I don't approve of violence in movies.'

'Well, at least there wasn't any sex,' her mother said defensively. 'I know you don't like him watching sex in movies. But then, neither do you,' she added with that look she always gave Lisa whenever sex was mentioned. As if she was a prude.

If only she knew, Lisa thought, several images flashing into her mind from the night before. The episode in the spa had been pretty incredible, but didn't compare with their raunchy encounter on the terrace, with her gripping the railing and Jack behind her.

Lisa's mouth dried just thinking about how *that* had felt.

'I don't mind a bit of sex in movies,' she said. 'Just not over-the-top stuff.'

You little hypocrite, came that brutally honest voice which kept popping into her head. But…remember that movie where they had sex on the kitchen sink? You haven't tried that yet. Or in the shower. People were always doing it in the shower in movies.

There was no doubt water felt very erotic, when you didn't have any clothes on.

'So what time did you get to bed?' her mother asked as she carried two steaming mugs of coffee over to the table.

'I'm not sure. Two-ish, maybe?' She just hadn't gone to sleep.

'I did try to call you around eleven this morning to ask if it was OK for Cory to go next door, but you didn't answer.'

'I was still sound asleep,' she replied quite truthfully.

'But your phone is right next to your bed.'

'I didn't sleep there. I crashed on the lounge downstairs.'

'Sounds like you had too much to drink.'

'The champagne was free.' And flowing right down her throat at a rate of knots.

'Lucky you. Was your boyfriend there?'

'Who? Oh, you mean Nick Freeman.'

'Yep. Nick Freeman. Did he win an award?'

'Yes. The Golden Gun award. For best thriller of the year. And you were right. That's not his real name. His real name is Jack Cassidy.' Lord, how cool she sounded. Was this what getting tangled up with a wicked man did to you? Made you into an actress as well as a nymphomaniac?

'Jack. Yes, that sounds right. That's a good name for a man of action. Is he good-looking?'

'Tall, dark and handsome. Though on the macho side. He's no pretty boy.'

'Sounds yummy. How old?'

'Mid-to-late thirties.'

'Girlfriend?'

'He came with a blonde.'

'Typical. Hal likes blondes.'

Lisa didn't like being reminded of that. Or how much Jack was like Hal.

Her mother sighed, rather like Jack's fans had last night.

'I'll definitely have to read all those books again one day,' she said. 'But not just yet. They're too fresh in my mind. Did you read any of *The Scales of Justice* yesterday?'

'No. I didn't get the time. But I will. I'd like to read the whole series again, too. Could you get the rest of them for me while I'm here?'

'Sure thing.'

'Are you going to read *all* those books, Mum?' Cory asked on the way home.

'Yes, Cory, I am.'

'But when? You never have time to do anything I want to do.'

Lisa rolled her eyes. Children. They always threw things back at you. 'I read when I go to bed at night, *after* you go to sleep.'

'I hate going to sleep,' Cory grumbled. 'You make me go to bed too early. I don't have to go to bed that early at Grandma's. We watched this beaut movie last night. It was all about... Oops.'

'It's OK, Cory. Mum told me all about it.'

Cory's big blue eyes grew into saucers. 'She *told* you? But she said she'd get into big trouble if you ever found out. Did you go mad on her?'

'Not really, Cory. But you know I don't like you watching violent movies.'

'It wasn't really violent, Mum. It was great. The hero was great. I'm going to be a soldier just like him when I grow up. Jason and I played soldiers today. Can I go back to Grandma's next weekend, Mum? She said I could. Jason's coming up from Sydney again and he wants me to come over and play with him.'

Was fate being kind? Or cruel?

'Please, Mum,' Cory begged.

'If you're a good boy,' she replied, trying to keep her excitement in check. 'And go to bed when I tell you to.'

'I promise, Mum. And I'll clean my teeth without you asking.'

'Now, that would be a first! OK, if you go to bed without whinging and clean your teeth without my telling you, then you can go to Grandma's next weekend.'

'Oh, wow! Wait till I tell Grandma.'

For the first time, Lisa didn't feel jealous over her son's obvious delight at spending more time at his grandma's. She was already thinking how this would leave her totally free to be with Jack again, for the whole weekend, without having to worry about Cory. She could leave her mother's hat off for a while and just be…what, exactly?

A budding nymphomaniac? Or just a girl who'd discovered her sexuality a little late in life and wanted to experience all she'd missed out on?

A third answer jumped into Lisa's mind, one which made her stomach turn over.

Maybe she was simply acting like a female who had finally fallen—not into lust—but in love. Maybe this sexually driven woman she'd become had nothing to do with hormones, but her heart.

Lisa felt sick at the thought she might have fallen in love with Jack. What a total waste of time that would be!

Still, she supposed being in love with the man was more acceptable than being a sex addict.

'Mum,' Cory suddenly piped up, 'you've gone past our street again.'

Lisa groaned. 'Sorry, love.'

'No worries.'

When she pulled into the kerb and waited for the traffic to clear, Cory smiled over at her.

'You look very pretty today, Mum.'

'Do I?' She didn't think so. But everyone was saying it. Jack. Her mother. And now her son.

'Yeah. You look great.'

'Thank you, Cory,' Lisa said, flushing with pleasure.

'When I grow up, I'm going to marry a girl just like you.'

Tears suddenly pricked at Lisa's eyes. It was the nicest thing her son had ever said to her.

'Mum, you're crying!' Cory exclaimed, looking shocked.

'Of course I'm not!' she denied as she dashed the tears away. 'I just had something in my eye.'

Cory looked unconvinced, and remained very quiet during the short drive home.

'I'm going to go upstairs and get ready for my bath,' he offered as soon as they were inside the door.

'What a good idea,' Lisa said with a weary sigh.

All of a sudden she felt very tired. And very fragile.

Hopefully, she would sleep well tonight. And hopefully, in the morning, she would find some much needed strength of character.

CHAPTER FIFTEEN

LISA found she could not go to sleep. Her mind would not relax, along with her body. In the end she sat up in bed, rereading *The Scales of Justice*, and trying to work out just how much of Hal Hunter was Jack in disguise.

Hal's parents were killed tragically, as Jack's had been, but not in a road accident. In a terrorist attack at a foreign holiday resort. Hal grew up obsessed with the idea of justice, but also revenge. He resolved never to feel as powerless as he did on the day his parents were killed, virtually in front of his fourteen-year-old eyes.

That was obviously how Jack had felt when his parents were killed, and when the man responsible didn't get the punishment he deserved. Jack couldn't do much about the situation at the time without breaking the law. But Lisa imagined he gained great satisfaction in giving his fictional male protagonist the ways and means to wreak havoc and revenge on all bad guys.

In the first book, Hal used his inherited fortune to learn everything he needed to know to become a successful one-man vigilante. The teenage Hal was already physically strong and mentally brilliant, but he developed those qualities further with hard work. He increased his wealth with clever investments and cultivated powerful friends, some good, some not so good. Politicians, as well as media magnates and takeover tycoons. He bought an international-news bureau so that he could find out exactly what was going on, anywhere in the world.

And all the while he was searching for the leader of the terrorist group who had claimed responsibility for the killing of his parents and a couple of hundred other innocent people.

Lisa knew from having read the book before that Hal finally found the leader, and killed him. Hal also seduced and then executed a female member of the terrorist gang, *after* finding out an address he needed.

Hal's ruthlessness where women were concerned had permeated the whole series so far, as had his abilities in the bedroom. He would use his sexual skills to find out information, and to exact revenge. He would often sleep with the mistresses and wives of bad guys, not turning a hair when some of these women fell in love with him. He never fell in love himself and never stayed with a woman for long.

Lisa was wondering how long *she* was going to last when the phone beside her bed rang.

For a second she hesitated, worried it might be Jack. She really didn't want to talk to Jack tonight. At the same time, she didn't want the rather loud ring waking Cory up. He was in the bedroom next to hers, after all.

Grimacing, she snatched up the receiver. 'Hello?' Her tone was quite short.

'Hi, Lisa. It's Gail. Sorry to bother you on your home phone on a Sunday night but I thought I should speak to you personally.'

'Oh? What's up? Your ankle not healing well?

'No. It's a lot better. But I still won't be able to clean Jack Cassidy's place next Friday. Or any other Friday, for that matter.'

'Why? What else has happened?'

'Nothing terrible. Phil's got himself a new job. The pay's very good and he said if I didn't want to, I wouldn't have to do cleaning any more. To be honest, Lisa, I hate cleaning. It's enough to do my own place. So I won't be back. I'm sorry. You've been very good to me and I don't like to let you down. But you should be able to find someone else before Friday.'

'Don't worry, Gail,' she said. 'Everything will be fine. And I'm pleased about your husband's job. You deserve a change of luck. If you ever want to come back, just give me a call.'

Gail laughed. 'I won't be doing that. Not unless Phil gets laid off again. Look, I'll probably see you up at the school tomorrow, but I thought I should let you know straight away. I did try and ring you last night, and again this morning, but there wasn't any answer.'

'I was out.' Plus she'd forgotten to put her answering machine on. Ever since Jack had come into her life she'd been in a spin.

'You know, you should marry again, Lisa,' came the unexpected word of advice from Gail.

The wave of dismay which suddenly washed through Lisa made her want to groan.

Because she knew what it meant. She was definitely falling in love with Jack. No use pretending—or hoping—that what she was suffering from was just lust.

Let's face it, Lisa, why else would you be devouring his books again, looking for answers to his complex and unusual persona? And why, most telling of all, would Gail's advice to marry again leave you feeling so suddenly bereft?

Because Jack will never marry you, that's why. All he wants from you is some company at best, along with lots of sex.

How perverse, Lisa thought, that her own discovering the pleasures of the flesh would come with the promise of future misery.

Her own.

'I don't think that'll ever happen, Gail,' she said a bit sharply. 'I'll see you tomorrow. Bye.'

She hung up just in time before tears flooded her eyes. Sighing, she jumped off the bed and hurried into her small *en suite* bathroom, snatching some tissues from the box on the vanity unit and blowing her nose furiously.

The sight of her distressed face in the mirror brought total exasperation with herself.

What's happening to me? I never cry. Now I've done it twice today. All because of that infernal man. I wish I'd never met him. Wish I'd never read his rotten books. I'll bet he's not sitting around his penthouse, blubbering like some baby. Or even giving me a second thought. He's probably sitting at his computer, thinking up more ruthless adventures for his cold-blooded alter ego. *And* giving him more silly women to seduce.

Blondes, of course!

As Lisa marched back to bed and snatched up *The Scales of Justice* once more, Jack was indeed sitting at his computer, attempting to start a new book. He still had one book to deliver on his present contract, a year from today. Which seemed a long time ahead. But Jack knew from experience that if he took too long a break from writing, he found it hard to get back into it.

Yet he hadn't typed a single word after 'CHAPTER ONE'.

Jack had writer's block as he'd never had it before.

'It's all that impossible woman's fault!' he declared, slamming his hands down hard on his desk and levering himself upright.

Why couldn't she be like other women he'd known? he thought irritably as he headed for the bar in the living room. Just when he thought she was putty in his hands, Lisa had pulled back and gone all ice princess on him again.

Jack knew she could have found time for him tomorrow. Even worse was his conviction that she *wanted* to be with him.

But no. The cold light of morning had brought with it a return to the old uptight Lisa. The passionate girl who'd thrilled to his making wild love to her on the terrace in the moonlight had been locked away again, not to be released till she decided it was the right time.

Lisa obviously had an obsession with control. Losing it frightened her.

Yet when she did…

Jack's body leapt at the memory of how she'd lost it last night. Not once, but several times. He loved seeing that glazed look in her eyes, and feeling her body tighten as it did just before she came.

He'd become addicted to making her come. Addicted to how she was with him afterwards, so soft and sweet and utterly his.

He hadn't liked it when she wouldn't go along with what he wanted today.

Not that he'd shown his displeasure. Jack knew that wasn't the way to win a woman like Lisa over. He'd pretended to go along with what she wanted, despite feeling quite desperate to make love to her again. In truth, Jack had found keeping his hands off her this morning a real struggle. Having her in his arms had become more than a need. It was now an obsession, with his increasingly demanding desires in danger of running amok.

From the moment he'd dropped her off at her house, Jack had begun working on a strategy to undermine Lisa's obvious resolve to keep a rein on her own desires.

Which was probably why he couldn't put his mind to thinking up a new plot. The plotting area of his brain was already in use, though not too successfully as yet.

A large Scotch might help, Jack decided as he picked up a fresh bottle of whisky, unscrewed the cap and filled half a glass. To that he added some ice from the bar fridge and carried it down to his home theatre.

Picking up the remote, he settled into the large leather sofa and switched on the TV, flicking through the selection of movies available, choosing a romantic comedy about a pair of mismatched lovers who finally got it together.

'With a bit of luck,' Jack muttered between deep swallows of whisky, 'it might give me some ideas.'

CHAPTER SIXTEEN

LISA sighed, then glanced at the small silver clock she kept on top of her computer. Only eleven.

The morning had seemed endless; she had been constantly tempted by the thought of being with Jack, a much more exciting prospect than doing the same tedious things she always did every Monday morning: take down all the messages on the answering machine and attend to them; update the files and rearrange any of the rosters which had to be rearranged; answer all the emails which had come in through her website; ring any potential clients who had left numbers...

She'd made it sound to Jack as if she'd be flat-out all day. But in truth, she was already on top of everything. She could easily drive out to his place after lunch. Or even before lunch.

He could have *her* for lunch.

Lisa's stomach crunched down hard at the memory of how he'd done that to her by the pool. Spread her out on the tiles and feasted on her till she'd come several times. He seemed to really like doing that to her. And she couldn't get enough of it. She groaned at the thought of him doing that to her right now. Making her forget everything but the pleasure of his tongue sliding over her, and into her...

Lisa shuddered, stunned that she was so turned on just thinking about it.

How easy it would be to ring him and tell him she was on her way over.

Easy, but pathetically weak.

Lisa didn't want Jack to see her as one of those women who came running whenever he snapped his fingers.

Which she could very well become.

Bad enough she was going to his place tomorrow on the pretext of cleaning his study. She knew very well there wouldn't be much cleaning done. And what about Friday? She'd be back there again, on Friday, once again with the excuse of cleaning his place.

Because no way was she going to let some other woman near him. Most of her cleaners were fairly young and some quite attractive. And sex mad, in her opinion.

A bit like you, came that brutally honest voice.

Her front doorbell ringing startled Lisa.

'Oh, lord!' she groaned, jumping up from her desk. 'Please don't let it be Jack.' Not whilst she was hopelessly turned on.

Running from the office, Lisa bolted along the hallway to the upstairs landing, where there was a window overlooking the street below.

The sight of a white van parked outside her house, and not Jack's black Porsche, brought relief and disappointment, Lisa's mixed emotions indicative of her torn frame of mind.

As she made her way more slowly downstairs, she wondered who it could possibly be. A lost tradesman perhaps?

No. Someone selling something more likely.

It was a young woman, holding the most glorious arrangement of red roses.

'Lisa Chapman?' she asked briskly.

'Yes. That's me.'

'Lucky you,' she said with a knowing smile as she handed her the flowers. 'There's a note attached,' she pointed out. 'Have a nice day.'

Lisa stared at the roses as she carried them inside, knowing before she glanced at the note who they were from. Her hands were shaking by the time she placed them in the middle of her dining table and detached the note.

'For a very special lady,' she read. 'Jack.'

Lisa's eyes immediately moistened.

She could not remember the last time she'd received flowers.

'Oh, Jack,' she cried softly as she lifted one of the red roses to her mouth, rubbing the dark, velvety petals back and forth across her lips. 'If only you knew how much I want to just say yes to anything you ask of me.'

Lisa was in danger of succumbing to tears again when her phone rang. She pulled a face, then pulled herself together. Her mother, no doubt. Not a day went by without her mother ringing her at some stage.

Poking the rose back into the arrangement, Lisa

walked back into the family room, where there was an extension on the kitchen bench. Scooping in a gathering breath, she picked up the receiver.

'Hello?'

'Did the flowers come?'

Lisa's heart stopped momentarily before lurching back into a quickened beat.

'Jack,' she said a bit breathlessly.

'The one and only. And the flowers?'

'They…they just arrived.'

'And?'

'They're beautiful.'

'Red roses, I hope. I ordered them over the phone first thing this morning. When I told the florist I wanted two dozen red roses delivered within two hours she said she couldn't promise. But she'd try.'

'They're here and they're exquisite,' Lisa said. 'But horribly expensive, I would imagine. Really, Jack, you shouldn't have.'

'I told you I wanted to spoil you rotten.'

Impossible not to feel ridiculously pleased. And flattered.

'I'll have to hide them, you know. I can't let Cory see them. Or my mother. She drops in sometimes. Unexpectedly.'

'I didn't send you roses for you to hide them, Lisa,' he said with exasperation in his voice. 'Why don't you say they're from a grateful client? It's close to the truth.'

'Two dozen red roses? You think my mother would believe that?'

'Truly, you're a difficult woman. OK, but I refuse to let you hide them. Bring them with you when you come tomorrow and we'll put them to good use.'

'What on earth are you talking about?' Lisa asked, perplexed.

'That's for me to know and you to find out.'

'Might I remind you that I'm supposed to be cleaning your study tomorrow,' she said archly, even whilst her body thrilled to the thought of him doing erotic things to her with the roses.

'And so you shall. You can even wear that adorable apron of yours. The one with the bib and the tie round the back. Though, of course, nothing else. Except perfume and shoes. Yes, high heels would look good. Stilettos, with open toes. And you should paint your toenails and mouth red. A deep red, like the roses.'

Lisa was horrified by the picture he was painting of her.

Horrified, but horribly excited.

'You don't honestly expect me to do all that, do you?'

'Expect? No. But a man can hope…'

'You're a wicked man, Jack Cassidy.'

'Not wicked, Lisa. Infatuated. With you.'

'Oh…'

'You took my breath away at the weekend, do you know that? I can't stop thinking about you. I want you every single minute of the day. I'm going insane with wanting you. I tried to write today but I couldn't. Because my mind is too full of you.'

'Please don't talk to me like this,' she begged, her head whirling with the wild passion in his voice.

'Why not? Why shouldn't I tell you how much I want you?'

'Because…'

'Because you want me the same way, don't you?'

'I…I…'

'I know you find it hard to admit. It's all too new. I could sense that in you yesterday. You wanted to run away from your feelings. You're scared. But you needn't be. I won't hurt you, Lisa. I promise.'

'Promises are just words, Jack. And words come cheap.'

'Not with me,' he ground out. 'My word is my bond. I never go back on my word.'

'Then promise me that you won't try to turn me into some mindless plaything with no will of my own.'

'Is that what you think I'm trying to do?'

'It's what I *know* you're trying to do. Why else would you suggest my cleaning your place in just an apron and stilettos? If you truly like me and respect me, it should be enough that I'm there, with you. You shouldn't need to dress me up like some whore.'

The sudden silence from the other end of the line brought a degree of panic. She'd done it now.

'I…I'm sorry, Jack,' she choked out. 'But that's how it sounded to me.'

'No, no, you're right. I keep forgetting that you're different.'

'Different from what?' she snapped. 'From your usual lay? I suppose you think I'm pretty boring.'

'I think you're very special. And not boring at all. But you are still slightly uptight about sex. Making love can be fun. It doesn't always have to be deadly serious. Dressing up is just a game, Lisa. I'm sorry you took offence at it.'

'No, no. I'm the one who's sorry. You're right. And yes, I am afraid. I'd really like to dress up like that for you, Jack. But I...I just don't have the confidence. Or the courage.'

'You have more courage than any girl I've ever met,' he said with flattering fierceness.

Lisa let out a long, shuddering sigh of surrender. 'You're too strong for me.'

'What do you mean by that?'

'Nothing. Everything. Please let me go now. I...I'll see you tomorrow.'

'What time tomorrow?'

'I'll come as soon as I've dropped Cory off at school.'

'I'm already counting down the hours. Take care, Lisa.'

'And you,' she replied, though a bit stiffly.

He hung up before her, Lisa staring into the dead phone for several seconds.

Slowly, and with a worried frown on her face, she shook her head from side to side. He *was* way too strong for her. Sexually, she was already his, till he decided otherwise. Which he would, one day. Men like Jack didn't stay loyal forever.

All she could do was keep him out of her son's life till that day came.

That part I *can* control, Lisa vowed fiercely.

And I will!

CHAPTER SEVENTEEN

'YOU didn't bring the roses,' was the first thing Jack said when he let her in the following morning.

Lisa swallowed as she gazed up into his eyes. She'd forgotten how good-looking he was. And how big.

He looked even bigger in the loose white trousers and sleeveless black T-shirt he was wearing, clothes which showed off the wearer's tan. And muscles, if he had them.

Jack had them. Oodles of them.

Despite his casual dress and bare feet, he had shaved that morning, she noted. And was wearing cologne, a sandalwood scent which she liked.

'I forgot them,' she replied.

A lie, of course. But how could she possibly put two dozen red roses in the car with her whilst she'd taken Cory to school? He'd have asked her about them. As it was, she'd had to hide them at the back of a high shelf in her walk-in wardrobe before he came home from school yesterday.

Lisa supposed she could have gone back home after dropping Cory off to get them, but she'd wanted to drive straight on here.

She hadn't, however, forgotten the apron. Or the high heels. White, they were. Backless, with open toes. She was wearing them, along with the same white Capri pants and brown singlet top she'd worn last Friday. She was also wearing her sexiest underwear, a cream satin half-cup bra and matching thong which she'd bought at a lingerie sale not long back and never worn.

Lisa had drawn the line at the red nails and lipstick, however, opting instead for a nice bronze colour.

'You've put your hair up again,' Jack said disapprovingly.

'I always put it up when I'm cleaning,' she told him.

His dark brows beetled together in a frustrated frown. 'Come with me.'

He grabbed her hand and pulled her down the hallway to the study door, which was open.

'Oh!' she exclaimed, once she'd looked into the room. 'It's all clean.' Not just clean but also perfectly tidy, with not a scrap of paper on his desk, or a book out of place on the shelves.

'I did it yesterday after our phone call.'

She turned and looked up into his eyes, her own carrying confusion. 'But why, Jack?' She'd spent all night screwing up the courage to clean his study wearing nothing but her apron, thinking that was what he wanted of her.

'Because I decided I didn't want you to spend one second whilst you were with me doing anything other than you making love to me.'

Lisa's relief was short-lived. 'Did you say *me* making love to *you*?'

'Absolutely.'

'But...but I won't know what to do!'

'You're a well-read girl, Lisa. You *do* know what to do.'

So it had come to that already.

Lisa tried to swallow the huge lump which immediately filled her throat, without much success.

'Shall we adjourn to the bedroom?' Jack suggested.

Lisa knew immediately she couldn't do this coldly.

'Would...would you kiss me first, Jack, the way you did the other night?'

Would he kiss her?

Jack suspected, if he started kissing her, he wouldn't be able to stop. He'd thought of nothing else but being with her since Sunday. By the time she'd arrived this morning, he'd resolved not to play time-wasting games. His intention had been to make immediate love to her, then keep her in bed with him most of the day, breaking only for lunch.

Why he'd challenged her to make love to him, he had no idea. That had come right out of left-field. But the idea excited him so much that he refused to back down.

'No,' he said firmly. 'You kiss me.'

She's not ready for this, his conscience castigated him when her already vulnerable blue eyes widened appreciably.

Too late, his male ego countered. The game had begun and he was on the field, making the play and thinking excitedly of the results.

If Jack was brutally honest, he'd wanted to break down all her defences right from the start. More than anything he'd wanted to see this beautiful ice princess lose that iron control which she prized so highly, but which had never brought her any happiness.

For a long moment she just stared up at him, but then the most amazing determination entered her wide-eyed gaze. With measured movements, she lifted her hold-all from her shoulder and walked over to put it on his desk. Then she turned and walked back to where he was still standing in the doorway of his study, her eyes having gone a dark, smoky blue. Once there, she startled Jack by taking his hand and leading him towards the bedroom.

'You're too tall for me to kiss you properly, Jack,' she said on the way. 'You need to be lying down.'

How cool she sounded! How in control!

Exasperation joined his frustration. Wasn't that just so typical of her?

By the time Jack lay down on the bed, his own normally excellent control was already teetering, his flesh under fire as hot blood pumped through him at a rate of knots.

He watched her with a drying mouth as she kicked off her shoes then stretched out beside him on one elbow, leaning over him till her mouth hovered just over his.

'Don't forget this was your idea,' she said, her suddenly trembling voice betraying her underlying nerves.

She kissed him. Very lightly, her lips brushing back and forth across his.

Such a ridiculously sweet kiss, yet it made Jack moan.

Her head shot up to stare down at him with anxious eyes.

'Did I do something wrong?'

'Not that I noticed.'

She smiled a sweet smile, then frowned, as though trying to work out something. 'I...I think I want you naked,' she said at last.

Now it was his turn to stare up at her. 'Naked?'

'Yes, please.'

She was saying please.

Jack scrambled out of his clothes with indecent haste, smothering a sigh of relief at the release of his pained flesh.

'Heavens,' she said when she glanced down at him.

'More like hell,' Jack returned drily. 'Now, how about you?'

She smiled. Not a sweet smile at all this time. A siren's smile.

'All right,' she agreed, climbing off the bed and stunning Jack by starting a slow striptease. Not clumsily, either. Very sexily, lifting her top off first whilst she moved her hips sinuously to some unheard music in her head.

Her cream satin bra was utterly delicious, just covering her nipples. Jack waited with bated breath for her to remove it next, but she didn't. She let her hair down first, finger-combing it sensuously over her shoulders before she finally unhooked her bra and tossed it carelessly aside.

During his days in the army, Jack had seen quite a few stripteases. Some by skilful dancers with incredibly voluptuous bodies. But none had done for him what Lisa's simple striptease was doing. When her hands dropped to her white hipster trousers, his loudly thudding heart literally stopped in his chest. By the time she was standing in front of him wearing cream satin panties which were even more provocative than her bra, Jack's desire had reached the point of no return. How he was going to stand it when she took that last scrap of clothing off, he did not know.

With a mad mixture of pain and pleasure, he soon discovered.

There was nothing ice princess about her now. She'd become one hot babe, half closing her eyes and running her hands over her naked curves in a way which made Jack struggle to stay silent and still on that bed.

Lisa could hardly believe she was doing what she was doing. Yet she thrilled to her own boldness. Thrilled at the way Jack was looking at her. As if she was the sexiest thing on the planet.

Lisa felt more than sexy. She felt wild. And wanton.

By the time she rejoined him on the bed and kissed his mouth once more, her hands had developed a mind of their own. And an independent agenda. They weren't shy at all. Or concerned by their own lack of experience. They seemed to know exactly what to do and where to go.

Maybe Jack was right. Maybe all those sex scenes she'd read in his books had been imprinted on her memory, the well-described techniques waiting to be recalled at this precise moment.

Her left hand cupped the nape of his neck whilst her right hand roved over his body, unerring in its sense of direction, faultless in its instinctive knowledge of just what he would like. It skimmed down his chest towards his stomach, just brushing the tip of his erection before moving over to caress his hip. Very slowly, it travelled down his outer thigh before drifting across between his legs then moving upwards.

His loud groan startled her, her mouth lifting from his.

'Don't stop,' he ground out.

She loved the wild look in his eyes, and the gravelly note in his voice.

She didn't stop, her hand turning over to trail her fingernails lightly over his groin. Her hand reached then encircled the base of his erection. She kissed it, then her lips instinctively parted. Surprisingly, the feel of Jack in her mouth didn't repulse her at all. She thrilled to the unexpected discovery that she *liked* it. Liked making love to him this way.

Because that was what it was. Making love. Giving him pleasure. She could hear his pleasure in the sounds he was making.

Her mouth moved up and down in a slow, sensual rhythm, her hands loving him at the same time. She did not stop when he cried out her name. Or when his hands wound into her hair. She knew he liked this. Hal always did.

I have to stop her, Jack agonised even as his will to do so was disintegrating.

His body was rushing towards a climax. She would hate that, he worried. And so would he.

Because she would think afterwards that he'd turned her into his whore. Yet that was so far from the truth it wasn't funny. She was the woman he loved. He could finally admit it. He loved her. This wasn't just lust. This was far deeper than that.

Lust would let her go all the way. Lust wouldn't care what she felt like afterwards.

His hands were a bit brutal as he yanked her up off him. But there was no time to waste. He rolled her over in a flash and surged into her, groaning as his tortured flesh became enclosed within her deliciously excited body.

He could not possibly last, his body like an active volcano which had been rumbling for far too long. He managed one stroke of his pained flesh inside her. Then two. And then an unexpected three. Maybe, if he concentrated on something else, he could get to five.

Her coming undid him totally, and he just let go, his orgasmic cry both loud and primal, his mind uncaring then of nothing but his own physical release.

Jack did not come back to awareness for quite some time, and when he did Lisa was pushing at his shoulders. More than pushing. She was hitting him.

'Get off me,' she cried. 'Get off!'

Bewildered by her sudden attack on him, Jack stayed right where he was, grabbing her flailing hands and trying to work out why she was reacting like this.

'Stop it, Lisa,' he said, spreading her arms wide and holding her still against the bed.

'But you didn't use anything,' she threw up at him, her face twisted with distress. 'You just went ahead and did it when you knew I wasn't capable of stopping you.'

Aah, so that was the problem. His not using protection.

'It was *me* who couldn't stop, Lisa,' he confessed. 'I was too turned on by what you were doing. I'm sorry. Truly, I am. But I was thinking of you.'

'Thinking of me? How you can say that!'

'I didn't think you'd want me to come in your mouth.'

'Oh, God,' she cried, her eyes squeezing shut as her still flushed face turned away from him.

'I promise you're not in danger of catching anything from me,' he said, upset by her upset. 'You have my word that that is the first time I've ever practised unsafe sex in my life.'

Her expression was pained when she opened her eyes and turned them back to look up at him. 'I could catch a baby.'

Jack withdrew from her abruptly and sat back on his heels, poleaxed. A baby!

'But you said the other night that you were protected from falling pregnant.'

'Not protected, Jack. *Safe.* But only the other night. It wasn't the right time in my cycle for me to conceive. Time has moved on nearly three days since then. I could fall pregnant.'

Jack tried not to panic. Panicking never achieved anything.

'I see,' he said. 'Would a bath help?'

Her look—then her laugh—was quite scathing.

'You don't know as much about a woman's body as you think, do you? No, a bath will not help. What will be, will be.'

Jack grimaced. Damn, but he wished he'd stopped

and put on a condom. But of course, he'd been way past stopping. Way past doing anything but coming.

'I still want to have a shower,' Lisa went on unhappily. 'I feel…yucky.'

Jack sighed as he withdrew. What a disaster!

She looked steadfastly away from his eyes as she scrambled out from under him and half ran to the bathroom, where she slammed the door after her, making him wince.

Jack climbed off the bed himself and pulled on his shorts.

A baby. Good lord.

He was sitting on the side of the bed, still cursing himself, when the bathroom door finally reopened and Lisa came back out, wrapped in a towel and looking very pale.

'So when is your next period actually due?' he asked straight away, trying to assess the risk.

'Sixteen days,' she said precisely. 'I have a twenty-eight-day cycle. Ovulation usually occurs twelve to fourteen days before a period starts.'

'So the odds of your falling pregnant aren't that high.'

'Too high for me,' she said dispiritedly as she started picking up her clothes.

When he tried to help her, she snatched her bra out of his hands and glowered up at him. 'I think you've done enough, don't you?'

'Lisa, don't be like this.'

'Don't be like what?' she snapped. 'You promised you would never hurt me. But you have, in the worst possible way. I don't want to have your baby, Jack. But if a baby does come out of this, then I'll have to.'

'You don't *have* to, Lisa. Not these days.'

'I knew you'd say that,' she threw at him with derision in her face.

'All I meant was that it's your choice, Lisa. It's your body.'

'But it would be *your* baby too, Jack,' she pointed out fiercely. 'I wouldn't be killing just my child. I'd be killing yours.'

Her arguments stunned Jack. Because he'd never looked at abortion like that before.

But she was right. The bottom line was that a life would be taken, a life he'd created. To terminate without any medical reasons for doing so was nothing short of murder.

'I would never ask you to do that, Lisa,' he told her sincerely. 'I've seen too many babies and children heartlessly killed to join that brigade. If you're pregnant, I will stand by you and the baby. I love you, woman, don't you know that?'

Lisa's whole body ceased to function for a few seconds. Her heart and her mind. They just shut down. But a burst of anger jump-started them again.

'Don't you dare say that to me! You don't know what love is, Jack Cassidy. Love would have protected me. Love would not have done what you did today.'

'That's not fair, Lisa. We were both responsible for what happened just now. You could have stopped me, but you didn't. You wanted me as much as I wanted you.'

'That's because you've done what I asked you not

to do. You've turned me into some mindless, sex-mad fool who can't even think straight half the time!' Tears suddenly flooded her eyes. Her head dropped into the clothes she was holding as her shoulders began to shake.

Her inconsolable weeping tore Jack apart. Love sure could make a man feel rotten, he conceded. But it also made him stronger, and more determined.

'Hush,' he said as he came forward and folded her against him. 'You're getting yourself into a right state. And there's no need to. Not yet, anyway. From what you've said, the odds of your falling pregnant are not that high.'

'But what if I am?' she wailed against his chest. 'What will I tell Cory? And my mother? And everyone else?'

'You'll tell them the truth. That you've fallen in love and you're going to have a baby.'

Lisa wrenched out of his arms and glowered up at him. 'I have not fallen in love. You spelt it out for me on Saturday night, Jack. I've fallen in lust, the same as you.'

'I won't argue with you now,' he said, though he didn't look all that pleased.

'I have no intention of arguing with you at all,' she shot back. 'I know what I know, and you won't convince me otherwise. Now I'm going to get dressed. And then I'm going home.'

'Wouldn't it be a better idea if I took you somewhere nice for lunch? Once you calm down, we can talk more rationally.'

'I'm perfectly rational. *Now.* Which is why I'm

going home. *Before* you start doing something to make me go crazy again.'

'All right. If that's what you really want.'

'That's what I really want,' she lied.

'I'll ring you tonight. See how you are.'

'Please don't.'

His eyes blazed like molten steel. 'Don't be ridiculous, Lisa. Call it what you will what's between us, but it's too powerful to ignore. Baby or not, I have to see you again. And if I'm not mistaken, the same applies to you.'

Lisa knew he was right. But be damned if she was going to be so easy in future.

'Cory's going to his grandmother's place again next weekend,' she said stiffly. 'I can see you then.'

'But that's days away!'

'If you love me, like you claim to, you'll be happy to wait.'

'I'm not a waiting kind of man.'

'Love is not selfish,' she argued.

'I just want to *see* you, woman. We don't have to have sex. Look, let me take you to lunch tomorrow. Is that too much to ask?'

'I do my food shopping on a Wednesday,' she said stroppily when she felt herself weakening.

'That's all right. I need to buy food, too. We can shop together, then we can have lunch.'

'All the cold things will melt.'

'In that case, we can have an early lunch, then shop afterwards.'

Lisa sighed. She might as well just say yes and be

done with it. But he wasn't going to get everything his own way.

'All right,' she agreed reluctantly. 'But I'm not going to Erina. I shop at Tuggerah.'

'Tuggerah's fine by me.'

'And I will drive myself in my own car,' she insisted. 'I'll meet you outside the library. At eleven.'

'I'll be there.'

'You have no idea where Tuggerah, or the library, is, do you?'

'I can find them. I'm a big boy.'

Yes, he was just that, she thought irritably. A big boy, wanting what he wants when he wants it. And wheedling and conniving till he gets it. His saying he loved her was just another ploy. Very much like Hal, who told women he loved them all the time to get what he wanted.

'I'm getting dressed now and going home,' she announced for the second time as she scooped up her shoes from the floor.

'I'll make you some coffee before you go,' he offered.

'No!' she snapped. 'No coffee. No food. No nothing!'

Jack stood at the terrace railing, his mind ticking over as he watched her drive off.

She was running for cover again, he realised.

But that was understandable. Everything had happened very quickly between them. Too quickly for a careful girl like Lisa.

Taking risks would worry her. A possible pregnancy would worry her a lot.

Jack had finally got his head around the fact he might have made a baby today. And strangely, now that he'd calmed down himself, he wasn't worried at all. In fact, he rather liked the idea.

Rather amazing for a man who'd thought he never wanted to bring a child into this world.

But that was before he'd met Lisa.

Falling in love with a wonderful girl like her had made him see that *he'd* been running for cover since he left the army.

But he no longer felt consumed with the bitter demons which had plagued him all these years, and which had made him seek a solitary existence, never becoming emotionally involved with anyone or anything.

His emotions were certainly involved now. With this very special and very challenging lady.

His next challenge where Lisa was concerned was to make her see that it wasn't lust binding them together, but love. He also had to make her see that he was husband material.

Oh, yes, he'd changed his mind about marriage as well.

It had been a truly amazing day!

CHAPTER EIGHTEEN

HE WAS already there, outside the library, when she arrived, right on eleven.

Once again, Jack's sophisticated appearance surprised her. He looked very handsome in trendy bone-coloured chinos, a cream and blue striped shirt and smart brown shoes. He was clean-shaven and smelt wonderful.

But it wasn't what he looked like which made her eyes cling to his. It wasn't just lust which swelled in her heart. It was love as well, Lisa had accepted overnight. Because once she'd recovered from the initial shock of possibly conceiving Jack's baby, she found herself secretly thrilled by the idea.

Lust would have been angry at being trapped with a playboy's unwanted child. She didn't feel angry today. She felt weirdly happy.

The depth of her feelings made Lisa extremely nervous, and vulnerable, and needy. She wanted to kiss him. Wanted to hold his hand. Quite desperately.

Instead, she kept her distance and said stiffly, 'You look very smart today.'

'And you look very beautiful,' he returned warmly.

More flattery? Lisa wondered. Or a genuine compliment?

She'd deliberately not gone to too much trouble, dressing in dark blue jeans, a simple white shirt and flat white sandals. She'd left her hair down, curled up slightly on the ends. Her make-up was minimal. The same with her jewellery. Just a gold chain around her neck and gold studs in her ears.

'Come on,' he said. 'Show me to the best eaterie in Tuggerah.'

When he took her hand, Lisa glanced around agitatedly unless someone was watching them. Someone who might know her. But she didn't try to pull her hand away. It felt too good nestled within his large, strong palm.

Still, if she wanted to keep their relationship a secret, she should have chosen a more private and discreet meeting place than a large shopping arcade. All she could do now was minimise the damage, taking him to a café at the other end of the shopping centre which was tucked away in a quiet corner.

Hopefully, no one would see her with Jack there. But to be on the safe side, she put her back to the open side of the café, so that passers-by wouldn't readily notice her.

'Got an email from my editor in London last night,' Jack said after the waitress had taken their order.

'Problems?' Lisa said, happy to discuss anything other than themselves.

'She's having kittens over my last chapter. Says Hal is getting too dark.'

'And is he?'

Jack shrugged. 'Hal's always been dark. So he

seduces a married woman. So what's new? She enjoyed it. And so will the readers.'

Lisa had to admit that they probably would. Hal's wickednesses with women were very exciting to read. Exciting when fiction became reality, too. Regardless of what eventually happened between them, Lisa could never regret her affair with Jack. It had been an incredible experience.

'I'm reading all your books again,' she confessed. 'I started the one set in Africa last night, where all those women and children got massacred and Hal reaps vengeance on their behalf.'

'I reread that one myself sometimes. I like the ending.'

'Did you witness something like that, Jack? For real?'

Jack didn't answer for a few seconds. 'Yeah,' he said, his voice rough. 'Yeah, I did.'

Lisa found his body language very revealing, and reassuring. It was a relief to discover that Jack, unlike Hal, still had a heart. She could see the hurt in his eyes, and hear the pain in his voice.

'How dreadful for you,' she said gently.

His eyes flashed. 'What was even more dreadful was that I couldn't do anything about it. I was ordered not to become involved, yet we were stationed there as a peace-keeping force. Fat lot of peace we kept. That bastard who was running the country at the time was nothing but a homicidal maniac. What I wouldn't have given to be able to shoot him down like the rabid dog he was.'

'So you had Hal torture and murder him instead,' Lisa said.

'Only fictionally. He's still alive somewhere, living off the rewards of his evil.'

'I think you've seen a lot of evil, Jack.'

'*Too* much,' he admitted. 'Not just in Africa, but in other war-torn corners of the world where people do unspeakable things in the name of power and greed. Unfortunately, most of the atrocities committed were against innocent women and children.'

'I can imagine seeing things like that would harden a man.'

Jack shot her a sharp look across the table. 'Let's just say by the time I left the army, I was a candidate for therapy.'

'And did you have therapy?'

Jack laughed. 'Are you kidding? Lying on a psychiatrist's couch isn't my style. Not only that, I'm not sure it would have done any good. Creating Hal became my therapy, just like you so cleverly deduced. He enabled me to give vent to my suppressed need for justice and vengeance. And to release all the hate and anger I had bottled up inside me.'

'I see,' she said, a quiet hope filling her heart. 'And has Hal finished his work yet? Are you feeling better?'

'Much better, actually. I didn't realise how much better till I met you. I'm no longer the emotionally dead man who left the army six years ago, Lisa. I'm no longer Hal, if that's what you're trying to fathom.'

'I suppose I was,' she said, though Lisa suspected there was still a fair bit of Hal left in Jack. Which was perhaps why she'd fallen for him.

Tall, dark and dangerous could be very attractive.

'Look, I understand why you're wary of me, and of letting me into your son's life,' Jack said suddenly. 'And I respect your decision. I can see how important Cory is to you and how protective of him you are. But I want to be more than your secret lover, Lisa. I want our relationship out in the open. Is that too much to ask?'

A great lump had formed in Lisa's throat with his speech. Maybe he did love her a little.

'I guess not,' she said. 'But I still don't want you staying over at my place. Or taking out my son. Or buying him things. Not yet, anyway.'

His face betrayed some annoyance at her demands. 'I'll hang on to that "not yet" bit. But I insist you tell your mother about me. Either that, or let me hire a babysitter occasionally for your son. I want to spend more time with you. I don't want to just snatch an hour or two whilst your boy's at school.'

'Not my mother,' she immediately rejected. 'I'll hire a babysitter myself. *And* pay for her.'

'Aah...Miss Independent.'

'That's the way I am, Jack. I can't help it.'

'It's all right. I like your independence. No one could ever accuse you of wanting me for my money.'

Lisa stared at him. 'Your money?'

'I do have a lot of it, Lisa. If it turns out you're expecting my baby, you can take me for a bundle.'

'How can you ever think I would do such a thing?'

He smiled. 'I don't. But other people might.'

'That's disgusting!'

'Hush up. People are looking over at our table. Which reminds me. When you were talking just then, there was a woman just over there, staring at us like we're visitors from another planet.'

Lisa's head swivelled round.

'No point in looking now,' he said. 'She's gone.'

'What did she look like?'

'Plump. Fiftyish. Attractive in an offbeat way.'

'Please don't tell me she had red hair.'

'Nope. No red hair. She was blonde. Sort of.'

'Thank goodness.'

'Your mum's got red hair?'

'The reddest.'

'Then it was definitely not her. Maybe it was one of your cleaners,' he suggested.

'No. None of them are that old. Could have been someone who thought she recognised you, Jack.'

'Maybe,' he said.

Their food arrived at that moment, two plates of quiche and salad, followed by huge mugs of steaming black coffee.

'It's difficult to keep a secret on the coast,' Lisa muttered after the waitress departed. 'If you go anywhere in public, someone you know is sure to see you.'

'That's why I don't want to keep our relationship a secret. Why not tell your mother and be done with it?'

'Because she thinks you're just it. I wouldn't be able to live with her if she found out about you and me.'

'But you don't live with her, Lisa. You live with your son.'

'She rings me at least once a day.'

'That much.'

'Yes. And drops in all the time. Look, I might tell her, eventually. I might *have* to,' she added, her stomach flipping over at the reminder that she might be pregnant. 'But not yet.'

Jack frowned. 'Is your mother strait-laced, is that it?'

Lisa laughed. 'Oh, no. Mum's had more lovers than you can poke a stick at. I suspect that one of the reasons I grew up frigid was because I didn't want to be like her in any way.'

'I see. Well, you're certainly not frigid any more. Which reminds me. Do you seriously expect me to wait till Saturday before I can see you again? In private, I mean.'

Lisa realised she was being pretty silly, trying to keep him at bay. At the same time, she didn't want him to think her weak.

'I have to come over and clean your place some time this week,' she said.

'No Gail?'

'She's left and I can't find a replacement that quickly.' Lisa tried not to look guilty, but suspected she failed.

'You're lying, Lisa.'

'OK, so I don't want to send you a new cleaner. I'd rather do it myself.'

'You don't trust me.'

'I don't trust other women.'

'You're jealous.'

'Yes, I'm jealous. And possessive. And crazy about you, all right?'

He grinned at her. 'Absolutely all right. So when can I expect you to come and clean? Tomorrow?'

Lisa knew if she raced over to his place tomorrow, nothing would get done for the rest of the week. Sandra always came to do the books on a Thursday and her own house desperately needed cleaning. She'd been very slack lately; too much time spent reading.

'I can't make it till Saturday,' she said.

'Saturday! What about Friday?'

'I do have other things to do, Jack. The business won't run itself.'

'Fair enough. But about Saturday…'

'What about Saturday?'

His eyes locked with hers, his expression passionate and masterful. 'Don't forget to bring that apron with you.'

Lisa had not long arrived home with Cory when her phone started to ring.

'You get on with your homework, Cory,' she instructed him. 'That's sure to be your grandma.'

'Can I talk to her, too?'

'When I've finished.'

He walked off disgruntedly as she picked up the mobile phone. 'Hello,' she said, and headed for the side-door. She would get the washing in and start folding it up whilst her mother chattered away.

'Lisa. It's your mother here.'

Lisa's step faltered. Her mother never called herself *your mother* like that. Not for years, anyway.

'Yes, Mum?'

'I won't beat around the bush. I saw you, Lisa. Today. At Tuggerah. With that man.'

The penny dropped straight away, along with Lisa's stomach. It *had* been her mother staring at them. She must have been to the hairdresser's and changed her hair colour. Again. She did that at least once every two years or so.

'Really? You saw me with my new client? Where?'

'Sitting having coffee in the middle of the mall. A new client, did you say?'

'Yes. He signed up with Clean-in-a-Day not long ago. He's filthy rich and owns a penthouse in Terrigal. Anyway, I ran into him whilst I was shopping and he asked me for coffee.'

'Oh. I thought for a minute there you'd been keeping secrets from me.'

'Mum! Surely you know me better than that.'

'Well, it's not like you to be happy for me to mind Cory two weekends in a row. So when I saw you today with a good-looking man, I thought—'

'You think too much, Mum,' Lisa broke in, then almost laughed. She was sounding just like Jack.

'Actually, he's *very* good-looking, Lisa.'

'I suppose he is.'

'Is he single?'

'Yes, Mum.'

'Did he ask you out?'

'Mum. Don't start.'

'I just want you to be happy.'

'Mum, can we talk about something else? Tell me what you were doing in Tuggerah.'

Thankfully, this launched her mother into a discussion over her change in hair colour. And Jack was forgotten.

But not by Lisa. He was never forgotten. Not for a single moment. He was there, in her head, all the time. Haunting her. Tormenting her.

Today had been very difficult, especially when they went food shopping together. She'd had difficulty keeping her hands off him, wanting to touch him all the time.

Saturday seemed eons away.

CHAPTER NINETEEN

'THIS is absolutely delicious,' Jack said as he put down his fork and picked up his glass of wine. 'You could be a chef, Lisa.'

'I did take a cordon-bleu cooking course,' she admitted, pleased that he liked the stir-fry she'd cooked him. 'I have this compulsion to do everything to the best of my ability. I think it's a hangover from my growing-up years. Like my cleaning fetish. Mum was not the best of housewives. Our house was always a mess. And meals were slapdash affairs. Often little more than snacks. Like baked beans or eggs on toast. Things haven't changed much,' she added with a wry smile. 'That's why Cory likes staying with her so much. Gives him a break from his pain-in-the-neck stickler of a mother.'

'I think his mother is fantastic,' Jack complimented with a sparkle in his eye. 'And I rather like her compulsion to do everything to the best of her ability. Especially in the bedroom.'

Lisa gave him a saucy look. 'I don't recall having been in your bedroom too much today.'

'A mere technicality. You know what I mean.'

Lisa did. Her behaviour from the moment she'd arrived at Jack's penthouse around ten this morning had been exactly as she'd feared. She'd done whatever Jack had demanded of her, starting with cleaning the place in nothing but an apron.

Looking back, however, she felt no shame over the episode. It had been exciting, and fun, Jack following her around and pouncing on her at regular intervals. Not once had they made love in or on his bed. Things had been far more imaginative than that. She had taken her apron off once, to clean his shower, with the water running full bore and Jack in there with her.

By the time the penthouse was thoroughly clean, their insatiable need for each other had been temporarily quelled.

When Jack proposed they go out for a drive, they'd ended up in Erina—a closer shopping centre to Terrigal— where Lisa had bought the ingredients to cook Jack dinner. When they'd returned, they'd made much more leisurely love for a couple of hours. But once again, not in his bed.

When Lisa had confessed to Jack that there'd been a time when she'd been repulsed by watching people make love in movies, he'd been amazed, but understanding.

That was one thing she really liked about Jack. How understanding he was of all her flaws and foibles. It encouraged her to confide in him. To keep nothing secret. She even told him that it *had* been her mother, watching them the other day. With new blonde hair.

'What did you tell your mum you were doing this

weekend?' he suddenly asked, almost as though he'd been reading her mind.

'I said I had a cleaning job today. I explained that Gail had quit without much notice and she had this extremely difficult client with very special requirements who would make a fuss if things weren't done right.'

Jack grinned. 'You're becoming a very inventive girl.'

The highly individual sound of Lisa's mobile phone ringing echoed through the penthouse, making Lisa drop her fork.

'My mobile!' she exclaimed, and jumped up from her chair. It had to be her mother. Lisa had told her to call her on her mobile if there was a problem.

Panic swept in as she raced over to where she'd dropped her hold-all on an armchair. Within seconds, her phone was at her ear.

'Yes, Mum?'

'Lisa…'

Lisa's heart squeezed so tight, she thought she was having a heart attack. In that one word, her mother had conveyed so much. There was a problem. And it was serious.

'What is it?' Lisa demanded to know. 'What's happened to Cory?'

'He…he went to play with Jason next door and he…'

Lisa listened with escalating fear whilst her mother explained that the two boys had been playing commandos in the forest up behind their properties. One would hide and the other had to find him. Just before Cory was due to come home, he hid, and Jason couldn't find him. It seemed he'd gone in too far and become lost. Jason had heard Cory yell out once and then nothing. The police had been called and they did search for a while. But darkness had fallen and they said it was pointless to continue, because there was no moon to help them. Cloud had come in late in the afternoon. The search was due to resume again at daybreak.

'I didn't want to tell you,' her mother said brokenly. 'But I knew you'd be very upset if I didn't. Although there's nothing much you can do tonight.'

'I'll be there as soon as I can,' Lisa said, sounding calm, but feeling anything but.

Jack had by then risen from his chair and was standing near by.

'What is it?' he asked as she clicked off and shoved the phone in her bag.

'It's Cory,' she said, then burst into tears.

Jack took her by the shoulders and shook her. 'Stop that,' he snapped. 'It won't do any good. Just tell me what's happened.'

She told him, gulping down sobs all the while.

'I see,' he bit out, and finally let her go. 'I'll drive. You're not fit. But first, I have to get a few things.'

'What things?' she threw after him as he ran off.

'I'll explain in the car,' he shouted back, and dashed down to his gym room, returning after a couple of minutes with a bag stuffed to the brim with who knew what.

By the time they were underway, Lisa was feeling physically ill. What if they never found Cory? Or if they did, what if he was already dead? What if a snake had bitten him? Or he'd fallen and hit his head? Why else would he not have answered everyone's calls?

'Don't start that catastrophic thinking, Lisa,' Jack advised her in the car. 'I'll find him. Trust me.'

'But how? It's a moonless night. And that bush is terribly thick.'

'Because I was trained in guerrilla warfare. I know how to operate in jungles at night. Plus, I have the right equipment for it. I kept all of it, after I left the army. Just as well I did.'

Jack probably broke the speed limit getting to her mother's place. But Lisa didn't care. The sooner they got there, the better. She also didn't give a damn about her mother finding out about her relationship with him. Nothing was important now but finding her son.

There were no police cars parked in the front yard of her mother's place. Everything looked very quiet. Jack screeched to a halt at the bottom of the front steps, then turned to her.

'I presume we're not going to have any nonsense about your mother knowing who I am, are we?'

'No. No, of course not.'

Her mother came out onto the veranda as Lisa leapt out of the car, her swollen eyes showing the depth of her own distress. Seeing them softened Lisa's underlying anger, for she knew how much her mother loved Cory.

'Oh, Lisa,' her mother cried, a bunch of damp tissues being wrung to death in her hands. 'I'm so sorry. I...I should have made him come home sooner.'

'It's all right, Mum,' she said, sounding a whole lot braver than she felt. 'Jack's going to find Cory for us.'

'Jack?'

Her mother frowned as she stared over Lisa's shoulder at Jack. 'But…I don't understand…'

Jack stepped forward and held out his hand. 'Jack Cassidy, Mrs Chapman. I'm the man you saw having lunch with your daughter the other day. And yes, I'm also Nick Freeman, the writer. But we haven't time for chit-chat at the moment. I need to change clothes quickly, then get you to show me exactly where Cory went into the forest. Here, Lisa, take this mobile phone and put your number into its menu under one. I'll call you as soon as I find Cory.'

'You're going to look for him?' Jill asked. 'Tonight? In the dark?'

'Too right I am,' Jack said as he drew a tracksuit and boots out of his bag. 'Got that mobile number in there yet, Lisa?'

'What? Oh. No. No, I haven't.'

'Then hop to it. Time's a-wasting. Mrs Chapman, could you get me a water bottle and something for Cory to eat, once I've found him? He'll be hungry.'

Both women were happy to be doing something constructive. Lisa even began to feel more hopeful. Jack had an air of competence about him which was very reassuring.

Once changed into his tracksuit and boots, he drew out a torch. 'I have special night glasses to wear later,' he explained. 'Meanwhile, we'll use this.'

Lisa went with them whilst her mother showed Jack where Cory had gone into the bush.

'Can you make it back without the torch?' he asked, and they nodded.

'Good. I might need it. Now, don't you go worrying, my love,' he said to Lisa as he put on the strange-looking night glasses. 'I'll ring you. And I'll find your boy.'

The bush had swallowed him up before Lisa realised she hadn't thanked him.

'Lisa,' her mother said quietly by her side, 'what's been going on between you two?'

Lisa sighed. 'Oh, Mum, please don't ask me that now. All I can think about is Cory at the moment.'

'But…but that's Nick Freeman. *The* Nick Freeman!'

'Oh, all right. I guess this will all be a lot easier if I tell you the truth. Come on, I'll fill you in on the way back to the house.'

Lisa would have liked a camera to record her mother's reaction when she did just that. Jill's expression was priceless. Lisa didn't even bother to water anything down. She told her everything. Even the fact that she'd fallen madly in love with the man. The only bit she left out was that she could possibly be pregnant. She couldn't even think about having another baby when her first precious baby, her darling Cory, was lost out there somewhere.

'I don't believe it,' were the first actual words Jill spoke.

By then they were back at the house, in the kitchen. 'Does *he* love *you*?' she asked.

'He say he does.'

'But you don't believe him.'

'I just don't know, Mum. He's Hal Hunter in disguise, and he wanted to sleep with me.'

'I see. Yes, I see. But Hal's not a bad man, Lisa. Underneath his hard outer shell, he's a hero. That's why

his readers love him, and care about him. It's obvious
all he needs is to meet the right girl. Which I have no
doubt he just has. You are a very special girl, Lisa. How
could any man help but fall in love with you?'

'Oh, Mum,' Lisa cried. 'What a lovely thing to say.'

Her mother smiled. 'Here. Give your old mum a hug.'

Lisa was enfolded against her mother's soft bosom
when her mobile phone rang. Her heart leapt as she
grabbed it off the kitchen table.

'Haven't found him yet, Lisa,' Jack said straight away.
'Thought I'd better check in and see how you're doing.'

'Holding on, Jack. I do feel better knowing you're
out there, looking for him.'

'Couldn't let the woman I love worry herself sick all
night now, could I?'

Lisa's heart turned over. Not a bad man, her mother
had said. A hero.

He was that to her at this moment. And more.

'Oh, Jack, I love you too,' she said, then burst into
tears again.

'Did I hear right? Did you just say you love me?'

'Yes,' she sobbed.

'Right. Get off this phone, then, woman. I have a job
to do here. I have to find our boy.'

Lisa clicked off and just stared at her mother, tears
running down her face.

'I think he does love me, Mum,' Lisa choked out. 'He
said he had to find our boy. *Our* boy.'

'Oh Lisa. That's wonderful.'

More than wonderful forty minutes later when her
phone rang again.

'I've found him, Lisa. He's all right. Just a badly sprained ankle and a big egg on his head. Tripped over a fallen tree trunk and knocked himself unconscious for a while. I'll have to carry him out, so I'd better stay put for the night. It's a bit hazardous in the dark. He wants to talk to you, but he's worried he's going to get into trouble. I told him no way, but he needs to hear that for himself.'

'Mum?'

Emotion grabbed at her heart and throat, almost choking off her voice.

'Cory,' was all she could manage in a strangled tone.

'I'm all right, Mum. Honest. But there's a rip in my shirt.'

'I don't care about your shirt, darling. As long as you're all right.'

'Yeah. I'm fine. Jack's looking after me.'

Lisa had to smile. So it was Jack, already.

'He said he's your new boyfriend.'

'That's right, Cory.'

'Cool! Did you know he used to be a soldier?'

'Yes, Cory.'

'Mum…'

'Yes, Cory.'

'I love you, Mum.'

Tears welled up in her eyes. 'I love you too, Cory. Could I speak to Jack again, please?'

'Sure.'

'Me here,' he said.

'Thank you,' she choked out.

'You don't have to thank me, Lisa.'

'Yes, I do. Not just for finding Cory, but for really loving me.'

'It wasn't very hard. Which reminds me. Would you reconsider your thoughts on our relationship? One where the girl wears a ring? Or two?'

'Jack! Do you honestly mean that?'

'You'd better believe it. So what's your answer?'

Lisa thought of how she'd only known him for nine days. But it felt like a lifetime. Maybe because she had got to know him so well through his books.

'He wants to marry me,' she whispered to her mother across the table. 'What do you think I should do?'

Jill looked startled. 'You're asking me for *my* advice?'

'Yes, Mum.'

'Go with your heart, daughter. Always go with your heart.'

'Jack?'

'Yes?'

'Yes,' she said. 'Yes, I'd like that very much.'

'Fantastic! We'll go ring-shopping tomorrow. And then I'll take you and Cory out somewhere for a celebration dinner. Is that OK with you?'

'Can I bring Mum as well?'

'Absolutely.'

Lisa sighed, then smiled. Now she knew what it was like to be happy. Really, really happy.

'Take care, Jack,' she said softly.

'I'll see you in the morning,' he returned, his voice all smiles as well. 'Have the coffee ready.'

CHAPTER TWENTY

THE Academy Awards, sixteen months later…

'Grandma! Helene! Mum and Jack are on the telly. They've just got out of the limo. Hurry!'

Helene ran into the hotel suite sitting room first, followed by Jill, who was carrying her five-month-old granddaughter in her arms.

'There they are!' Cory pointed out excitedly.

'Don't they both look absolutely stunning!' Helene exclaimed.

'Like movie stars,' Jill agreed.

Jack took Lisa's elbow as they walked down the red carpet, cameras flashing in their faces all the time. He felt supremely proud of the woman by his side. Dressed in a long, floaty lavender gown, his beautiful wife outshone everyone else, in his opinion.

'Jack! Over here!' an interviewer called out.

When Jack saw the man was from Australia, he guided Lisa towards his microphone.

'How do you feel about *The Scales of Justice* being

nominated for so many awards, Jack?' came the inevitable question he'd been asked all week.

'Very surprised,' Jack replied. 'Action thrillers don't usually rate so highly with the Academy.'

'Aah, but your story is not just a thriller, Jack. It's a character study.'

'That's very perceptive of you,' Jack complimented. 'Not everyone sees that.'

'I've heard rumours that you won't be writing any more Hal Hunter stories, is that right?'

'Yep. The last one has just gone to the publisher and will be out for the American summer.'

'Everyone wants to know if you killed Hal off.'

Jack grinned. 'Sorry. That's a trade secret.'

'Mrs Cassidy! Can you give us any clues?'

Lisa smiled up at Jack. 'Let me just say that you're in for a surprise.'

'Doesn't sound like he gets killed off, everyone,' the man announced into the microphone. 'Which will be a relief to all the Hal Hunter fans out there. Before you go, Jack, can you tell us what the new book is called?'

'*Retribution and Redemption*. And that's all we're going to tell you.'

'Your female fans aren't going to like Hal getting married, Jack,' Lisa whispered to him as they walked on.

'I don't think they'll mind.'

'But to a cleaner?'

'A beautiful blonde cleaner,' Jack pointed out. 'Who had his secret love-child two years before.'

'It reads more like a romance than a thriller.'

'But it *is* a romance, my darling. With a happy ending. Just like us.'

Her smile, when she glanced up at him, was why Jack had no need to write Hal Hunter books any more. His life had different needs now. And different goals.

'Have I told you that you look incredibly beautiful tonight?' he said.

'Only about twenty times so far. Do you think we might win tonight, Jack?'

'Never in a million years.'

The Scales of Justice took out every award it was nominated for, including best movie, best director and best screenplay.

Jack and Lisa didn't go to any of the glamorous after-awards parties. They went straight back to the hotel, where Jack's first action was to go in and look at his sleeping daughter.

Lisa hadn't fallen pregnant that first time. So they'd waited till they married before taking any more chances.

Jack had been besotted with his daughter even before she was born. He'd almost cried at Lisa's ultrasound when he saw life moving inside her. The day Jessica had been born, he *had* cried.

'She's like you,' he told his wife when she joined him by the cot.

'With that chin? She's a female image of you, Jack. And just as stubborn.'

'She's an angel,' Jack murmured.

Lisa laughed. 'And I thought you were going to be a firm father.'

'I will be,' he said, taking his wife into his arms, 'once Jess starts dating. I certainly won't let her go out with anyone like me.'

'There are worse things that can happen to a girl,' Lisa murmured, her eyes going all smoky.

Jack kissed her. Then he kissed her again.

Nine months later, Cory had a little brother to go with his little sister. They named him Hal.

CHAPTER ONE

Sydney airport. Eight o'clock.
One Friday evening in March.

'THANK YOU for flying with us, Mr Armstrong,' the female flight attendant purred as Sebastian disembarked through the first class exit.

He nodded and hurried on by, anxious to get out to the taxi rank before the hordes descended. Thankfully, he'd only brought a cabin bag with him and didn't have to collect any luggage.

The warm air outside the air-conditioned terminal came as a shock and Sebastian was glad to step into a taxi with minimal delay. He momentarily thought of ringing Emily to let her know he'd caught an earlier flight, but decided against it. It wasn't as though he needed her to cook him dinner, and really, he wasn't in the mood to talk.

All he wanted was to get home...

Emily's hands trembled as she picked up her resignation letter from the computer printer and read it through.

Just a few simple sentences, yet it had taken her over an hour to compose.

But it was done now. Her decision had been made.

'And it's the right decision,' Emily muttered to herself as she propped the envelope against her desk calendar. 'The *only* decision.'

For how could she continue as Sebastian's house-keeper, now she realised she'd fallen in love with him?

When he returned home tomorrow morning, she would hand him her resignation, then, first thing next Monday morning, she'd ring the employment agency and tell them she was accepting the job she'd been offered that afternoon.

In truth, Emily had been taken aback at securing such a plum position after just one interview: assistant manager at an exciting new conference centre on Sydney's prestigious Darling Harbour. Which was why, when the agency had rung her just after five today, she'd asked for the weekend to make up her mind.

But she hadn't needed the weekend. Just a couple of hours of soul-searching, plus listening to her head instead of her foolish female heart.

Of course, Sebastian's being away had helped with her decision making. She certainly wasn't looking forward to his return tomorrow, especially after he found out she was leaving.

He was not going to be pleased. Not pleased at all.

Emily knew that Sebastian liked her. Made no secret of his liking her. That was what made it all so hard, her heart squeezing tight as she recalled the many evenings he'd invited her to sit with him over dinner, or a night-cap, clearly enjoying her company.

But not as much as you enjoyed his, came the timely warning. What Sebastian likes most about you, my girl, is the smoothly efficient way you run his house.

Sebastian liked employees who did what he wanted, when he wanted, the way he wanted. When his much valued PA had tendered her resignation last year, Sebastian had offered her every incentive to make her stay with him. More money. Better working conditions. Even a different title.

Nothing had worked. The woman had left anyway and Sebastian had been in a black mood for days. No, weeks!

Emily quivered inside at the prospect of her boss's reaction to her own resignation.

No doubt he would first offer her more money.

But more money would not persuade her to stay.

Better working conditions would not be possible either, she thought as she glanced around her beautifully furnished bedroom. The desk she was sitting at was made in rosewood, with the most elegantly carved legs. And her four-poster mahogany bed had once been slept in by a European princess. The rest of the one-bedroomed flat which came with her present position was just as exquisite, full of even more antiques, plus many elegant little touches that any female would love. She especially liked the flat's position above the garages, which meant she had total privacy from the main house.

Emily shook her head regretfully. She was really going to miss living here.

But not enough to make her stay.

As for offering her a new title…

There weren't many other ways of describing a housekeeper.

Domestic goddess, perhaps? Emily ventured wryly.

A musical chiming coming from the adjoining living room had Emily glancing at her watch. Eight o'clock. Time to go over to the house and check all the doors and windows, a job she always did every evening around this time when Sebastian was away. She found it impossible to settle down for the night till she felt certain everything was safe and secure.

Picking up her set of keys from where they lay on her desk, Emily headed for the front door of her flat, startled to find, once she stepped outside, that the night air was still very warm. Obviously, the predicted southerly change hadn't arrived yet.

She stood there for a long moment, staring over at Sebastian's house, saddened by the thought that this might be the last time she would do this.

It was such a beautiful house, a Georgian style sandstone mansion sitting on an acre of land on the Hunter's Hill peninsula overlooking the Parramatta River. Originally built in eighteen eighty, the house had been in serious disrepair when Sebastian had bought it several years ago. He'd had it lovingly restored, filling the grand rooms with antiques and adding a conservatory and heated swimming pool.

Upstairs, there were four spacious bedrooms and two bathrooms, one being the private domain of the palatial master bedroom. Downstairs, all the rooms had French windows leading out on to coolly shaded verandas. On the left side of the hallway as you entered, sat a formal reception room which led into

an equally formal dining room, which in turn led
into the sunny and much more casually furnished
conservatory. On the right side of the front hallway,
the first door opened into a billiard room. Next along
was Sebastian's study-cum-library, followed by the
kitchen and utility room.

Out the back was a sunny flagstoned courtyard, a
perfect setting for the new swimming pool. On the
courtyard's left was a row of golden pines, which
gave privacy and acted as a wind-break. On its right,
set back a little from the house, were the garages,
Emily's flat above reached by way of a flight of steps
attached to the side of the stone building, with a
small landing at the top on which Emily was currently standing.

Beyond the pool, the beautifully kept lawns fell
away in a gentle slope to the river bank, where there
was a boathouse and a jetty. Beyond the bank at this
point, the river widened into a great expanse of water.
In the distance, directly opposite Sebastian's
property, the arch of the Gladesville Bridge formed
a wonderful backdrop for what was already a magnificent view. At this time of night, the lights on the
bridge, and the city lights beyond, created a magical
and rather romantic atmosphere.

Emily had fallen in love with the place on her
very first day.

Falling in love with Sebastian had taken longer,
she conceded as she started walking slowly down the
steps. In truth, Emily hadn't realised she had till he'd
announced one day about a month back that he and
his supermodel girlfriend had parted company, with

Lana planning to marry an Italian count whom she'd met during a recent fashion week in Milan.

Emily's over-the-top pleasure at this news had been very telling, as had her fierce regret that she'd down-played her looks to secure the job as Sebastian Armstrong's housekeeper. At the time, she'd desperately wanted *any* job and had been advised that Australia's most eligible bachelor was unlikely to hire a thirty-three-year-old blonde with a pretty face and a provocative figure.

Apparently, the mobile phone magnate had been trying to find a suitable housekeeper for some weeks and had expressed his displeasure at the number of applicants so far who'd waltzed into their interviews looking far too glamorous and sexy!

Putting her age up a couple of years, dyeing her hair back to its natural mid-brown, donning glasses and wearing loosely fitting clothes had done the trick: Emily had secured the job.

She'd managed to get rid of the glasses after a few weeks, pretending to take Sebastian's advice to have laser treatment on her eyes. But she'd kept the brown hair, with its plain, pulled-back style, along with the sensible clothes.

Till this last week.

Emily knew better than to go to an interview for a job in the corporate world looking dowdy. So she'd had her shoulder-length hair expertly blow-dried and styled for the occasion. And she'd bought herself a figure-hugging power suit in camel suede, teaming it with a cream cami which showed a hint of cleavage.

Sebastian would hardly have recognised her.

Maybe if she…

'No, no,' Emily muttered to herself as she marched along the covered walkway which skirted the pool and led to the back of the house. 'He'll never look at you in that way no matter what you do, so don't go there.'

Emily valiantly put aside all thought of Sebastian—plus her non-existent chances of attracting him—till she found herself upstairs in his bedroom. Hard not to think of the man when faced with the intimate setting of his love life, not to mention the lingering scent of the woman responsible for her boss's absence.

Ever since Emily had been in Sebastian's employ, there'd only been the one woman in his life: Lana Campbell. In her late twenties, Lana was currently at the height of her modelling career, in great demand for catwalk work, especially in Italy. A natural redhead, she was statuesque and curvy. The Italians did not like skinny models. Although not traditionally beautiful, Lana was exotic-looking, with startling green eyes and a sultry mouth. She was also extremely intelligent, with a sharp wit which could tip over into sarcasm if she didn't like you.

She didn't like Emily, for some reason. Though she'd been clever enough to hide that dislike from Sebastian.

She also had a temper. In the weeks leading up to their break-up, Emily had often overheard Lana being very vocal in her complaints about their relationship.

Sebastian didn't love her, she'd screamed at him on one occasion. If he did, he would marry her. Or at least let her move in with him.

He wouldn't do either, for whatever reason. Neither would he be provoked.

Sebastian was not a man to ever raise his voice. He had other ways of showing his displeasure. Whenever Lana made a scene, he would look at her coldly and then walk away, after which she would inevitably storm off.

But Emily felt certain that Sebastian did love Lana, a fact confirmed when he'd flown to Italy five days ago, clearly in an attempt to get her back. Not successfully, as it had turned out.

Lana's wedding to the Italian count had gone ahead a couple of days ago, and had been extensively covered by the media.

Sebastian had emailed Emily the following day, his message curt and brief.

Landing Mascot Saturday morning at seven. Home by eight.

Usually his emails to Emily were a bit more friendly. Clearly, he was going to be in a difficult frame of mind when he returned. Not a pleasant prospect.

Still, losing the woman he loved to another man was never going to sit well with him. Although heaven only knew what Lana saw in that Italian count. Compared to Sebastian, he was downright ugly: very short and decidedly overweight, with a weak fleshy face and beady black eyes.

Of course, he had a title. And he *had* presented Lana with a wedding ring.

Sebastian couldn't really expect a girl like that to

settle for less. Lana probably wanted children as well as marriage. Clearly, Sebastian didn't.

It was obvious to Emily that her forty-year-old single employer liked his life the way it was. Liked his space. Liked being alone sometimes. Australian men could be like that.

Italians, however, were a very gregarious race, renowned for their sense of family and love of children.

Thinking about family and children reaffirmed Emily's decision.

Yes, it was definitely time to leave. Time to actively pursue the future Emily also wanted for herself. Which was a husband and at least one child before she was too old.

Eighteen months ago, Emily hadn't given a damn about marriage and babies. Or about men. She'd still been grief-stricken over her mother's death from cancer. And devastated by the discovery of her father's betrayal.

But time had a way of changing your mind about things; wounds could heal and priorities change. Emily could understand why Lana had left Sebastian to marry her Italian count. Passion and sex were not the be-all and end-all to a woman, although Emily would have found it extremely hard to leave Sebastian's bed.

'Just as well you've never been in it, then,' she snapped irritably to herself when her eyes kept being drawn to that very bed. 'You're having enough trouble leaving the man as it is!'

But leave him I will, Emily vowed, as she hurried from the room.

No more being a martyr for you, my girl!

Okay, so she was in love with the man. Big deal. She'd been in love before. With that rat, Mark, who'd jumped ship when she'd gone home to nurse her mother.

Surely she could fall in love again, she reassured herself as she headed down the stairs.

First, however, she had to get herself out of here and out there, into a different world than the cloistered environment she was currently living in. A conference centre would bring her into contact with oodles of eligible executive types every day. If she had her hair dyed an eye-catching blonde again and invested in a new figure-hugging wardrobe, she was sure to attract plenty of male attention. It would just be a matter of weeding out the creeps and finding a quality man with a good job who was capable of true caring and a solid commitment.

And if he wasn't quite as impressive as Sebastian, then that was too bad. Not too many men were.

Sebastian was a man amongst men. Strikingly handsome, with a brilliant mind, a great body, and more passions than any man Emily had ever met. Aside from his various business achievements, he was an accomplished sportsman, as well as an expert in antiques, and wine, and whatever subject currently took his fancy. His library was extensive, with books on a wide variety of topics, along with a huge array of biographies. He'd told her once that he found inspiration from reading about the lives of successful people: people who'd forged their own paths and made their own luck in life.

'And that's just what *I'm* going to do, Sebastian,' Emily announced as she locked the back door. 'Forge my own path and make my own luck!'

Despite all her common sense lecturings and brave resolves, by the time Emily reached her flat, her insides were totally twisted up into knots. Going to bed was not an option. Too early. Neither was watching TV. She'd grown bored with the television lately, becoming sick and tired of reality shows.

Reading didn't appeal, either.

Perhaps a swim...

She'd already had a swim earlier in the afternoon, Sydney having experienced the longest, hottest summer on record. Today it had been thirty-one degrees, despite summer having given way to autumn three weeks back. The water in the solar-heated pool would still be warm, and very inviting.

Emily made her way straight to the bathroom, where she stripped off all her sensible housekeeping clothes and reached for her black one-piece swimming costume, which was draped over the claw-footed bath. It was still wet and Emily grimaced at the thought of dragging the wet Lycra over her warm body.

The temptation to go skinny-dipping popped into her head.

Strangely enough, Emily had never been skinny-dipping. Yet she'd been a bit of a wild child in her teens, and a real party animal in her twenties.

What had happened to that girl? she wondered as she pushed the temptation aside, then started to step into the wet swimming costume.

'She's in danger of turning into an old maid, that's what,' Emily muttered. 'And an old fuddy-duddy to boot!'

That did it!

Throwing the damp costume back across the bath, Emily snatched down the white towelling robe which she kept on a hook high on the bathroom door. Rebellion fuelled her actions as she shoved her arms into the roomy sleeves and sashed the robe around her naked body.

But her courage faded once she was out by the pool and faced with the prospect of actually taking that robe off. She stood there for ages, reassuring herself that the pool had total privacy from prying neighbours and there was no one else in the house to see her.

Sebastian didn't like his household staff to live in. Only Emily. A cleaner came in on Mondays and Fridays to do the heavy cleaning. And Emily hired casual staff to help her whenever Sebastian entertained. A local garden and landscaping service looked after the grounds and a pool man came in once a week to keep the water sparkling clean.

Emily had no reason to feel nervous about having a dip without any clothes on. No one was going to pop up unexpectedly, especially her employer.

In Emily's experience, Sebastian was a very predictable man, addicted to routine and punctuality. If he said he would arrive in the morning, then that was when he would arrive.

Yet when Emily finally took off the towelling robe, her eyes kept darting up to the blackened windows of the house, worried that a light would suddenly snap on upstairs and Sebastian would be standing there at his bedroom window looking down at her.

Agitated by this thought, Emily swiftly stepped up to the side of the pool, stretched out her hands and dived into the water, not surfacing till she was half-way up the thirty-metre pool. As she slicked back her hair with her hands, she once again glanced ner-vously up at Sebastian's bedroom window, relieved to find it still in darkness.

The pool was not in darkness, however; some subtle underwater lighting shone through the crystal clear water. Emily felt both vulnerable and exposed as she began the rather amazing experience of swimming in the nude. The water was like warm silk caressing her unclothed flesh, bringing an acute awareness of her female body.

Swimming breast-stroke was a definite turn-on, something Emily didn't need at that precise moment. Because being turned on made her think of Sebastian and the sexual longings he'd begun to inspire in her.

Lately, she'd found herself day-dreaming about him all the time, wondering what it would be like to be his girlfriend, to have him look at her the way she'd seen him look at Lana—with white-hot desire blazing bright in his brilliantly blue eyes.

Emily abruptly changed to the more vigorous overarm, swimming with rapid strokes and her head down till she reached the far end of the pool. Gripping the curved terracotta tiles at the edge, she sucked in some much-needed air, once again lectur-ing herself on the futility of her love for her boss.

The sooner she was away from that man, the better!

Emily pushed herself back from the side of the pool, staying on her back, gently moving her arms to stop herself from sinking. Floating that way was not quite so erotic, providing she didn't look down at her generous breasts and their disturbingly erect peaks. Impossible to blame their state on being cold. More likely she was too hot from thinking about Sebastian.

Emily directed her gaze steadfastly upwards, at the night sky above. It was inky black and star-studded. The moon was only a quarter, but how brightly it shone. A night for lovers, or for witches.

The security lights near the house suddenly snapping on had Emily jerking upright with a gasp. Spinning round in the water sent a great mass of wet hair across her face, so she couldn't make out who it was standing at the edge of the pool. But she recognised his voice from the very first word.

'What in the hell do you think you're doing, Missie, swimming in my pool without any clothes on?'

CHAPTER TWO

SEBASTIAN. Oh, my God, it was Sebastian!

What cruel twist of fate would bring him home early on the one night she'd decided to go skinny-dipping?

Emily didn't know what to do. Whether to use her hands to cover her breasts, or push the hair off her face, so that he could recognise who it was swimming in his pool.

'I'm waiting for an answer, Missie,' Sebastian snapped.

His calling her Missie like that evoked some much-needed resentment that she'd been put in this humiliating situation. Was it her fault that he'd come home early?

Absolutely not!

Piqued, Emily dipped her head forward in the water, then threw it backwards, the action sending her hair flying back off her face and plastering it to her bare back.

Fortunately, she was far enough away for the spray of water created not to hit Sebastian, who was standing at the edge of the pool, his trousered legs wide apart, his dark suit jacket pushed back, his hands on his hips.

He still didn't seem to recognise her, despite her whole face now being exposed.

Understandable, Emily conceded ruefully, considering he was glaring down at what else was exposed.

'It's only me, Sebastian,' she said, sounding much cooler than she felt.

Sebastian's eyes jerked up to hers, his darkly frowning expression immediately changing to bewilderment, before settling on shock.

'Emily? My God, it *is* you!'

Emily's face flamed when his eyes dropped back down to her naked breasts. She valiantly resisted the urge to cover them, pride demanding that she brazen things out rather than start acting like a shy, simpering virgin.

Besides, there was something satisfying in seeing Sebastian stare at her like that. Emily knew she had a good body. Now Sebastian knew it too.

But it was a perverse satisfaction. Because it inevitably turned to distress.

'I didn't expect you home,' she said somewhat stiffly, pained at the way he couldn't seem to take his eyes off her breasts.

Men could be so shallow when it came to sex, she thought bitterly. Even Sebastian.

'Obviously not,' he said, his gaze drifting even lower in the water.

Her chin tilted upwards as defiance kicked in. 'I'd like to get out now,' she threw at him.

'Pity. I was just thinking of joining you.'

'*What?*'

'Nothing like a relaxing swim after a long flight.'

His sudden shrugging off of his jacket and tossing it carelessly aside brought Emily close to panic. Surely he couldn't mean to strip off and go skinny-dipping with her. Surely not!

'Have…have you been drinking?' she blurted out shakily.

He smiled a slightly crooked smile as he dispensed with his tie, then attacked the buttons on his blue business shirt. 'First class flying does come with the very best of wine.'

So he *had* been drinking. Which accounted for this most uncharacteristic behaviour. In all the months she'd worked for Sebastian, he'd never crossed that invisible line between employer and employee. Even when she'd sat with him at dinner time, they hadn't talked of personal or private things, their conversation restricted to more general topics. He'd never said or done anything which could have been misconstrued or would give offence.

Clearly, he wasn't himself tonight. Losing Lana must have unhinged him.

'It's never a good idea to drink and swim, Sebastian,' she pointed out, not unkindly.

'You'll be here to save me.'

'No, I won't. I just told you. I'm getting out now.'

'What if I ask you to stay?'

Emily groaned. If only he knew how much she'd like to stay.

But she wasn't about to be used, not even by him.

'I'm not comfortable with this, Sebastian,' she said quite sharply.

He stopped undressing, his eyes narrowing on her. His sigh, when it came, sounded weary.

'You're right,' he said. 'I'm behaving badly. Please forgive me.'

Before she could utter a single word of forgiveness, or anything else, he snatched up his jacket from the ground, whirled on his heel and was gone, disappearing through the back door.

Emily wasted no time, swimming over to the side of the pool, scrambling out and dragging her robe on over her dripping body. She flew across the pool surrounds and along the flagstone walkway, running up the steps and inside her flat, slamming the door behind her.

Only then did she realise she was shaking. Not from fear. From how incredibly stupid she'd just been!

She clasped her hands to her head as she realised how close she'd just come to having her wildest fantasy come true—that of having Sebastian make love to her.

If and when a male and female went skinny-dipping together, it was never a platonic activity. Sebastian might not have looked at her with quite the same passion as he'd once looked at Lana, but there had definitely been desire in his eyes as they'd raked over her naked body. No doubt about that!

Okay, so it would have been nothing but sex on his part, Emily conceded. She would have just been a substitute for Lana, a salve for his male ego.

But so what? her love-sick soul protested. She

would have known what it was like to be in his arms, to have him kiss her and touch her. She could have *pretended*, at least for a little while.

And now?

Now, all she had was frustration and regret. And her stupid bloody pride!

Tears rushed into her eyes. Why, oh, why couldn't she have thrown caution to the wind? Why did she have to be so damned self-righteous?

Any other female would have taken what was on offer. And who knew? Something might have come of it, something special. She had a lot to offer Sebastian.

But he has nothing special to offer you in return, the voice of reason intervened. Not love…Or marriage…Or children.

Only sex.

You had a lucky escape tonight, my girl. Now hand in your resignation in the morning, then get the hell out of here!

CHAPTER THREE

THE pre-set alarm on Sebastian's bedside clock went off at ten to six. He woke with a start, followed by a groan.

Despite having found oblivion the moment his head had hit the pillow last night, and sleeping a good nine hours, he'd resurfaced this morning with a slight hangover, his first in years.

Still, he only had himself to blame. He'd drunk far too much during the flight home, though goodness knew he'd had to do something to block out the memory of what had happened in Milan.

It had worked too.

By the time the plane had landed at Mascot, Lana had been consigned to history and all he'd wanted was to get himself home.

And what had happened?

He'd arrived to find his ladylike housekeeper skinny-dipping in his pool, showing off the sort of body which he'd always found a serious turn-on.

Not that he'd recognised her at first. He'd thought

she was some wild young chicky-babe from the neighbourhood.

The moment he'd realised it was Emily, however, he should have reined in his galloping hormones. Instead, his behaviour had bordered on sexual harassment.

Fortunately, his very sensible housekeeper had put him right back in his place, saving him from the embarrassment of doing something he would very definitely have regretted this morning. As much as he had been momentarily struck by desire for Emily, he valued her far too much to risk losing her.

Thankfully, she'd noted that he'd been drinking and hadn't seemed too offended. Though she'd made him feel like a naughty schoolboy with her rather pointed remarks.

He still felt chastened this morning. And somewhat perplexed. How could he not have noticed those incredible breasts before?

As Sebastian threw back the bed-clothes and struggled out of bed, he wondered if she did that kind of thing often. Went skinny-dipping, that was. It seemed extremely out of character.

Still, she had every right to do as she pleased when he was away. And every right to expect her employer to always act like a gentleman around her, no matter what the circumstances. Or the provocations.

Although apologies did not come easily to Sebastian's lips, he decided to say sorry again over breakfast this morning.

In the meantime, he had to get himself dressed and down to the river. It was time for his morning exercise.

Exercise always cleared his head. That, and the two painkillers he intended to take right now.

Emily stood at her bedroom window, watching Sebastian as he strode down the path which led to the boathouse, his black wetsuit protecting him from the cooler air which had swept into Sydney shortly after midnight. Dawn was just breaking, the sky turning from purple to that soft blue-grey which often preceded the sun bursting over the horizon.

Emily admired Sebastian's dedication to his morning fitness regime, but she sometimes wondered if he bordered on being a bit obsessive. One would think that after yesterday's long flight home—plus a possible hangover—he might have given it a miss this morning.

But no! There he was, striding forth down to the water's edge, as he did every morning right on six.

Clearly, he'd slept well last night and wasn't suffering any jet-lag, or other after-effects. His broad shoulders were back, his handsome head held high. He looked simply superb.

'Oh, Sebastian,' she murmured, before turning abruptly away from the window.

How could just *looking* at the man give her pleasure? It was perverse in the extreme, as perverse as the pleasure she'd felt when he'd looked at her last night.

Love did make fools of people—women, especially.

Thinking such thoughts gave Emily the courage to go through with what she'd decided to do last night. And to face the inevitably unpleasant confrontation with Sebastian after she'd tendered her resignation.

An hour later she was in the process of setting the breakfast table in the conservatory when she heard the back door open and close. The master of the house had returned as he always did right on seven. Fortunately, he always went straight back upstairs to shower and shave. In thirty minutes, however, he'd be back downstairs and she'd be facing the music.

Her stomach tightened as she anticipated Sebastian's reaction to her resignation letter. She'd weakly decided to put it on the breakfast table, rather than hand it to him personally.

At seven-thirty Emily was standing next to the coffee percolator, rehearsing her speech over why she was leaving when the hairs on the back of her neck suddenly stood up. She knew, before she spun around on her sensible trainers, that Sebastian would be standing in the doorway.

He was, looking his usual sophisticated self, in smart fawn trousers and a long-sleeved black and cream striped shirt.

Emily tried to stop her stupid heart from pounding at the sight of him. But without much success.

'Yes?' she said a bit sharply, thinking irritably that no man had a right to have so many attractions.

'I wanted to apologise again about last night,' he said in his richly masculine voice. 'I was way out of line.'

'It's okay, Sebastian,' she returned somewhat stiffly. 'No harm done.'

His dark brows drew together into a frown. 'Are you sure? You seem a bit…out of sorts…this morning.'

'I'm just embarrassed.'

'You have nothing to be embarrassed over.'

'You weren't supposed to come home till this morning,' she said, half accusingly.

'I caught an earlier flight than I intended.'

'You shocked the life out of me.'

'I was pretty shocked myself, to find a naked nymph in my pool. I didn't recognise you without your clothes on.'

Emily winced. 'Please, Sebastian, couldn't we just forget about last night?'

'If that's what you want…'

'It is.'

'Fine,' he said matter-of-factly. 'I won't be having a cooked breakfast this morning. Just toast. Bring the coffee in as soon as it's ready, will you?' he added. And was gone.

Emily closed her eyes and waited for the summons which she knew would come very very shortly.

'Emily, would you come in here, please?' came the gruff call from the conservatory less than thirty seconds later.

Leaving the coffee to perc by itself, Emily straightened her shoulders and headed in the direction of the conservatory, her hands curling into fists by her sides.

Don't let him talk you out of leaving, she lectured herself as she made her way through the dining room. *Keep focused. And strong.*

The double doors which separated the dining room from the conservatory were wide open, as they always were every morning. Sebastian's back was to her as she walked through, but the set of his head and shoulders were intimidating, to say the least. Emily knew, before she saw the formidable expression on his face, that he was not happy.

But that was no surprise.

'What's the meaning of this?' he snapped as soon as she moved into sight. Her resignation letter was in his right hand, opened and obviously read. 'I thought you said you were okay with last night.'

Emily scooped in a deeply gathering breath, exhaling slowly as she uncurled her fists and looped her hands together in front of her in an attitude of superbly feigned composure.

'My resigning had nothing to do with last night, Sebastian,' she told him calmly. 'I had already typed out that letter *before* you came home. I've been offered another job and I've decided to take it.'

'Another job?' he repeated, managing to sound both startled and affronted. 'What other job? I sincerely hope none of my so-called friends have poached you from me,' he added, his eyes the colour of a stormy sky.

'I have not taken another housekeeping position,' Emily was relieved to inform him. 'I'm to be the assistant manager at a new conference centre at Darling Harbour. If you recall from my résumé, I have a degree in Hospitality Management. I also worked for several years at the Regency Hotel on their front desk, and in their PR department, so I am well qualified for such a position.'

He looked at her hard for several seconds whilst he slowly slapped her letter against the palm of his left hand. Finally, he stopped the irritating action and placed her letter down on the table whilst his lips made tight little movements back and forth, outer evidence of an inner anger which he was battling to contain.

'And how did this offer come about?' he asked in clipped tones.

'I put my name down at an employment agency. They sent me for an interview on Thursday, then rang me yesterday afternoon to offer me the job.'

'On just the one interview? You must have impressed them.'

'Apparently so.'

'You've been planning to leave for a while, I take it? From what I know of the corporate world, you don't even get an interview like that overnight.'

'I've been looking for another position for a few weeks.'

'Why, Emily? I thought you were happy here.'

'I have been happy here.'

His expression showed confusion. 'Is it the money, then? You want more money?'

'No. I don't want more money.'

'You want more time off?'

'No. I have plenty of time off, Sebastian, with you being away on business every second week or so.'

'Then what is it that you want, Emily? You must know I'll do anything in my power to keep you.'

Emily had known he'd take this tack. But she was ready for him.

'You can't give me what I want, Sebastian.'

'Try me.'

'I want to marry and have a family before I'm too old. I'll be thirty-five next birthday, and…'

'Wait a minute there,' he interjected brusquely. 'If

I recall rightly, you were already thirty-six when you applied for *this* job. That makes you going on thirty-eight, not thirty-five.'

Emily sighed. Trust her to make that mistake. But the cat was out of the bag. No point in trying any further cover-ups.

'I didn't think you'd hire me if you knew I was only thirty-three. So I increased my age by three years.'

'I see. And what other subterfuges did you do to get me to hire you?'

Emily pulled a face. What did it matter if she told him the total truth now?

'I was advised by the agency not to look too glamorous, so I dyed my hair a mousy brown and wore glasses. And yes, I lied to you about having laser treatment later. I found I simply couldn't stand wearing glasses.'

'Understandable. That's why I had laser treatment on my own eyes.'

When he leant back in the chair and began studying her rather closely, Emily had to use her well practised—and often pretend—composure to stay calm and still. But inside she wanted to run from the way his eyes travelled over her. Because they were undressing her, stripping her of her loosely fitted navy tracksuit and seeing her as they'd seen her last night. Without a stitch of clothes on.

It took all of Emily's will power not to blush.

'So what *is* your natural hair colour?' he asked at last.

'Actually, mousy brown *is* my natural hair colour,'

she said, proud of her steady voice and direct gaze. 'But I've been dyeing it blonde ever since I was sixteen.'

'I see. Presumably, before you came to work for me, your wardrobe was somewhat more flattering as well. As much as you might want me to forget last night, it was impossible not to notice that you do have a very…delectable…shape.'

Heat zoomed into her cheeks. She couldn't help it.

'I didn't care what I looked like at the time.'

'But you do now…'

'Yes. Yes, I do now.'

'Because you want to find yourself a husband.'

'Yes.'

'You feel you can't do that while you work for me?'

'Come now, Sebastian, I'll *never* meet a potential husband if I stay here, in this job. Maybe you haven't noticed, but I don't have a social life. I don't have any friends. That's been my choice up till now, I admit. When I took this job, I needed to retreat from the outside world. I needed time to heal.'

'I presume you're talking about your mother's death.'

Emily frowned before recalling she'd mentioned her mother's death at her initial job interview. She'd had to explain what she'd been doing during the years leading up to her applying for the house-keeping job.

'That,' she said, 'and other things.'

'What other things?'

Emily was beginning to find his persistence very annoying. 'That's my private and personal business.'

His face reflected some hurt at her curtly delivered

rebuke. 'I thought we'd become friends during your time here, Emily,' he said with disarming softness.

Emily squirmed a little. 'Please, Sebastian, don't make this harder for me than it already is.'

'You don't really want to leave, do you?'

Emily tried not to let him see the truth in her eyes. But she suspected she failed.

'I don't want you to leave either,' he said. 'You are the best housekeeper I've ever had. You make it a pleasure for me to come home.'

Oh, God…

'I *have* to move on, Sebastian.'

'Rubbish!' he said, snapping forward on his chair. 'You don't have to do any such thing. There must be a way around this problem where we can both have what we want.'

'I don't see how.'

He stared at her for a long moment before a light suddenly switched on in his blue eyes. The sort of light which came with an idea.

'We'll talk about it over lunch,' he announced.

Emily sighed an exasperated sigh. 'Sebastian, you are not going to get me to change my mind.'

'Give me the opportunity to try.'

'If you insist.'

'I insist.'

Emily's teeth clenched hard in her jaw. He really was an impossible man!

'What would you like for lunch?' she asked coolly, determined not to let him rattle her.

'I'll be taking you out to lunch, Emily.'

She blinked, then just stared at him whilst her

heart flipped over inside her chest. So much for her resolve not to be rattled.

'And I want you to dress the way you dressed when you got that fancy new job,' he added, his eyes taking on a knowing gleam.

'*What?*'

'I'm sure you didn't snare such a position looking the way you look this morning. Now, I have some business to attend to in the city after breakfast, but I'll be back by noon. We'll leave at twelve-thirty.'

'You're wasting your time, Sebastian,' she said, desperate now to hold on to what little of her composure was left.

'I never waste my time, Emily,' he returned in a voice which sent an odd chill running down her spine.

Suddenly, she was afraid. Afraid that by the end of lunch she would forget her own sensible plans and do exactly whatever Sebastian suggested.

'That coffee smells good,' he went on abruptly and picked up the morning paper. 'You'd better bring it in before the percolator boils dry.'

CHAPTER FOUR

BY NINE o'clock Sebastian had left for wherever he was going in the city. Probably his office, Emily reasoned, since he drove off in his car, a silver Maserati Spyder which matched its owner for style and power, but required careful parking, especially in the city.

The office of Armstrong Industries was situated in a high rise building in the middle of Sydney's CBD, which had its own underground car park and which supplied a number of parking spaces to the lessees of its office space.

The executives at Armstrong Industries didn't have to catch trains and buses to work. Nor did they have to pay the exorbitant fees charged by public car parks in the city. Their jobs came with their own personal car spot as a highly prized perk.

As CEO and owner of the company, Sebastian had two private parking spaces.

Emily knew this because Sebastian had offered her the use of one of them last year, not long before Christmas, after she'd complained about the horrendous parking situation in the city. When she'd thanked him for his kind offer, Lana—who'd been staying over at the time—had caustically remarked that Sebastian's occasional bursts of generosity always had an ulterior motive and she'd better watch herself.

Whilst Emily could not possibly see what ulterior motive Sebastian could have had on that occasion, she had to privately agree that her boss was basically self-absorbed, as a lot of successful men were.

So she knew Sebastian's reasons for taking her to lunch today would be entirely selfish ones. He didn't really care about what she wanted. Only about what *he* wanted. Which was her, staying on as his housekeeper.

His asking her to doll herself up for their lunch date was a puzzle, however. Unless he didn't want to be embarrassed by being seen in public with a woman who looked downright dowdy. Which she did this morning, in her less than flattering tracksuit and with her hair pulled back into a knot.

What would Sebastian think, Emily wondered as she completed her household chores, when he saw her wearing her smart new suede suit and with her hair done properly and full make-up on?

Would he be shocked?

She hoped so. She hoped he'd be stopped in his tracks.

Emily craved the opportunity to show him that she was an attractive woman. Maybe not as glamorous or as sexy as Lana, but still capable of attracting male attention.

As nervous as she was about this lunch, she now had her chance. And she aimed to make the most of it!

Noon saw Emily looking the best she could without going blonde, but with more butterflies in her stomach than when she'd gone for her job interview the other day. She kept worrying over what arguments Sebastian was going to employ to persuade her to stay, her improved appearance no longer the main focus of her thoughts.

The sudden sound of the garage door opening underneath her flat sent her running towards the window which overlooked the driveway. She reached it just in time to see the top of Sebastian's sports car disappearing into the garages below, the heavy door automatically coming down behind it.

His putting his car away brought confusion and dismay. Did that mean he'd changed his mind about taking her to lunch? Had he decided she wasn't worth the effort of trying to change her mind?

Emily was still standing at the window, feeling totally crestfallen, when there was a knock at her door. It would be Sebastian, of course, she thought unhappily, come to tell her lunch was off.

Steeling herself not to act like some disappointed fool, she went to answer it. But inside, Emily fiercely regretted the time she'd taken to painstakingly blow-dry her hair the way the hairdresser had the other day, practically strand by strand. It had taken ages. So had her make-up. What a waste of time!

After scooping in one last calming breath, she swept open the door, her face an impassive mask.

Sebastian wasn't exactly stopped in his tracks by the sight of her.

But he did take a long look.

'Just as I thought,' he said, his eyes showing satisfaction as they raked over her from top to toe. 'You're no plain Jane, are you, Emily? Not that I ever thought you were. Impossible to hide your lovely skin and eyes. As for your stunning figure…I confess you have hidden that extremely well these past eighteen months. But last night rather put paid to that little subterfuge.'

Emily struggled to prevent an embarrassing blush from spoiling her resolve to remain cool and calm, no matter what.

'It's nice to finally see your curves shown to advantage,' he added, his gaze dropping to the hint of cleavage displayed by the lowishly-cut camisole.

Emily froze when her nipples tightened alarmingly within the silk confines of her strapless bra. No, she thought angrily. No, no, no!

Time to stop this little scenario before it became seriously humiliating.

'Thank you,' she replied frostily. 'I take it you've changed your mind about lunch?'

Her assumption surprised him more than her appearance had, his head jerking back as his brows drew together in a startled frown. 'Why would you say that?'

'You put your car away.'

'Aah. I see. No, I've ordered us a taxi. Easier than trying to park at the Quay. It'll be here at twelve-thirty, so I'd better away and change into something more suitable for lunching with such a beautiful lady.'

It was no use. This time she did blush. And it irritated the life out of her. As did the degree of her relief—and delight—that their lunch together was still on.

'Flattery won't change my mind, Sebastian,' she said sharply.

'Thank you for warning me. But I would never rely on flattery for something so important as keeping you, Emily.'

Emily squared her shoulders in defiance of the supreme confidence she saw in his eyes. 'There's no point in offering me more money, either. Or better working conditions.'

'Look, let's leave this discussion till later. The taxi is due in twenty minutes. What say we meet on the front veranda just before twelve-thirty?'

Emily sighed. 'Very well.'

'There's no need to sound so put out. At worst, you will have a free lunch. At best...' He shrugged, obviously not willing as yet to reveal his battle plans. 'Must go. See you shortly.'

Emily shook her head as she closed the door behind his departing back. Sebastian meant to persuade her to stay. How he aimed to achieve that goal was the unsettling question.

As the minutes ticked down to their arranged meeting on the front veranda, the thought haunted Emily that there was no such thing as a free lunch.

At twelve twenty-five, she picked up the camel-coloured handbag which matched her suit, locked her apartment door, then made her way downstairs, each step reminding her of the tightness of her skirt and the height of her heels.

Whilst more than happy with her smart city-girl look, Emily was relieved that her suit jacket covered most of her breasts, and her still erect nipples.

Thankfully, the morning had not warmed up too much, despite the sky being clear and sunny, so she could keep the covering jacket on without feeling too hot.

Locking the back door of the main house on her way through didn't take long, Emily telling herself all the time to keep calm and not let Sebastian change her mind about leaving, no matter what he said.

But it wasn't what he would *say*, came the unsettling realisation when she walked out on to the front veranda to find him already waiting for her. It was the way he could make her *feel*.

Emily already knew that just looking at him gave her pleasure.

Being taken to lunch by him, however, was a whole different ball game. She would have to keep her wits about her.

He looked superb, of course, dressed in an elegant grey business suit, his shirt blue, his tie a silvery grey. His slicked-back dark brown hair looked faintly damp, suggesting he'd had a quick shower. He might have run a razor over his chin as well, as the skin on his face looked very smooth and sleek.

'I love a lady who knows how to be on time,' he said with a quick smile. 'Did you lock the back door?'

'Of course,' came her cool reply.

'Of course,' he repeated. Not nastily. Or sarcastically.

But it annoyed her just the same.

'The taxi's here,' she pointed out, nodding towards the front gates, which were shut. Sebastian often caught taxis but never let them come inside. He valued his privacy, and his security.

Understandable, considering the extent of his wealth.

'I'll just lock the front door,' he said.

Emily practised some deep breathing while he did so.

When he turned and took her arm, she flinched before she could stop herself.

'Come now, Emily,' came his smooth rebuke. 'I'm not going to bite.'

The penny dropped. So this was how he was going to persuade her to stay. By using his not inconsiderable charm. His demanding that she get dressed up was an underhand but clever way of making her more aware of her femininity, thereby lowering her sexual defences.

And it was working, of course.

'I still can't get over how amazing you look,' he continued as he steered her down the front steps and along the front path. 'But you're right, I think you'd look even better with blonde hair. One of those short sexy styles which would show off your swan-like neck.'

The deviousness of his tactics inspired rebellion, as did the traitorous heat which his touch was sending through her entire body.

'I'll keep that in mind before I start my new job,' she told him in a brilliantly blithe tone.

Not with much effect, however, because he laughed. 'You know, I realised when you were talking this morning that you were just like me.'

'Like *you*?' she threw up at him, stunned by such an unlikely observation.

'Absolutely. You do what has to be done. You don't fantasise or romanticise. You're a realist.'

Their arriving at the front gates stopped Emily from blurting out that he knew nothing about her at all. She'd been fantasising about him for weeks!

Getting through the gates and into the taxi gave her a few moments to become what Sebastian thought she was. A cool-headed realist.

Till they were under way.

Finding herself sitting so close to the man she loved in the confined space of the taxi was not conducive to sensible thinking. The lack of conversation didn't help, either. Suddenly, there was nothing to distract her heated imagination, or to stop it from running amok.

Could he possibly be planning to seduce her? came the horribly exciting thought. Would he go that far to keep her? And if he did proposition her, how would she react?

Last night, she'd regretted not going skinny-dipping with him.

Today, she suspected she might be putty in his hands.

In all seriousness, however, Emily could not believe Sebastian would go that far. He was not a callous womaniser. Or a cold-blooded seducer. He was a gentleman through and through. That was why she'd been so shocked last night when he'd suggested joining her in the pool.

'Have you officially accepted that new job offer?'

Sebastian's unexpected question whipped her head around, her rapidly blinking eyes taking a moment to focus on his face.

Something in her own face must have betrayed her.

'You haven't, have you?' he said, sounding pleased.

Emily adopted what she hoped was a totally un-
ruffled expression. 'I intend ringing the agency first
thing Monday morning to accept.'

'Why didn't you accept the offer straight away?'

'I don't like to rush any decision,' she told him
coolly and he nodded.

'Sensible girl.'

'That doesn't mean I didn't decide later,
Sebastian,' she went on, hammering home her stance.
'That's why I resigned as your housekeeper this
morning. In three weeks' time I will no longer be
working for you. Trust me on that.'

'I believe you.'

'Then what is the point of this lunch?'

'I intend to make you a counter-offer.'

'What kind of counter-offer?'

He placed his index finger against his lips. 'When
we're alone,' he murmured.

She stared at his finger, then at his lips.

Sebastian had a very sensual mouth, in contrast to
the rest of his more harshly sculptured features. His
lips were soft and full, whilst his cheekbones were
sharply prominent, his nose long and strong, his chin
squared and stubborn.

But it was his eyes which dominated his face and
inevitably drew one's own eyes. Deeply set and a
bright blue, with a darker blue rim, they were
piercing and quite magnetic.

Emily found herself looking up and into them;
found herself thinking she would do anything he asked,
if only he would keep looking at her like this. As if she
were an attractive woman. No, a *desirable* woman.

She could not tear her eyes away from his, no longer caring about anything but this moment, this precious, private, impossibly romantic moment.

'Whereabouts around here do you want me to drop you off, mate?' the taxi driver asked.

Sebastian looked away and the moment was gone, torn from Emily with the wrenching pain of a suddenly amputated limb. Reality returned with a rush, making her face the fancifulness of her interpretation of what had just happened, plus what she was secretly hoping might happen later on.

Sebastian was not going to seduce her. He was going to offer her more money.

Her boss was a man who found practical solutions to problems he encountered, not ones which could cause him even more problems. Seducing his housekeeper would be an extremely hazardous solution, especially for a wealthy man. Sebastian would not risk his reputation—or a sexual harassment lawsuit—to keep her in his house. She wasn't *that* valuable to him.

'Just here will do,' Sebastian told the driver, and the taxi slid over to the kerb just outside the ferry terminals.

From there, it was only a short walk down to the restaurants and alfresco cafés which lined the quayside and which all provided their patrons with splendid views of the harbour, the bridge and the Opera House.

Emily had no idea where Sebastian was taking her but she couldn't imagine it being anything less than the best.

Having lunch with him, however, had now totally

lost its lustre. She'd be relieved when it was over. *Very* relieved when he graciously accepted her decision to leave.

Emily opened the door and climbed out of the taxi, not waiting for Sebastian to do it for her.

No more mooning over him, she lectured herself as she stood on the pavement and waited for him to finish paying the driver. No more foolish fantasies. No more saying she was going to do one thing whilst dreaming about another.

Be the realist he thinks you are.

'Emily?'

A startled Emily turned at the sound of her name being called out from behind her.

'So it *is* you,' the owner of the male voice said as he strode over to her, his good-looking face breaking into a warm smile. 'I didn't recognise you at first with brown hair.'

CHAPTER FIVE

EMILY could not believe it! Fancy running into Mark, of all people.

Still, he did live at Manly and had always caught the ferry to and from work. And he often worked on a Saturday, being one of the partners in a high-powered stockbroking firm.

She supposed it wasn't all that much of a coincidence.

But still...

'You're looking very well,' Mark went on, his eyes fairly gobbling her up.

'You too,' she replied, privately wishing that he might have grown fat or bald in the four years since he'd dumped her. But no, he looked even better than ever.

Not as tall or as impressive as Sebastian, but extremely attractive. And very well dressed—Mark had always had style. And an eye for the ladies. He was eyeing her up and down right now, his dark eyes glittering in that way she'd once loved, because she'd thought his desire had been just for her.

In hindsight, Emily suspected that he probably

looked at every fanciable female with I'd-love-to-take-you-to-bed eyes.

'I've often thought of you, Emily,' he said, lowering his voice in the way she now realised was a ploy he used to sound sincere.

'And I you, Mark.'

He didn't seem to notice the chilly note in her reply.

'Good heavens!' he suddenly exclaimed, his eyes having abruptly moved from her face to a spot over her shoulder. 'That's Sebastian Armstrong over there.'

Emily spun round to see that Sebastian was finally getting out of the taxi.

'Yes, it is,' she agreed coolly. 'He's taking me to lunch.'

Emily enjoyed Mark's shocked expression. 'You're moving in pretty rarefied circles these days.'

'Sebastian's my boss.'

'No kidding. The great man himself. Look, can I give you a call? It'd be great to catch up.'

Emily found it difficult to hide her fury at Mark imagining for one moment that she'd want him calling her. Or catching up with her.

'I don't think so, Mark,' she said frostily.

'No? Oh, well, I suppose you've got better—and bigger—fish to fry,' he said nastily with a sour glance Sebastian's way.

'He's just my boss, Mark.'

'Then why isn't he looking too pleased with your talking to another man?'

'Really?' Now it was Emily's turn to be shocked.

Actually, Sebastian did look a bit annoyed as he

stepped up on to the pavement. By then, Mark had gone, like the coward that he was.

'Damned driver pretended he didn't have the right change,' Sebastian muttered as he joined her. 'In the end I gave him a fifty dollar note. Which I suppose was what he was angling for from the start. But I do resent giving large tips to people who do nothing for them.'

Emily castigated herself for entertaining the ridiculous notion that Sebastian could possibly be jealous. Her imagination was really working overtime today.

But that was becoming a habit whenever she was with Sebastian.

'This way,' he said, taking her arm and steering a safe path through the people hurrying to and fro.

Circular Quay was always busy, even on a Saturday, being a popular spot for tourists who flocked to see Sydney's most famous icons, its Harbour Bridge and Opera House, which admittedly were both unique and very beautiful.

Emily hadn't been in this part of the city for years, but she was familiar with the area. She had, after all, once been a working girl in the city. She'd lived with Mark in his apartment at Manly as well, catching the same ferry he caught every morning, just so she could spend every possible moment with him.

What a romantic fool she'd been back then!

Maybe she was still a romantic fool.

But not for much longer!

'So who was that man you were talking to just now?' Sebastian asked as he guided her along the sun-drenched quay.

'And don't lie to me, Emily,' he went on before she could even open her mouth. 'I'm a good judge of body language and I know when a man and a woman have once meant something to each other. He couldn't take his eyes off you. And you…you looked almost murderous at running into him. If looks could kill…'

Emily supposed there was no reason not to tell him the truth. Though really her private life was none of his business.

'Mark's an old boyfriend,' she admitted.

'How old?'

'What do you mean?'

'How long ago did you break up?'

'About four years, give or take a month.'

'What happened?'

'My mother got cancer, that's what happened,' she said sharply, giving vent to some of the bitterness she'd bottled up for years. 'Mark didn't like my decision to go home and look after her. Prior to that, we were living together. But he couldn't cope with a girlfriend who wasn't there for him, twenty-four seven.'

'He obviously didn't care for you very deeply.'

'I did come to realise that,' Emily said with a sigh. 'But it was very hurtful to be dumped at such a distressing time.'

'You loved him a lot, didn't you?'

Emily wished she hadn't. But she had. And there was no point in denying it. 'Yes,' she said simply. 'I did.'

'He's the reason you haven't had a boyfriend since, isn't he?'

Emily began to feel uncomfortable with Sebastian pursuing this line of personal probing.

Grinding to a halt, she speared him with a firm look. 'Could we talk about something else, please?'

'I'm just trying to get to know you better,' he said.

'Why? So you'll know what buttons to push to persuade me to stay?'

He smiled a wry smile. 'You don't pull any punches, do you?'

'I just don't like being taken for a fool.'

'It would be very difficult to fool you, Emily.'

No, it wouldn't be, she thought as she glowered up at him. I've been made a fool of before. By Mark. And my father.

You could make a fool of me too. More easily than you know.

'I would hope that you wouldn't try,' she said in all seriousness.

He frowned, his eyes thoughtful. 'I would hope so too.'

'So what is this counter-offer you're going to make to me?' she asked, sick of not knowing. 'We're alone now, so there's no reason why you can't tell me.'

'I think we should get to the restaurant first,' he replied, 'before they give our booking to someone else.'

Emily smothered her irritation at yet another delay with some difficulty. Sebastian led her down to a nearby Thai restaurant which had an alfresco section outside that captured both the splendid view and the warm autumn sunshine. By the time they were settled at one of the brightly umbrellaed tables, and the drinks waiter had taken Sebastian's wine order, her patience was wearing very thin. Her stomach had begun churning with nervous anticipation, but her resolve to move on had grown stronger than ever.

'No more hedging, Sebastian,' she insisted. 'Out with it.'

'Very well,' he said, his piercing blue eyes locking with hers. 'I must warn you, however, that you'll probably be taken aback at first. Promise me that you will give my proposal due consideration. Don't reject it out of hand.'

'Your proposal of what?'

'Of marriage.'

Emily knew that if she'd been holding a glass of wine at that moment she would have dropped it, or spilt wine all over herself.

Taken aback did not begin to describe her reaction. Shocked was also inadequate. Stunned came close, but still fell short of capturing the emotions which crashed through her.

'In case I haven't made myself perfectly clear,' he swept on, 'I'm not proposing some kind of business arrangement, or a marriage in name only. This would be a real marriage in every sense of the word. I'm well aware you want at least one child, Emily, and I'm prepared to give you what you want.'

He couldn't be serious, she thought dazedly as she stared at him.

And yet he *was* serious!

She could see it in his eyes.

'I...I don't know what to say,' she choked out.

'Yes would be acceptable,' he replied with a small smile.

She stared at his smiling mouth, her own mouth

still open and rapidly drying. She closed it and licked her parched lips, then shook her head, not in rejection, but in bewilderment.

'You don't propose marriage to your housekeeper, Sebastian, just to stop her from leaving. That's a crazy thing to do, especially for a man who's made it perfectly clear he never wanted to get married. Or become a father.'

She'd overheard him say as much to Lana. Loudly and firmly.

'I haven't up till now, that's true. But then I hadn't met a woman I wanted to marry. I want to marry you, Emily.'

'But *why?* You don't love me. You still love Lana. I know you do.'

'Then you know differently to me,' he stated quite coldly. 'I do not still love Lana. I never did.'

'Then why did you chase after her?'

He shrugged. 'There were things left unsaid which had to be said. My going to Italy was more a matter of curiosity. And closure.'

Emily was not in any way convinced. If that was the case, then why had he over-indulged in alcohol on the flight home? That was not like him at all. Sebastian liked a couple of glasses of wine with his meals, but she'd never seen him as intoxicated as he'd been last night.

He could say what he liked. He *had* loved Lana and he wasn't over her. Not by a long shot.

The drinks waiter arriving with the bottle of white wine Sebastian had ordered put paid to their conversation for a while, giving Emily the opportunity to get a grip on her emotions and think more rationally about Sebastian's marriage proposal.

It was utterly outrageous, of course.

But a very Sebastian thing to do.

In one fell swoop, he would solve both his current problems. Keep his housekeeper, plus fill the empty space Lana had left in his bed.

Thinking of filling Lana's space in his bed, however, sent Emily's head into a whirl. As much as she secretly thrilled to the prospect of Sebastian as her husband and lover, she could not discount the awful thought that if she married him she would always be a second-choice substitute for the woman he really wanted. What would happen when he got over his hurt and realised he'd married a woman who couldn't possibly fire up his passions the way Lana had? Would he want a divorce, or expect his wife of convenience to play the little woman at home whilst he took a mistress? Or two?

As much as Emily was madly tempted to still say yes, yes, yes and be damned with the consequences, her bitter experiences in the past kept warning her to stop and think. Did she really want to let herself be used by another man? Her father had used her, till her services were no longer required. Mark had done the same.

Could she rely on Sebastian being any different?

If anything, he might be worse, given his extreme wealth. Billionaires were used to getting their own way. Just because she thought the sun shone out of Sebastian didn't mean he didn't have a dark side. All men did.

By the time the drinks waiter left, Emily's head felt as if it would burst with the torment of her emotional dilemma.

For how could she possibly say no? She loved him and she wanted him.

It was the wanting which was the most difficult to resist. Last night she'd run from the chance of having Sebastian make love to her. How could she run from it again and not regret it till her dying day?

'Have a sip of the wine,' Sebastian suggested as soon as the drinks waiter left, 'and tell me what you think of it.'

Emily gripped her wineglass tightly lest her hand begin to shake. She brought it to her lips and sipped, then put it down carefully.

'Very nice,' she said.

'Have a guess where it comes from.'

Emily felt like throwing the wine in his arrogantly handsome face. But such overt tantrums weren't in her nature.

'New Zealand,' she answered. 'The Marlborough region.'

It was a game he played with her sometimes. Like most men, he liked to show off his own knowledge on a subject. But she knew her wines, her father having always kept an extensive cellar. Mark had been a wine buff as well so she'd had a very good schooling on the subject.

'Damn. I thought you might say Western Australia.'

'I've always liked New Zealand whites.'

'They do go well with Asian food. Have you decided what you're going to eat?' he added when another waiter materialised by their side, holding an order pad.

Emily had glanced at the menu sitting in front of

her, but very blankly. Since Sebastian had dropped
his bombshell, her mind had been on other things.

'Why don't you order for me?' she suggested,
not really having much appetite. She was also beginning to feel quite warm, with her shoulders and
arms in the sun.

Sebastian ordered a couple of noodle dishes, after
which he stood up and took off his own suit jacket,
draping it over the back of his chair.

Emily had seen him wearing a lot less. She
already knew he had broad shoulders, a flat stomach
and slim hips. So why did she have to stare at him
the way she did?

Perhaps because she was already anticipating that
moment when she would see him wearing absolutely
nothing. Which she would, if she became his wife. He
would be hers to look at. To kiss. To make love to.

The thought was mind-blowing. And a serious
turn-on.

When his eyes met hers across the table, heat
zoomed up her throat into her face.

'You should take your jacket off as well,' he said,
thankfully misinterpreting the pink in her cheeks.
'You're looking hot.'

'Here,' he said, when she tried to struggle out of
it whilst sitting down. 'Let me help you.'

She had to stand up, holding herself stiffly whilst
he peeled the jacket back from her neck and lifted it
up off her shoulders. Was she imagining it, or did he
deliberately allow his fingertips to brush against her
skin as he slid the jacket down her arms?

'I'll bet that feels better,' Sebastian remarked as

he draped her jacket across the back of the chair next to her.

She sat down again and leant back in her chair, making a conscious effort to relax. Not an easy thing to do when her nipples were like bullets and her whole body was on the verge of spontaneous combustion.

She managed a small smile as he sat back down. 'It's turned out hotter today than I thought it would.'

His gaze flicked over her bare arms and shoulders, then back up to her face. His expression was guarded, his eyes unreadable. But the air between them crackled with an unspoken tension.

'Have you had enough time to think about my proposal?' he asked, his voice calm but his eyes watchful.

'Yes…'

'Good. Then what's it to be, Emily? Yes? Or no?'

Emily's head shouted no at her whilst her heart screamed yes.

At the last moment, she realised she didn't have to say, either. Let him wait for her answer. And work a little harder for it.

'As I said earlier, Sebastian,' came her cool sounding reply. 'I don't like to rush my decisions. Could you give me the rest of the weekend to think about it?'

'The rest of the weekend,' he repeated slowly, looking not at all pleased by her answer.

'Yes. I'll let you know by Sunday night.'

'I would prefer to know where I stand today,' he ground out. 'Is there anything I could say, or do, to make up your mind a little earlier? Perhaps we could discuss your concerns over lunch, whatever they are.'

What a cold-blooded devil he was, Emily realised. No wonder Lana had left him. He had no idea how a woman felt. Or what a woman wanted.

Time to set him straight.

'The thing is, Sebastian, I always hoped that I would marry for love.'

'You loved your Mark,' he pointed out impatiently. 'If you'd married him, do you think you would have been happy?'

'Perhaps not.'

'Love as a basis for marriage is seriously over-rated,' he argued. 'Just look at the divorce rate in the Western world where most marriages are love matches. Caring, compatibility and commitment are much better bets.'

'But what if we're *not* compatible?'

'But we already are,' he said. 'We get along very well together, Emily. Surely you can see that.'

'In a platonic fashion. But what about sexually?'

Her question startled him, his brows drawing together in an almost affronted fashion. 'You think I can't satisfy you in bed?'

'I don't know. That's the point. I would never marry a man who was inadequate in the bedroom,' she answered with a superbly straight face. 'For all his flaws, Mark was an excellent lover.'

He stared at her long and hard across the table till she wished she hadn't dared challenge him in such a silly fashion. He was not a man you threw down the gauntlet to.

But perhaps that was why she'd done it. Because subconsciously she knew he'd pick it up.

'If that is your main concern,' he said, his eyes clashing boldly with hers, 'it can be easily dispensed with. Spend tonight with me. Find out for yourself what kind of lover I am.'

Emily stopped her mouth from gaping open this time, her pride demanding she not betray herself by suddenly acting like some love-struck fool. Though possibly she was more lust-struck at that moment.

'You're very sure of yourself, aren't you?' she said with deceptive calm. If he could see her insides, he'd know the truth.

'I know what I'm good at.'

'But what about me? What if you find out *I'm* hopeless in the bedroom?'

His eyes searched her face. '*Are* you?'

'I guess that depends,' she said, 'on whom I'm with.'

'You like to be in love with your lovers?'

'I like to believe they love me.'

'Love and great sex do not have to go together, Emily. I could prove that to you tonight.'

No, you won't, she thought despairingly. Because I already love you. Having you make love to me is going to feel great, no matter what you do.

'I…I'll think about it,' came her slightly shaky answer.

Suddenly she couldn't bear to sit there any longer. She had to get away from him for a while. Had to have a few moments to herself.

'If you'll excuse me, Sebastian,' she said, putting down her glass and scooping up her handbag from the adjacent chair, 'I need to go to the ladies'.'

CHAPTER SIX

SEBASTIAN watched Emily flee the table. And him.

Not that she ran. She walked. But he could see flight in her body language.

Things were not going as he'd anticipated.

He had expected her to be surprised by his marriage proposal. But he'd also expected her to say yes, once it sank in what marriage to him would give her.

A beautiful home she'd always admired. A husband who liked and respected her. Plus a lifestyle which would make her the envy of every woman in Australia.

What more could a girl like Emily want?

He was even prepared to give her a child.

And what had she focused on?

Love. And then sex.

That had seriously surprised him. When his practical and pragmatic housekeeper had outlined her husband-hunting plans this morning, she hadn't mentioned craving love and sex. Just a husband and a child before she got too old.

Sebastian had never imagined for one moment that Emily was a closet romantic.

His right hand reached into his jacket pocket, his fingers wrapping around the box which contained the very expensive engagement ring he'd bought this morning.

For a moment he contemplated taking it out and presenting her with it on her return. There was something about a huge diamond which usually melted a woman's resistance.

Unfortunately, Emily was not a usual woman.

She was different from every other woman he'd ever known. Right from the first moment he'd met her, he'd recognised that she was unique, projecting an air of capability and maturity far beyond her years. No wonder he'd believed she was older than she really was.

Within no time she'd brought an organised and peaceful atmosphere to his home which he'd come to rely on.

No, not just rely on. Which he needed.

He needed Emily in his life, a lot more than he'd ever needed Lana. When Lana had left, he'd been angry and frustrated. Sebastian was a possessive man who didn't like to let go, or to lose. But his drinking too much on the flight home yesterday had not been the result of a broken heart but a case of self disgust. The only good thing to come out of his chasing after Lana was finding out he never wanted to see her ever again.

When Emily had announced she was leaving him, however, Sebastian had known within seconds of reading her resignation letter that he would do anything to keep her. Anything at all!

When the idea of marriage had first popped into his

mind he'd honestly believed he'd come up with the perfect solution. What woman in her right mind would say no to the most eligible bachelor in Australia?

Emily Bayliss, that was who.

So much for Lana snidely remarking one day that his housekeeper had a crush on him. She couldn't have been further from the truth.

Which left Sebastian no alternative but to move on to Plan B.

The only problem was he hadn't worked out what Plan B was as yet.

But he would think of something.

He'd be ruthless if he had to be.

By the time Emily emerged from the ladies' room, she had come to a decision.

It was a very bold decision, and one which left her quaking inside. But she simply could not go to her grave regretting that she'd knocked back the chance to go to bed with the man she loved.

So she would accept Sebastian's offer to spend the night with him.

But she would not marry him.

Of course she would not tell him that in advance, otherwise he might retract the offer of sex. She would let him think her saying yes to his suggestion was likely to lead to her saying yes to his proposal.

Emily could only hope and pray that when the morning came she would have the courage to say no and walk away.

Because to marry Sebastian would be setting herself up for future misery and heartache. And she'd had enough of that in her lifetime already. She wanted a marriage which would bring her peace and contentment, not emotional turmoil.

No doubt Sebastian could provide her with every material comfort, and possibly a great amount of physical comfort. But no comfort for her already damaged heart and her long-suffering soul.

Their meals had arrived, she noted as she returned to the table, which was good. She could talk about the food, thereby hiding her growing tension.

'This smells delicious,' she said as she sat down quickly and picked up her fork.

'They're called drunken noodles,' he informed her, then smiled. 'I thought it was an appropriate choice, given my appalling state last night.'

Emily might have relaxed at this point if she hadn't known what was ahead of her.

One part of her wanted to get it over and done with, that terrifying moment when she'd have to look him in the eyes and say, *By the way, Sebastian, I think it's a good idea, our going to bed together tonight.*

But she simply could not find her tongue, her eyes dropping to her food.

'You know, Emily, you have a very beautiful body.'

Her eyes jerked upwards at his softly delivered words.

No, not softly. Seductively. As seductive as his eyes which were travelling slowly over her body now, implying that his offer to sleep with her was not just to prove a point but because he desired her.

Her mouth dried as her heart thudded within her chest.

'Thank you,' she choked out.

'You are a very beautiful woman all round,' he went on mercilessly. 'Please don't think I asked you to marry me just because I wanted you to stay on as my housekeeper. I'll hire another housekeeper, if and when you marry me.'

'But I wouldn't like that,' she blurted out before she could think better of it.

'You prefer to take care of me and my home yourself?'

'No…Yes…I mean…'

'You can do whatever you want, Emily,' he interrupted in that soft, silky voice. '*Have* whatever you want. I am a very wealthy man, as you know.'

Suddenly she saw what he was doing. He was trying to seduce her. And corrupt her.

Emily knew exactly what Sebastian wanted. For the status quo in his household to stay the same, even if he had to give her the title of wife, plus give her a bit of something else as well.

Emily could not help feeling cynical about all of Sebastian's proposals. And about the so-called desire she'd seen in his eyes just now.

Let's face it, girl, she told herself. He hadn't wanted to marry you before today, had he?

'I think we're getting ahead of ourselves,' she said firmly. 'I won't be rushed into something as serious as marriage, Sebastian. But I do think your idea of our spending tonight together is a sensible one.'

His eyes widened slightly at her cool acceptance of his sexual proposal.

For a long moment he stared at her, his gaze

thoughtful and probing. But she held her ground, and her outer composure.

It was just as well, however, that he could not see her inner turmoil.

Or was it excitement making her heart race and her stomach churn?

'I trust you haven't changed your mind about that,' she added in a challenging tone.

The hint of a smile pulled at the corners of his mouth. 'Absolutely not.'

'That's good, then,' she said matter-of-factly. 'Now, I think we should get on with our drunken noodles before they get cold.'

Emily fell to eating with apparent gusto. But in fact she had to force every mouthful down. A lump seemed to have lodged in her throat.

Whenever she stopped to take a gulp of wine, Sebastian glanced up from his meal to gaze at her with those far too intelligent eyes of his.

What was he thinking? she kept wondering, and worrying.

As much as Sebastian tried, he could not quite grasp what was going on in Emily's head.

But he had to admire her. What other woman would react as Emily had today?

Her lack of enthusiasm for his marriage proposal, then her amazingly cool agreement to spending tonight with him had certainly put him on the back foot, a position which he did not like.

Sebastian enjoyed being the boss. At work, at home and in the bedroom. *Especially* in the bedroom.

Time to take the reins again.

'Mountains or the ocean?' he asked when she next reached for her wineglass.

Her glass froze in mid-air, her expression confused. 'What?'

Sebastian picked up his own glass and took a leisurely swallow.

'Which do you prefer?' he asked smoothly. 'The mountains or the ocean?'

'Um... The ocean.'

'Then the ocean it is.'

'I have no idea what you're talking about.'

'Where we will spend tonight. I'll find us a nice hotel on the south coast. Which means I won't be able to drink too much more of this wine. Not if I have to drive. You can have my share.'

'But...do we *have* to go away? Why can't we just stay home?'

'Come now, Emily, I wouldn't expect you to share the bed I shared with Lana.' He'd noticed this morning that it still smelt of Lana's perfume, a powerfully exotic scent which seemed to have seeped into the mattress. Maybe even the carpet as well.

Now that Lana was definitely out of the picture, Sebastian planned on having the whole room refurbished. He wanted nothing left to remind him of that bitch.

'But I...I don't have any nice clothes for going away,' Emily protested. 'Other than what I have on.'

'Which will be highly suitable for arriving and leaving in,' he said. 'Between those times, you won't be needing many clothes.'

At last he got the reaction he wanted.

Heat zoomed into her cheeks, giving him a glimpse of the woman she might become in his arms.

His own body responded, reminding him of the way he'd felt last night, when he'd watched her swimming naked in his pool. *Before* he'd known it was Emily. He'd been transfixed by her voluptuous body...and turned on to the max.

Tonight, that same highly detectable body would be his to make love to.

It was a tantalising and very arousing thought.

Sebastian had deliberately kept his proposal of marriage very businesslike, because that was what he'd believed would appeal to Emily. But there'd been several moments already today when he'd been tempted to cast aside pragmatism in favour of the caveman approach.

When she'd shown up for lunch looking absolutely gorgeous, he'd wanted to do more than take her elbow. He'd wanted to pull her into his arms and kiss her till she was incapable of saying anything but yes to whatever he wanted, whenever he wanted it.

Then, in the taxi, he'd found it extremely hard to keep his hands to himself with her sitting so close to him. Only the fact that they were not alone had stopped him from pouncing.

Tonight, however, they would be alone, with no one to stop him.

Yet his mission was not to satisfy his own, surprisingly intense desires, he reminded himself. But to give Emily the night of her life.

Sebastian had no idea what she liked, sexually.

But he knew what just about every woman in the world liked.

Romance.

He intended to give her that. In spades.

CHAPTER SEVEN

'WHAT on earth have you done?' Emily asked the flushed face in her bathroom mirror.

She kept shaking her head at herself, all her earlier boldness nothing but a dim memory.

The rest of their lunch had passed in a bit of a haze, as had their taxi ride home. She hadn't spoken much. But then, neither had Sebastian. Not till they'd emerged from the taxi.

'Give me some time to organise things,' he'd said as he'd walked her up to the house. 'It's just gone three. I'll come and collect you around four. Like I said, don't pack a lot. A change of underwear and some toiletries. Maybe something casual, in case we go for a walk at some stage.'

Emily had managed to appear as cool as Sebastian till she'd reached the privacy of her apartment, at which point she'd rushed to the bathroom for a desperate call of nature.

Now here she was, on the verge of tears.

Till she suddenly thought of Mark. Then her father. Would they cry in her situation?

Never in a million years!

If Mark had been a woman, he'd have been jubilant. Though, come to think of it, he wouldn't have been in her situation, because he'd have agreed to marry Sebastian like a shot.

Money was Mark's god.

Emily wished she could think more like a man. They could separate love and sex so very easily. They compartmentalised.

Emily couldn't do that, although she was quite adept at hiding her feelings. When she'd been nursing her terminally ill mother, she'd become an expert at the brave face, and on putting a positive spin on the most depressing reality.

Thinking about her mother's death brought some perspective to Emily's thinking. Her situation with Sebastian, whilst upsetting, was hardly tragic. At least she was getting the opportunity to have the man she loved make love to her. How bad could that be?

Emily held on to this new, more positive attitude whilst she went and packed, as ordered. A change of underwear and toiletries were no problem. Choosing a casual outfit proved a little more difficult, because there wasn't much to choose from in her 'housekeeper' wardrobe.

She finally selected a pair of stretch jeans which she'd only worn when Sebastian had been away, a simple white T-shirt, a dark blue jacket and a pair of black shoes.

Her packing complete, Emily stripped off and had a quick shower, careful not to mess up her hair. Afterwards, she swiftly reapplied her make-up, then sprayed herself all over with the only perfume she owned, a light flowery scent which her mother had always worn and which brought fond memories of the hugs they'd shared.

It was nothing like the heavy musky scent Lana had practically bathed in. But then, she was nothing like Lana, except perhaps in bust size.

Lana had been a curvy girl too.

But not quite as curvy as me, Emily thought with secret satisfaction. She had not forgotten how Sebastian had stared at her bare breasts in the pool last night. Not with disgust. With desire.

What will it be like tonight, she wondered, when he saw her again without any clothes on? How would it feel when he touched her? Kissed her? Entered her?

A low moan escaped her lips at this last thought, her hands shaking as she stepped into her cream satin bikini pants.

This was why she'd made the bold decision she had, Emily accepted anew as she dragged on her panties, and then the rest of her clothes. Because she simply had to be with this man. It was a craving which would not be denied.

Once dressed, Emily came to another bold decision. She would not worry about the morning-after any more, would not stew over the consequences of tonight.

For the rest of today, she was going to compartmentalise her thoughts, blotting out all female emotions and focusing on one thing and one thing only.

The pleasure of the moment.

Looking at her completed appearance in the

mirror gave her pleasure. Thinking of tonight as an exciting adventure, rather than being fearful of it, sent extremely pleasurable quivers rippling all through her.

If this was what a man's thinking was like, Emily decided, it was much better than a woman's. She vowed to keep it up for as long as she could.

The doorbell ringing two minutes later rattled her resolve momentarily. But then she squared her shoulders, picked up her overnight bag and went to answer the door.

'Oh!' she exclaimed when she opened it and saw Sebastian standing there. 'You've changed your clothes.'

'Only partially,' he replied as he took the bag out of her hands. 'The suit's the same. Just the shirt and tie have gone.'

They certainly had, replaced by a sexy black crew neck top.

Emily had always thought Sebastian a handsome man. But she'd never thought him overwhelmingly sexy till she'd realised she'd fallen in love with him. It was as though, with this discovery, her eyes finally saw what her heart had subconsciously seen from the word go. That her boss possessed a physical magnetism which was totally irresistible.

To her, anyway.

Her blood charged around her veins as her gaze travelled over him from top to toe. What a stunningly sexy man he was. And tonight he was hers, as she was all his.

Emily could not wait to give herself to him. But not as some kind of sacrificial lamb. Tonight she would take as well as give, without the emotional turmoil which a one-sided love might have brought to their lovemaking.

'Have you got everything you want in here?' Sebastian asked, nodding down to the bag in his hands.

'I hope so.'

'Let's go, then.'

'I have to get my handbag.'

'I'll walk down and put this in the car. You lock up and meet me in the garage.'

A minute later Emily was running down the stairs, her pulse rate as excited as she was. She told herself to slow down and not start acting like a giddy school-girl on her first date.

But that was exactly what she felt like.

But then Sebastian wouldn't date schoolgirls.

Sebastian was standing by the passenger door of his magnificent silver sports car in the garage, his face breaking into a smile when she hurried in.

'You're my kind of girl, Emily,' he said as he opened the passenger door and waved her inside. 'You don't keep a man waiting.'

Lana had, Emily recalled, as she lowered herself into the leather bucket seat. All the time.

Emily frowned. Darn. She hadn't wanted to think about Lana.

Still, he hadn't asked Lana to marry him, had he, came the reassuring thought.

When Sebastian closed the passenger door after her, Emily's nostrils were immediately assailed with the smell of new leather. The car was only a couple of months old, Sebastian's previous vehicle of choice having been a more sedate BMW.

'I like the smell of new cars,' she remarked when Sebastian climbed in behind the wheel.

'You sound like you've got a lot of experience,' he said as he fired the powerful engine.

Emily shrugged. 'My father's always trading in his car and getting a new one.'

Sebastian glanced over at her with curious eyes. 'You've never spoken of your father before.'

'He's not exactly my favourite person,' came her clipped reply.

Sebastian's eyebrows rose. 'I suspect he might be a subject best left to another day.'

'I suspect you could be right.'

'In that case I will keep our conversation to more pleasant topics.'

'Please do.'

Sebastian stopped talking long enough to back out of the garage, swinging his car sharply right once they had cleared the door. It closed automatically, after which Sebastian reefed the wheel to the left and accelerated up the driveway. The large security gates forced a stop, though Sebastian didn't have to get out to open them. He had a remote control which he always carried with him. Emily had one too, which she kept in the glove box of her car.

'You smell very nice,' he said whilst they sat there, waiting for the gates to open wide enough to drive through.

Emily's initial reaction to his compliment was negative. Because she didn't think it could be sincere. Clearly, Sebastian would have liked Lana's heavier perfume, and her own was very light by comparison.

But she swiftly pushed aside such thoughts. Today was for positive thoughts, not negative.

'You do too,' she returned with a smile.

Her own compliment startled him. But then he smiled as well, a wickedly sexy smile, which sent a tremor running down Emily's spine.

The gates finally open, Sebastian zoomed through, not waiting till they were fully shut behind them before he turned left and sped up the tree-lined avenue.

'Where, exactly, are we going?' she asked at the first set of lights.

'North Wollongong. To the Norfolk. It's a newish hotel right on the beach. I stayed there last year.'

Emily winced. Not with Lana, she hoped.

'No,' he said straight away. 'Not with Lana.'

Her head whipped around. 'How did you know what I was thinking?'

'I know how women's minds work.'

Emily could imagine that he did, given he must have had relationships with dozens of women during his adult life. Being such a perfectionist, he would have learned all he could about the female psyche, along with their bodies. Clearly, he had no doubts or worries about his performance tonight.

Still, Emily found Sebastian's sexual confidence a turn-on.

Not that she needed a turn-on where Sebastian

was concerned. He only had to be in the same room with her these days and she was turned on.

Being in the same car with him, especially such a sexy one, was doing things to her that were positively indecent. She could hardly sit still in her leather seat.

No wonder men of the world always drove sports cars, Emily decided with a mixture of admiration and cynicism. They made foreplay almost unnecessary. She suspected that by the time they arrived at that hotel on the south coast she would be in a seriously excited state.

Emily had always liked sex. Mark had not been her first lover, by any means. But she had never craved it as she craved it at this moment. Had never wanted the kinds of things she was suddenly wanting with Sebastian.

She hoped he would not be gentle with her. Or sweet. Or, heaven forbid, loving. She wanted it rough, and wild.

The first time.

After that, she wanted it slow and sensual, so that she could wallow in the experience. Finally, she wanted the opportunity to give, rather than receive. She could see herself now, stroking him all over, kissing him all over, forcing him to lie back whilst she made mad passionate love to him.

Emily's heartbeat took off at the images which flooded into her mind.

'You're very quiet,' Sebastian said. 'You don't get car sick, do you?'

Emily swallowed, taking a moment to clear the breathtakingly exciting fantasy from her mind.

'Not usually. But you do drive fast, Sebastian,' she added as he zipped around a corner and down a narrow side street.

To be honest, Emily had no idea where she was. She never did in Sydney if she didn't stick to the main roads. Which Sebastian obviously hadn't.

'I'm an impatient person by nature,' he replied.

'Really? I wouldn't have said you were.'

'Most people wouldn't. But I am. I just hide my flaws better than most. I'm very impatient, and inclined to lose my temper far too quickly.'

'You never have with me.'

'No one could lose their temper with you, Emily.'

Emily wasn't so sure that was a compliment. It made her sound very boring. And lacking in passion.

'Unlike Lana, you mean,' she couldn't help saying.

'Lana who?' he quipped.

'Oh, I see,' she said. 'So that's how it is with you, is it? Once out of your life, a person doesn't exist any more.'

'That's right.'

Emily shook her head. 'I wish I could do that.' As much as she tried to hate her father, she knew she didn't. She still loved him. And whilst she didn't love Mark any more, she would never forget him, or the callously insensitive way he'd treated her.

'It takes practice,' Sebastian said so coldly that it sent a shiver down Emily's spine.

How bitter he sounded. And ruthless.

It was at that point she realised how little she actually knew about Sebastian. Oh, she'd read the articles about his brilliant business acumen, and seen a short segment on TV outlining how his career had got started; how he and a friend had started up one of the first Australian mobile phone companies when they'd been in their early twenties. Sebastian had had the brains and his wealthy friend had provided the backing, Sebastian revealing during that programme that, unlike his rich business partner, he'd had to work his way through university, his family being very working-class.

Both young men had made an absolute fortune when their chain of Mobilemania stores had been bought out by an international conglomerate. His friend had disappeared from the business scene after that. But Sebastian had started up his own company, Armstrong Industries, developing a wide range of business interests, from holiday resorts to day-care centres to cattle stations and even pine forests.

Sebastian had made the Richest Two Hundred in Australia list by the time he'd been thirty. Recently he'd made the top ten, one of only a select number of billionaires.

The public at large knew about his bank balance, and his single status. But what did they really know—Emily included—about his background?

Very little.

Maybe the media would have dug deeper if he'd been the kind of man who sought publicity.

But he didn't. He kept a very low media profile for a man of his wealth and power.

Emily did know he'd been an only child, courtesy of a remark he'd made during her initial interview when she'd said she was was one too. But she knew nothing of his parents, or his extended family, except that they never visited him.

Presumably his parents were dead.

Although curious, Emily was not about to ask.

Because today was about the pleasure of the moment, not bringing up awkward subjects.

'Now I know where I am!' she exclaimed when Sebastian finally directed his car out on to a main road. 'That's the Olympic stadium over there.'

'Did you go to the Olympics?' Sebastian asked.

'No. I wanted to, but my boyfriend at the time wasn't into sport.'

'Are you talking about that Mark fellow?'

'Er…no. The one before him.'

His eyes speared her for a brief but intense moment. 'You're not the quiet little mouse you've been pretending to be, are you?'

'I haven't been pretending anything,' she said defensively. 'I simply needed to withdraw from relationships for a while.'

'And now you're ready to go back into them?'

'Yes.'

'Complete with a new look.'

'Well I wasn't about to snare myself a husband looking the way I did, was I?'

'I don't know about that. You captured my interest.'

'Oh, don't be ridiculous, Sebastian. You hardly recognised me as a woman till you saw me in my birthday suit.'

'You'd be wrong there. But you did change my perspective on your personality when I found you skinny-dipping in my pool.'

'You didn't think I had it in me?'

'I thought it was out of character.'

'Well. Just shows you that you don't know everything. Even if you think you do,' she added saucily.

He laughed. 'You delight me, Emily.'

'I'm not trying to.'

'I know. That's what delights me. Do you have any idea what most women would do, if they were in your circumstances today?'

'I can guess. But I have a different agenda to most women.'

'Would you care to elaborate?'

'No.'

'Damn it, Emily, I might be tempted to lose my temper with you after all!'

'Won't do you any good.'

'No,' he sighed. 'I dare say it wouldn't. You wouldn't want to marry a man who yelled at you.'

'Absolutely not. And I wouldn't want to marry a man I didn't know, either. When I marry, I want to feel secure in my choice. I don't want any nasty surprises.'

'But you *do* know me. Hell, Emily, you've been my housekeeper for eighteen months. You've seen me in all sorts of situations and moods. More importantly, I haven't been trying to impress you, or hide things from you. My life is an open book. How long do you think it'll take you to get to know whatever new man you're going to meet at that conference centre? Years, if you want to know everything about him. By the time you feel secure enough to marry, your biological clock will be well and truly at midnight. And a baby is what you want more than anything, isn't it?'

Emily's heart lurched. What she wanted more than anything was his baby! To go along with his love... One without the other would be too bitter-sweet for her.

'Agree to marry me,' he swept on before she'd answered him. 'And we could start on the baby-making project tonight.'

Emily gasped, her head snapping round to stare at him.

'You are a truly wicked man, Sebastian Armstrong.'

'A determined man, Emily Bayliss. So what do you say?'

'I'm positively speechless.'

'That's a cop-out. Tell me what you're thinking.'

'I'm thinking I made a big mistake being here with you,' she snapped. 'I should have known you'd know exactly what buttons to push to try to force my hand and get your own way. You're a clever man, Sebastian. But a far too cold-blooded one. I wouldn't want such a man as the father of my children.'

CHAPTER EIGHT

EMILY'S vehement criticism of his character stunned Sebastian.

He'd honestly thought she liked and respected him.

His shock swiftly gave way to angry frustration. What was the point in going on if that was the way she felt? Clearly, she wasn't about to say yes to his proposal of marriage, no matter how good a lover he was.

Sebastian came to a quick decision, zapping his car around the next corner, before braking to a sharp stop at the kerb.

'It's very easy to fix your big mistake, Emily,' he ground out as he glared over at her startled face. 'I'll take you back home.'

Her expressive eyes betrayed an intriguing truth. She didn't want him to take her home.

Which meant only one thing.

She might think he was a total bastard. But she still wanted him to take her to bed.

Sebastian's eyebrows arched. Maybe he wasn't the only one in this car who was a bit on the cold-blooded side.

Still, he understood full well the perversities of sexual attraction. He'd wanted Lana from the first moment he'd seen her. Had wanted her, despite knowing she was a vain, shallow, temperamental creature of whom instinct warned he should steer well clear.

It was damned hard to act sensibly when your hormones were up and running.

'You don't want me to take you home,' he stated baldly, and watched her reaction.

She looked away, as a lot of women did when they were faced with an unpalatable fact.

'There's nothing wrong with wanting sex, Emily,' he argued. 'From what you've told me, you've been without a man for four years. That's not natural, not for a woman who's had an active sex life, which I gather you did have, once. Look, we'll forget about marriage and babies for tonight and just have a good time together.'

Slowly, very slowly, her head turned back. Sebastian was taken aback to see that her eyes were glistening.

Her distress upset him, far more than Lana's copious tears and tantrums ever had. This was no cold-blooded creature sitting next to him, he realised, but a deeply feeling, highly sensitive woman.

Her eyes dropped to her lap as she shook her head unhappily from side to side.

'I won't let you run away from your feelings, Emily,' he persisted. 'You might not like me, but you need me.'

Her head jerked up and round to glare at him. '*Need* you? I don't *need* you,' she threw at him as she dashed her tears away with the back of her hands.

'Yes, you do. Well, maybe not me, especially. But

you need a man. Someone who can get rid of that build-up of sexual frustration you're obviously suffering from. Someone who can show you that you don't need love to enjoy sex.'

'You have absolutely *no* hope of doing *that*, Sebastian.'

Sebastian was not a man to take a challenge lightly.

'Really,' he grated out. And, before she could do more than blink at him, he leant over and kissed her.

When Sebastian's lips crashed down on hers, Emily tried not to moan. Or to melt. Or, heaven forbid, open her own instantly treacherous mouth.

But it was like offering a starving woman a delicious dish of food and expecting her only to have a tiny taste.

So she moaned… And melted… And opened her mouth…

And it all felt fantastic. His lips, his tongue, his hand curving possessively around her throat, pushing her back against the leather seat, holding her captive.

How passionate he was, she thought with an almost delirious joy. How masterful. Exactly as she'd imagined in her fantasies.

When the pressure on her mouth eased, Emily's left hand instinctively lifted to cup the back of his head and keep the kiss going. She didn't want him to stop. Ever.

Sebastian groaned as he battled to gain control of himself.

Who would believe that kissing Emily would do this to him?

If he didn't stop kissing her soon, he'd be forced to do something he hadn't done in years. Have sex in the front seat of a car. In broad daylight.

This was not what he'd planned.

Still, nothing had gone as he'd planned.

If only she'd stop making those sexy little noises—stop squirming…stop digging her nails into him.

Hell on earth, he was dying to touch her, as well as kiss her. She wanted him to. He could tell.

But if he did…

Sebastian reminded himself of what was waiting for them at that hotel: a luxury suite, a king-sized bed, champagne on ice, chocolate-dipped strawberries and candles around the spa bath.

He'd left no stone unturned in providing the most romantic atmosphere for tonight, his mission not just to seduce Emily sexually, but to put her in the right frame of mind to accept his proposal.

If he went ahead with what he was doing right at this moment, she wouldn't be impressed afterwards. She'd be disgusted with herself, and with him. He'd hardly get her to change her mind about his character—and his offer of marriage—if he took cruel advantage of her sexual frustration.

With Emily clearly in desperate need of some lovemaking, Sebastian's goal of making her his wife was back on the agenda, no longer a mission impossible but a definite possibility. By her own admission, Emily was the type of girl who had difficulty separating sex and love. If he satisfied her in bed, she might surrender her heart to him, as well as her body.

This last thought held a lot of appeal. A woman in love was often willing to do things which her head warned her against.

No, he had to stop. And he had to stop right now!

No, don't stop, Emily screamed silently when Sebastian wrenched his mouth away.

He removed her hand—the one which was still caressing the back of his head—and pressed it forcibly down into her lap.

'This is not the place for this, Emily,' he ground out. 'Not nearly enough room. But no more nonsense now. I'm driving us down to that hotel and you're not going to say a single word the whole way. Conversation with you, I can see, is a risk. So zip that lovely mouth of yours up and keep it for what it does very well indeed. And no, I don't want any more of those shock-horror looks either. We both know you came with me today to be kissed, and a whole lot more.'

Emily opened her mouth to voice some kind of lame protest. But closed it again when he pressed two fingers against her lips, his eyes filling with a dark warning.

'Speak, and I promise you I will make you do things in this car which will truly horrify you afterwards.'

Emily almost laughed. Dear heaven, if only he knew...

Her lips parted slightly against the flesh of his fingers, her heart pounding within her chest. Her earlier qualms about coming with Sebastian today had been well and truly routed with his hungry kisses, all doubts replaced by a desire so intense she wasn't sure she could bear any more delay.

'I'll put the radio on,' he said, abruptly withdrawing his hand and doing just that, the car filling with music, a popular song about love lost.

'I suggest you lie back and get some rest,' he said as he gunned the engine once more. 'Because you're going to be damned busy from the moment we reach the privacy of our room.'

A highly erotic quiver rippled through Emily. She'd always known Sebastian would be a passionate lover. And an imaginative one. When Lana had stayed over, she'd always come down to the breakfast table smiling like a cat who'd got the cream.

Her heart suddenly squeezed tight behind her ribs, her eyes darting over to Sebastian, who was busy doing a U-turn.

Is he really over that woman? she agonised. Or will he be thinking of her whilst he's making love to me? Comparing us, perhaps.

'We'll soon be on the freeway,' Sebastian told her as he rejoined the traffic on the main road. 'We should be pulling up at the hotel in just over an hour. Now close your eyes,' he ordered. 'And relax.'

His telling her to relax reinforced to Emily just how different men were from women. Maybe he could relax after what had just happened. But she found it almost impossible.

Still, it came to her that he probably wasn't thinking of Lana at all. She was being ridiculously insecure and jealous.

Men lived in and for the moment, which was what she was supposed to be doing today. Living for the pleasure of the moment and not worrying about anything else, especially Lana.

Which was fine in theory, Emily had come to realise. Not so easy in practice. For her, anyway.

It was as well that Sebastian had taken command of the situation. Because he'd been so right. She hadn't wanted him to take her home. She wanted to have this one night to remember for the rest of her life.

For Sebastian, it would just be a night of no-strings sex, the kind men obviously enjoyed. For her, it would probably prove to be a bitter-sweet experience. But one which she would never regret.

If the effect of his kisses was anything to go by, she was going to have a fabulous time, sexually. Her whole body quivered just thinking about it.

Of course, the morning after was going to be difficult.

Despite what he'd said, Emily was not convinced that Sebastian had given up his quest to stop her from leaving him. He was an extremely stubborn man, and a super rich one, grown used to having his way.

She wouldn't mind betting he still thought he could seduce her into doing what he wanted.

Emily could not deny that when he was kissing her just now, all sensible thought had flown out the window. But he couldn't make love to her all the time. She would have some moments of respite, such as now.

Finally, Emily closed her eyes, leant back in the seat and focused on some sensible survival mantras.

Don't forget he doesn't love you, no matter what his lovemaking is like.

Don't forget he's only taking you to bed to get his own way.

Don't forget it's just sex to him. Nothing more.

CHAPTER NINE

EMILY couldn't really relax, of course. She just pretended to so that Sebastian would leave her alone. After a while, she turned her head and shoulders to face the passenger window so that he couldn't see when she opened her eyes.

By then, they were on the freeway. The southern Sydney suburbs had been left behind and they were speeding along the multi-lane highway which cut its path through national forests.

Thick bushland edged the road on either side.

Not the most distracting of views.

Emily hadn't been down to the south coast in years. She and Mark had always headed north when they'd wanted to go somewhere for the day, or a weekend. But she'd had a boyfriend once who lived in Campbelltown, and he'd often taken her down to Austinmere, a cute little beach on the south coast which had a sea pool. He'd also taken her to Thirlmere, which was more of a surfer's beach. She'd never actually been to Wollongong, which was the largest of the south coast towns. A city, really.

Once they were on the freeway, there were two ways of reaching their destination. You could get off the highway and go down the Bulli Pass, then follow the road south along the coastline to North Wollongong.

That was considered the tourist route, providing spectacular views.

The Bulli pass, however, was a formidable descent, with lots of hairpin bends.

Alternately, you could keep on the Princes Highway till you reached Wollongong proper. This was a faster route, with a more gradual descent from the hills to the coast, but less interesting.

When the sign for the Bulli Pass exit came up, Sebastian stayed in the centre lane, clearly going for the faster route. Fifteen minutes later, the bushland receded and Wollongong came into view below.

Emily actually spotted their hotel as they made their way down the escarpment, the tall white building standing out from its surroundings, the last rays of the setting sun just catching the upper floor windows. But she didn't realise it was the Norfolk till Sebastian turned his car into the circular driveway which led up to its equally impressive entrance.

'Wow,' Emily said, sitting upright in her seat. It was the first word she'd spoken since Sebastian had ordered her not to.

His sidewards glance carried a self-satisfied smile. 'You approve?'

'It's stunning.' And very expensive, by the look of it.

Emily knew her hotels. And this one would rival the very best in Sydney.

A parking valet pounced immediately they alighted, as well as a porter to take their two small bags. Sebastian cupped her elbow and led her through the revolving glass doors into the hotel proper, Emily doing her best to act as if this was what she did most weekends—stayed in five-star hotels with one of Australia's wealthiest and most eligible men.

The lobby was enormous, with marble floors, vaulted ceilings and some serious chandeliers which would not have looked out of place in a European palace.

The blonde behind the reception desk nearly fell over herself attending to Sebastian, Emily mentally shaking her head over the girl's gushing manner. During the time she'd worked the desk at the Regency, they'd had presidents, pop stars and even a sheikh or two staying there and she hadn't gone gaga over any of them.

The blonde even had the hide to cast an askance glance Emily's way when Sebastian was busy signing in, as though she could not understand what on earth he was doing with such an ordinary-looking girlfriend.

Emily squared her shoulders and speared the receptionist with dagger-like eyes until the girl flushed and looked away. By the time Sebastian led Emily over to the lift wells, she had her dander up, which was much better than succumbing to the butterflies gathering in the pit of her stomach.

'Do women always act like that when you're around?' she asked when he let go of her arm to press the up button on the wall.

His shrug was dismissive. 'In the main.'

'No wonder you're arrogant.'

Sebastian's eyes turned dark and thoughtful. 'Are you deliberately trying to provoke me, Emily?'

Was she?

Guilt consumed Emily once she realised she'd been trying to sabotage tonight one last time. Possibly because of fear.

'I'm sorry,' she said. 'That was rude of me.'

'Yes, it was.'

'I'm not usually rude.'

'I know. So why were you just now?'

'I guess it's because I'm nervous,' she confessed.

'Nervous?' he repeated, as though unfamiliar with such a condition.

'It's so silly,' she blurted out. 'It's not as though I'm a virgin.'

'Maybe not,' he said, his eyes soft on her. 'But it will be your first time in a long time. And your first time with me.'

'Yes,' she whispered through parched lips.

The lift doors opened and a couple came out, putting a stop to their intimate conversation. But not to Emily's rapidly escalating heartbeat.

When Sebastian took hold of her hand an electric current raced up her arm. Apprehension gave way to anticipation, doubt replaced by the most overwhelming need, not to be made love to, but to be totally ravished. Her head turned and her eyes locked with his.

'Don't be gentle with me,' she heard herself say.

He stared at her for a long moment, then nodded. 'Your wish is my command.'

'But I'm not usually like this,' she said shakily.

'You don't have to make excuses to me,' he replied darkly as he ushered her into the lift, then used his key card to gain access to their floor. 'I am well acquainted with the perversities of the flesh.'

Neither of them said anything during the brief ride upwards. Neither did they touch each other.

By the time the lift stopped and the doors opened, Emily felt close to fainting. When she swayed on her high heels, Sebastian scooped her up into his arms and carried her from the lift.

No one was in the waiting area to stare at them. Neither did they encounter anyone walking along the hotel corridor.

Not that Emily would have cared. Not with Sebastian's arms around her. She wrapped her own arms around his neck, her handbag hanging down his back.

When he reached their door, he moved his hold from behind her knees to just underneath her bottom, taking her full weight with that one arm whilst he used the hand which had been around her waist to open the door. Once inside, he kicked the door shut before carrying her past their bags—which had preceded them—striding through the spacious lounge room straight into the luxuriously appointed bedroom, which had a sitting area of its own and a king-sized bed covered by a cream lambswool spread.

Emily was not surprised that he'd booked what was probably one of the most expensive suites in the hotel. Men like Sebastian always travelled in style.

But she was taken aback by what she knew were

not customary accoutrements, unless one asked for them. Patrons of such a suite could expect a complimentary bottle of champagne on arrival. But not a magnum, or chocolate-dipped strawberries, presented exquisitely on a delicate crystal plate.

'No,' he said brusquely when he spotted the direction of her eyes. 'None of that till later.

'I won't be long. But before I go…' Cupping the back of her head, he planted a brutal kiss on her mouth, ravaging her orally for several seconds before wrenching his mouth away. 'You could hurry things along by getting undressed,' he told her gruffly, before spinning on his heel and stalking off into the adjoining *en suite* bathroom.

Emily stared after him, her heart thudding loudly in her chest.

She supposed she was getting what she'd asked for. But, for some weird and wonderful reason, she no longer wanted rough sex.

But she could hardly complain now. He would think she was crazy, going hot and cold on him all the time.

Not that she'd gone cold. She hadn't; her body was on fire.

But she wanted Sebastian to make love to her. Her stomach flipped over. If he came out and found that she hadn't even started undressing, he might think she'd changed her mind again.

Exhaling a shaky sigh, Emily placed her handbag on the seat of a nearby chair before removing her suede jacket and draping it over the back. Despite the pleasant temperature in the room, she suddenly broke out into goose-bumps and was standing there, rubbing her upper arms with her hands, when Sebastian emerged from the bathroom.

Their eyes met, Emily's gaze pleading with him not to do what she'd asked earlier. She needed him to be gentle with her. To be tender and romantic. She needed to pretend.

No woman had ever looked at Sebastian the way Emily was looking at him at this moment.

His bed-partners of choice in recent years had invariably been beautiful and provocative creatures, confident in their bodies and their sexual know-how. He'd never been attracted to shrinking violets, or blushing virgins.

Not that Emily was either of these things. He'd discovered for himself last night, and again today, that his seemingly reserved housekeeper could be as bold as the best of them.

She was, however, extremely vulnerable at this time in her life; it shone through in her worried, wide-eyed gaze.

He supposed it could not be easy to go to bed with a man after a break of four years. Or to strip off in front of him the way Lana would have done.

Sebastian decided that a change of tack was called for.

'There's a couple of complimentary robes in the bathroom,' he said straight away. 'Why don't you get undressed in there and put one on?'

Her relief was touchingly transparent as she swept up her handbag and hurried into the bathroom.

She was sweet, yet so damned sexy.

Sebastian hummed as he swiftly opened the magnum of champagne, poured two glasses and carried them over to the bedside table. After that, he returned to the living room, where he extracted some condoms from his overnight bag. Back in the bedroom, he put the foil packets into a bedside drawer.

Better to be safe than sorry but, with a bit of luck, by morning, Emily might be swayed into accepting his proposal and the use of protection could be dispensed with.

Of course, he'd have to impress her tonight if that was to happen.

Sebastian had no doubt he could deliver, sexually. He had every confidence in his bedroom know-how. The problem would lie with Emily's emotions. She was far more complex than he'd imagined. Far less pragmatic. And far more sensitive.

Sebastian didn't have any personal experience with soft, sensitive women.

The bathroom door opened quietly, Emily emerging wrapped from neck to ankle in a voluminous white towelling robe. Her face looked almost as white as she walked slowly back to the bed.

'Oh,' she said, her pale skin brightening once she sighted the glasses by the bed. 'You opened the champagne.'

Good move, Sebastian.

'It seemed mean not to,' he replied smoothly. 'And not very romantic. Now, why don't you slip out of that robe and pop into bed, beautiful?'

When she hesitated, he reached to undo the sash

at her waist, watching her eyes whilst he parted the robe and pushed it back off her shoulders.

Sebastian thought he knew what to expect from her body. He'd seen her naked in the pool, hadn't he? He already knew she was full-breasted and much slimmer than her loose-fitting clothes had indicated.

He almost didn't glance downwards as the robe fell from her shoulders, not wanting to embarrass her at this stage.

But when her eyes dropped away from his, he automatically looked down.

Sebastian was a connoisseur of female beauty, nothing attracting him more than a woman who looked like a woman. He did not agree with the fashionable idea that a woman could never be too thin. Neither did he like females who sported pumped-up or sinewy muscles.

Emily had everything Sebastian liked and which rarely came in one package. Magnificent breasts. A tiny waist which he could put his hands around. Great child-bearing hips which balanced her bust. And long shapely legs with slender ankles and small feet.

She possessed an hour-glass figure at its best, further complimented with a gently rounded stomach and the kind of soft clear skin which would feel great to touch.

By comparison, Lana had no mystery about her. She was a whore, Sebastian had finally come to realise. A heartless, gold-digging whore.

But not this lovely creature standing nervously before him. She couldn't be bought. That much was already obvious.

Which made Sebastian want her all the more, not just for tonight, but for the rest of his life.

So he'd better make sure he did this right.

'You are beyond beautiful, Emily,' he said softly. 'Come here…' He moved away from her to drag back the woollen spread and the crisp white bed-linen. 'Cover that far too tempting body up while I get myself undressed.'

CHAPTER TEN

A FLUSHED Emily found herself sitting up in the middle of the king-sized bed, the sheet clutched modestly over her breasts whilst she watched Sebastian undress, not in the privacy of the bathroom as she had done, but right in front of her.

His removal of his suit jacket didn't overly quicken her heartbeat, but when he yanked his black top out of the waistband of his trousers and reefed it up over his head, her pulse-rate went into overdrive. Which was ridiculous, really. She'd seen him bare-chested many times before, when he went swimming, and of course she already knew that his body was simply superb: broad shoulders, slender hips, a six-pack stomach, courtesy of all that rowing he did, and his skin was silky smooth and beautifully bronzed.

To look at him, you'd never believe he was forty.

Looking at him now, however, felt very different from looking at him around the pool, because of where it was heading—to total nudity, and him in this bed with her, touching her, kissing her, making love with her.

Emily gulped, then grabbed the champagne glass from the bedside table. A few drops spilled as she swept it up to her lips, because her eyes were not on what she was doing. They were fixed on Sebastian's hands, which had just unsnapped his waistband and unzipped the zip. Emily tried not to stare as he pushed his trousers down over his hips. But when his rough action took his underpants with him, her mouth went bone-dry.

'Better take these off too,' Sebastian said with a quick smile, then sat on the side of the bed and disposed of his shoes and socks.

'You're looking much more relaxed,' he said as he dived under the covers with her. 'Must be the champers. Give me a bit of yours.'

Both his hands closed over hers as he brought the glass to his lips. Emily stared deep into his eyes as he took a hefty swallow, an incredulous feeling rushing through her.

'This is just so crazy,' she said shakily.

Sebastian took the glass out of her hands, downed the rest of the contents, then placed it back on the bedside table. When he turned back to face her, he cupped her cheeks with his hands.

'Crazy can be good,' he said, pushing her back down on to the pillows. 'Crazy can be fun. How long is it, Emily, since you've had fun?'

'Too long,' she whispered just before his lips met hers.

Emily closed her eyes, then moaned, a low soft moan which echoed the rush of emotion which threatened to overwhelm her. Because it was finally happening. Sebastian was making love to her. Really making love to her.

His mouth was gentle. Not rough at all. And his hands. Oh, goodness, his hands...

One lifted to stroke the hair back from her forehead whilst the other travelled down her throat, over a breast, her ribs, her stomach, his touch slow and sensuous. Her skin tingled wherever he went, the rest of her body dying to have him touch her there.

But he took his time, making her wait, making her whimper each time his fingers grazed far too briefly over a stunningly erect nipple.

That roving hand finally made more intimate inroads, sliding down between her legs, bringing a tortured gasp to her lips.

Oh, no, she thought despairingly when he honed in on her most erotic zone. If he kept doing that she was going to come! And she didn't want that. She wanted him inside her. Wanted to hold him close. Wanted to be as one with him.

All her muscles stiffened, her mind desperately trying to stop the inevitable.

His withdrawing his hand brought a raw groan of relief. When his head lifted, her eyes clung to his in a mad mixture of adoration and gratitude.

He smiled down at her, then gave her a soft peck on her still parted lips.

'Won't be a sec,' he said huskily, then rolled away, yanked opened the top drawer of the bedside table and extracted a small foil packet.

His stopping to protect both of them brought another rush of relief and gratitude. Because Emily had been way past caring if he wore a condom or not. If he'd asked her to marry him at this moment, she would have said yes like a shot.

'Now where was I?' he murmured when he rolled back.

'No, don't,' she gasped when that wickedly knowing hand swiftly re-entered the danger zone.

'You don't like that?' he questioned, his expression surprised.

'I like it too much,' she choked out.

Sebastian smiled. 'What would you like me to do, then?'

'Just do it, for pity's sake.'

His laugh was soft and wry. 'And there I was, thinking all these months that my wonderful cool and calm housekeeper was the epitome of patience. No no, don't turn your face away, Emily. I like the wild passion in your eyes. It excites me. Here, feel what you've done to me.'

His pressing her hand against his stunning erection was like opening the lid on Emily's desire. With a naked groan, she encircled him, holding him tightly whilst she caressed his rock-hard flesh.

His muttered swearword showed she'd taken him by surprise.

'Stop that,' he growled and, grabbing both her hands, drove them high against the pillows above her head. The action sent him looming over her, his naked chest rubbing against her throbbing breasts, his erection pressing into her stomach.

'Put your legs up around me,' he ordered roughly.

Once she did, he let her hands go, trusting perhaps

that she would now lie still for him. But more likely because he needed his own hands elsewhere.

Emily would never forget the moment he first entered her, the rush of emotion far overwhelming any physical sensation.

Her heart lurched, but so did her body, shattering apart in an instant orgasm which was as perversely pleasurable as it was dismayingly premature. Her head whipped from side to side, her eyes squeezing tightly shut as her body trembled from top to toe.

Oh, Sebastian, she cried silently, tears welling up behind her eyelids. *My darling. My love.*

Sebastian didn't know what to do.

If he wasn't sadly mistaken, Emily was crying.

Should he ignore the fact and just continue?

His own body was screaming at him for release. At the same time, it seemed insensitive not to stop and see what was wrong. Though he suspected he already knew.

'No, no,' she choked out when he began to withdraw.

Sebastian sank back into the still throbbing depths of her body with a relieved sigh. At the same time, he did lever himself up on to his elbows so that he could see if his suspicions were correct.

Yes, she was crying, damn it. Not hysterically. Very quietly, silent tears running down her cheeks.

'You're not thinking of that fool, Mark, are you?' he asked with a touch of exasperation. Why was it that the really sweet girls in this world always fell for selfish creeps?

'Mark?' she said blankly, her eyes blinking open. 'No. No. I...I'm not thinking of Mark.'

'What, then?'

'Can't...can't a person cry with happiness?'

'Happiness?'

'Yes. It...it's such a relief to know I can enjoy sex without love after all.'

Sebastian couldn't work out why this discovery of Emily's didn't please him as much as he thought it would. Maybe because he'd been secretly hoping she would fall in love with him, once he made love to her. It would have made his marriage mission a lot easier.

Still, it was good that she was enjoying herself and not pining after some idiot.

'Okay for me to continue then?' he asked even as he was already moving inside her.

She didn't say anything, but her mouth fell open and her eyes glazed over. She sucked in sharply when her body started gripping his, a sure sign that she was far from finished.

Sebastian was suddenly seized with the urge to show Emily that if she married him, her sex life would not be restricted to once a night, or the missionary position. He would make love to her often, and in all sorts of ways.

Starting now!

She moaned softly when he withdrew, but made no protest when he flipped her over and pulled her up on to her hands and knees. Doing it this way had always been one of Sebastian's favourite positions. Perhaps because it practically guaranteed a woman's pleasure and satisfaction.

Sebastian prided himself on his sexual expertise and control, but Emily was proving to be a strangely difficult partner for him to keep his head with.

If only she'd stop rocking back and forth on her hands and knees, stop pressing her deliciously rounded bottom hard up against his groin.

His hands reached up to cup her breasts in a vain attempt to still the rest of her body, but it was too late. He'd reached the point of no return, his head bursting with stars as his body exploded deep inside her.

He didn't expect her to come with him, but astonishingly she did, heightening the thrill of his release when her flesh started spasming around his, over and over and over.

Sebastian tried not to groan. He was not normally a noisy lover. But groan he did. And it felt wonderful.

He decided not to be so silent in future.

Carefully he withdrew, not surprised when Emily collapsed, face down, on the bed, her arms outspread, her shuddering sigh that of a sated woman.

Sebastian smiled a darkly knowing smile. If she thought the sex was over, then she was very much mistaken. It had only just begun.

He stroked a possessive hand down the lovely curve of her spine, then trailed the back of his fingers over her peach-like buttocks, pleased with the tremors that rippled through her.

Sebastian now wanted to marry Emily more than ever. He would have the best of both worlds with this woman. A peaceful life, and passion as well. What more could he want?

The thought of her accepting that job next

Monday then leaving him could not be tolerated. He had to find a way to keep her with him, to make her marry him. Satisfying sex alone might not be enough to achieve that. Emily might still think she wanted love as well.

An idea popped into his head which was rather ruthless.

Could he get away with it?

Sebastian slid his hand down between her legs and played with her there till she squirmed, then moaned.

No trouble, he thought with a rush of heady power. No trouble at all.

CHAPTER ELEVEN

I MUST keep my head. I must keep my head. I must keep my head.

This mantra kept running through Emily's mind as she leant back in the spa bath, a chocolate-dipped strawberry in one hand and a fresh glass of champagne in the other.

Difficult to keep one's head, however, when one was this tipsy, and this much in love.

It was Sebastian who'd run the bath, and lit the candles, and arranged everything in here for them to eat and drink. Sebastian who'd thoughtfully given her five minutes privacy before he'd joined her in the bubble bath. Sebastian who was being so wonderfully attentive to her that if she didn't know him better, she might think he was in love with her as well!

But she understood that this was all part of his seduction routine.

'What time is it?' she asked before taking a delicious bite out of the strawberry, then following up with a sip of champagne.

'Around seven, I think,' he replied nonchalantly.

'Maybe a bit later. Are you hungry? Do you want me to order dinner from room service after we get out of here?'

'No. Not yet. I think all these strawberries have ruined my appetite.' She popped the last one into her mouth and washed it down with more champagne.

'We'll go for a walk later. Then you might feel like something more substantial than strawberries.'

Emily couldn't think of anything she'd like to do less than get dressed and go for a walk.

'Couldn't we just stay here?'

'You mean in this bath?'

'No. I'm getting a bit pruny. I was thinking that maybe…if it's all right with you…we could…um…I mean…I could…um…'

It was hard to just come out with what she wanted to do, despite being tipsy!

'Emily,' Sebastian said with that look he always got on his face when he was frustrated with something, or someone. 'Stop stammering and just say it.'

Emily took another mouthful of champagne. 'All right. I want to go back to bed and make love to *you*.'

His eyebrows lifted. 'You like being on top?'

'Well I…sometimes,' she said, even though it was a lie. She'd never overly liked that position. But she'd fantasised quite a bit lately about making love to Sebastian that way, and this might be her only chance to make that fantasy come true. It wasn't the being-on-top part she craved so much but the experience of touching him all over, and kissing him all over.

His blue eyes twinkled at her. 'Emily Bayliss, you are constantly surprising me today.'

'That's because you don't really know me. Just as I don't really know you.'

'Are you warning me again that you won't change your mind and marry me?'

Emily's hand tightened around her champagne glass. 'You promised we wouldn't talk about that tonight.'

'So I did,' he muttered. 'More fool me. But I'll be bringing the subject up again tomorrow.'

If he asked her whilst they were down here, in this romantic environment, she'd probably say yes. She could already feel her resolve to walk away weakening appreciably.

'Not till we leave here,' she asked him. 'Please, Sebastian.'

If he waited till they were on their way back to Hunter's Hill, she'd be back in reality again.

'Why's that?'

'Because I'm having a lovely time and I don't want to argue with you.'

'I can't imagine you ever arguing with anyone. Not seriously.'

'In that case, you *really* don't know me. Just before I came to work for you, I argued with my father and I haven't spoken to him since.'

Sebastian frowned. 'What on earth did you argue about?'

Emily regretted bringing her father into their conversation. Talk about an instant dampener. Although perhaps it was a timely reminder of how men used the women who loved them for their own ends. She had to be careful that she didn't let

Sebastian become the third man in a row to make her into a victim.

Time to take control of your life again, Emily. Time to have what you want, even if it is only for tonight.

'Would you mind if I deferred any disclosures of family feuds to some other time?' she said, sliding forward to take the almost empty champagne glass out of Sebastian's hand. 'I don't think this is the time or the place. Now…'

She stood up carefully in the bath, thrilling to the look in his eyes as he glanced up at her unfolding nudity.

'I'll just get out and put these glasses down. You stay where you are till I'm nice and dry. Then I'll see to you.'

Wow, Sebastian thought as he watched Emily towel herself down, one sensual bit at a time. This is one sexy woman.

By the time he climbed out of the bath, he was fiercely erect. By the time she finished towelling him down, he wished he hadn't agreed to her taking charge of their lovemaking. The urge to hoist her up on to the vanity unit and plunge into her right here and now was so intense he had to battle for control.

Returning to the bedroom—and the bed—gave him a brief respite. But he still extracted a condom from the drawer straight away and handed it to her, hoping she'd take the hint.

She smiled a saucy little smile, then placed it on the other bedside table.

'We won't be needing that just yet,' she purred, then

snuggled up to his side, her head on his right shoulder, her left hand resting in the middle of his chest.

'You're not to do a thing,' she instructed him as the hand on his chest began to move downwards in slow, tantalising circles.

Sebastian's stomach muscles tensed as she moved inexorably closer to his erection.

Her head lifted from his shoulder and she stared down at him for a long moment whilst her fingertips traced the muscles between his ribs. Her eyes were glazed, her expression almost wistful.

'You have a magnificent body, Sebastian,' she said at last.

'I work hard at it,' he replied, whilst thinking that Lana had never once given him a compliment like that. She'd been the one who expected all the compliments.

'What are you going to do in the morning with no river to row on?' Emily murmured.

'The same thing I do when I'm away.'

She glanced up at him, her hand stilling once more. 'Which is what?'

'A hundred push-ups and a five kilometre run.'

'You're kidding me.'

'No.'

'That's a bit obsessive, don't you think?'

'I *am* obsessive. How else would I have been the success I've been?'

'Maybe it's time for you to relax a little and enjoy the fruits of your labour.'

'Difficult to relax right at this precise moment,' he said with a stifled groan when the side of her hand brushed the tip of his erection.

'Poor darling,' Emily said throatily.

Sebastian knew where she was heading when she sat up and wriggled around to lie sidewards on the bed, both her head and hands having easy access to his lower body. Clearly, she meant to go down on him. Maybe even go all the way.

Strangely, Sebastian wasn't that fond of fellatio. He'd never been really convinced that a woman enjoyed doing it. Since becoming rich, he'd had any number of women all too eager to go down on him.

And, whilst he could not deny it gave him physical pleasure, he always felt mentally distanced from the act, his one overriding emotion being cynicism.

But as Emily caressed him intimately, then put her lips where her hands had been, Sebastian's heart squeezed tight. Impossible to feel cynical about this woman's lovemaking. Emily had no materialistic motive in giving him oral sex. There was no artifice in her, or cold-blooded ambition. She was doing this for pure pleasure. His and hers.

He moaned under the impact of the soft kisses she rained up and down his shaft, stunned by the feelings she evoked in him. When she finally sucked him deep into her mouth, he was propelled into a maelstrom of sensation and emotion which was totally alien to him.

He could hardly think. Hardly breathe.

Coming was only a heartbeat away when she stopped, pushing her hair out of her face as she looked up at him with a heavy-lidded gaze.

'I won't stop if you don't want me to,' she said.

Sebastian stared at her wet lips. At her flushed face. At her fiercely erect nipples.

'It's up to you,' he replied thickly.

'I'd rather do this,' she whispered, and moved to straddle him, her hands shaking as she angled his aching flesh into her body.

He groaned at the heat of her. And the wetness. She sank down upon him to the hilt, then began to rise and fall in a most abandoned rhythm.

Sebastian could see that she'd forgotten all about protection. She was lost to her passion and her need. Lost to the heat of the moment.

He wasn't far behind.

He momentarily thought of his earlier ruthless resolve to have unsafe sex with her before the night was out, to do his best to make her pregnant, thereby ensuring that she would marry him.

All of a sudden, however, it didn't seem right to try to trap her. Or to let her trap herself. Emily deserved better than that. So did any child they might or might not have in the future.

Sebastian frowned, his mind swinging abruptly to the serious subject of procreation.

He'd shied away from having children in the past, mostly because he'd needed all his focus and energy to make a success of his life. But partly because he'd never had a relationship with a woman he'd felt confident of being a really good mother.

Whilst he knew Emily was just such a woman, he still wanted her to be his wife before she conceived. He never wanted any child of his to have any reason to criticise his parents. Or to feel the kind of negative emotions he'd felt whilst growing up. A child deserved to be wanted and loved right from the beginning, not used as an instrument of emotional blackmail.

Which left Sebastian no option but to revert to his original plan, that of binding Emily to him sexually this weekend so that she could not possibly say no when he asked her again to marry him. It was obvious she was enjoying being on top, but that was not the kind of sex which would achieve his aim. He needed to take command again, needed to give her a level of pleasure which she'd hopefully never experienced with any other man.

When he took her forcibly by her hips and lifted her right off him, she cried out. Whether in surprise or protest, he wasn't sure. But it really didn't matter.

'Time for a change, beautiful,' he growled as he tossed her on to the bed, then loomed over her, bending his head to one of her fiercely erect nipples, licking it, then tugging at it with his teeth. She sucked in sharply, then moaned with pleasure, reminding him of what she'd said to him earlier in the afternoon.

'Don't be gentle with me…'

He aimed to take her at her word this time, moving over to her other breast, where he gave her eagerly awaiting nipple the same rough treatment. Only when her breasts had to be burning did he abandon them, sliding slowly down her body, sucking and biting her stomach as he went.

Even before his mouth reached its destination, her legs had fallen wantonly apart, evidence of her fever-pitch arousal. When he stabbed his tongue against her swollen clitoris, she immediately splintered apart, crying out her release.

'No, no,' she whimpered when he kept going, a sure indication that no man had done this to her before, taken her beyond that moment when she thought she wanted him to stop, propelling her to a blissfully erotic place where her mind was no longer connected to her body, where her flesh reacted instinctively, like an animal in heat.

She came and she came, moaning softly each time, till at last she lay still, totally spent. Or so she thought.

Sebastian immediately knelt up between her thighs, leaning over to snatch up the condom from the bedside table. She cried out when he pulled her up from the bed and slid her roughly across his thighs. Cried out again when he drove into her.

Her big blue eyes met his, their expression dazed.

'No more,' she said brokenly. 'No more...' And her head flopped forward against his chest, her arms dangling limply by her sides.

He ignored her, cupping her buttocks with his hands and rocking her back and forth upon him, clenching his teeth hard in his jaw in an effort to harness his rapidly disintegrating control.

A sigh whispered from her lips, but she did not protest, her body deliciously soft and compliant. He knew he could not possibly last long. Yet somehow he managed to hold on whilst his mind willed her to respond. Because he knew if she did...if she could not resist...if her body could be made to crave yet another orgasm, then she would be his.

Her arms were the first part of her to come to life, lifting from her sides to wrap around his back. Then it was her lips nuzzling at his neck. Then her internal muscles, clasping and releasing him in that way women's bodies did when they were well on their way to orgasm.

Finally, she began digging her knees into the bed and grinding herself against him. Her head jerked up and tipped back, her spine arching, her mouth gasping wide open as she took him with her in a release which had him bellowing like a bull.

Sebastian had never experienced anything like it.

Clutching her tightly against his chest, he buried his face in her hair, his flesh finally free to lose itself in hers. Which it did, for what felt like an interminable time, his spasms not stopping till long after hers.

Her having fallen asleep in his arms went unnoticed till he called her name and received no answer.

Sebastian smiled a triumphant smile, then lowered her gently back to the bed, satisfied that his mission had just about been completed.

Not that he intended to rest on his laurels.

Emily was not the sort of girl whose mind could be easily swayed or changed. He would have to reinforce his sexual hold over her when she woke, his ultimate mission being to make her totally addicted to his lovemaking before this night was out.

Not an unpleasant prospect, he conceded as he withdrew. Emily was proving herself to be a very intriguing bed partner. Marriage to her would certainly be more than a marriage of convenience. It would be both relaxing and exciting at the same time.

She sighed in her sleep when he stroked a soft hand over her breasts, her belly, her bottom. Sighed, then quivered.

A new wave of triumph washed through Sebastian
as he realised she was responding to him, even when
her mind was completely shut down. He might have
played with her further if he hadn't been exhausted
himself. Frankly, he needed a rest if he was going to
keep proving himself the exceptional lover he'd
bragged about being.

But Sebastian found it difficult to take his hands
from her body, difficult to leave her.

Emily *had* to marry him, he decided fiercely
when he finally forced himself to rise and head for
the bathroom.

Come tomorrow, he would not take no for an
answer!

CHAPTER TWELVE

'ANOTHER cup of coffee?' Sebastian asked Emily as he picked up the stainless steel pot and poured himself some more.

They were sitting out on the sun-drenched balcony, wrapped in matching robes, having just finished the very substantial breakfast Sebastian had ordered the night before and which had been delivered to their suite on a beautifully appointed trolley.

'Yes, please,' Emily replied, thinking to herself that Sebastian was still pulling out all stops to impress her. She'd never seen him once offer to pour Lana more coffee.

There again, he'd never wanted to marry Lana.

But does he still want to marry me? came the sudden thought.

Sebastian hadn't brought the matter up again this morning. And he would have if he wanted to, regardless of her asking him to leave any discussion of marriage till they left here. Maybe, after last night's performance, he didn't think he had to offer marriage to stop her from leaving. Maybe he believed she'd settle for being his mistress instead.

Which she probably would, Emily conceded unhappily.

'That's enough, thank you,' she said when her coffee cup was three-quarters full. Ironic words, ones which she wished she'd been capable of saying a couple of times last night.

Emily had known she was taking a risk agreeing to spend the night with the man she loved. She hadn't realised, however, how great a risk it was. By the time she'd woken this morning, any resolve she'd had to just walk away had well and truly dissolved, replaced by an all-consuming need to just be with him, no matter what.

Emily shivered at the memory of everything she'd experienced in his arms. She'd thought Mark had been good in bed. By comparison, Mark had been a novice, with limited imagination and stamina. Sebastian had shown her that a night spent with him went way beyond the romantic fantasy she'd envisaged.

Emily had never known such a dominating and demanding lover. He had not just made love to her countless times in countless ways. He'd skilfully seduced her mind along with her body till she wanted him continuously, unable to say no to anything he suggested.

Even now, sitting here, sipping coffee, she wanted him. Yet less than half an hour ago they'd been making love, on the vanity unit top, her body still dripping wet from the erotically charged shower they'd just shared.

She should have been satisfied. Instead, she wanted more.

Sebastian had uncovered a level of sensuality in

her which she'd never known she possessed. And now…now she was totally at his mercy.

Her only defence was pretence. So she was doing her best to act like a sophisticated woman of the world who'd been there, done that.

Who knew? Maybe she would still find the courage to walk away.

But she seriously doubted it.

The room telephone suddenly ringing brought a scowl to Sebastian's face. He put down the coffee pot and stood up, retying his towelling robe as he did so.

'I hope that's not reception forgetting we have late checkout,' he muttered as he headed inside.

Emily stood up also, but not to go inside. She walked over to the balcony railing, taking her coffee with her, sipping it slowly as she tried to find distraction from her worrying thoughts by surveying the picturesque view.

It looked spectacular in the morning light, the ocean sparkling under the rising sun. From the height of their floor, she could see above the tops of the Norfolk pines which lined the beach below, right out to the distant horizon.

It was inevitable, however, that her gaze was drawn down to the path which followed the pines and along which they'd walked the previous evening. They'd not long shared a lovely meal—brought by room service, of course—when Sebastian had suggested a stroll along the harbourside paths. She'd jumped at the chance, because by then she'd started to be consumed by the disturbing need to have him inside her all the time. She'd hoped that time away from that seductive hotel suite might break the cycle of need.

Wishful thinking…

Emily stared down at the path, wondering which pine tree it was that he'd pulled her over to, leaning her back up against the trunk whilst he'd kissed and fondled her. They must have looked like necking teenagers, or possibly honeymooners, unable to keep their hands off each other. The shadow of the tree had provided some privacy from passers-by. But people could probably have still seen them.

Yet Emily hadn't cared. She'd thrilled to his hands on her breasts, her bottom. Only when he'd reduced her to begging him for more intimacy, did he lead her back to the hotel for more.

'Damn and blast!' Sebastian muttered as he strode back on to the balcony, looking irritated and exasperated.

'What's wrong?'

'That wasn't reception. It was John.'

'John? Oh, you mean your PA.'

'I told him where I was heading in case I didn't come back. I always tell someone my destination when I drive off somewhere. I usually tell you, but you were coming with me. Not that I told him that.'

Emily wondered why not, if he was serious about marrying her.

'He couldn't contact me on my mobile, since I turned it off, so he had to ring here.'

'A business emergency, I presume?' she ventured.

Sebastian was a hands-on company owner who didn't delegate well. He was always being rung at home by various company executives, who all seemed to work seven days a week.

'There's a problem with a retirement village I'm building in Queensland,' he explained, frustration in his voice and in his face.

'What kind of problem?'

'What? Oh, nothing to worry your pretty little head about.' His frown cleared, his mouth curving into a sexy smile as he walked over to her. 'Mmm… You do look delicious in this robe,' he said, moving around behind her and wrapping his arms around her waist. 'But you look better without it.'

Emily could not believe it when he started undoing the sash. 'Sebastian! Stop that!' she protested, panic-stricken at the way her heart immediately started to race. 'Now look what you've done. You've made me spill my coffee.'

'Drink it up, then.'

'How can I possibly drink coffee with you undressing me? Sebastian! Someone might see!'

'Would you like that?' he purred into her ear as he opened the robe wide then cupped his hands over her breasts. 'Does that turn you on, Emily? The thought of having someone watch me make love to you? It turned you on last night, down there, against that tree.'

'You're a wicked man,' she choked out, clasping the mug more tightly between both hands.

'You're the wicked one,' he growled. 'You, and this provocative body of yours. It does things to me, Emily. *You* do things to me. I can't get enough of you.'

'You shouldn't say such things.'

Or *do* such things, she thought breathlessly. He'd retied the robe, but lifted the hem at the back and tucked it into the sash at her waist.

'Why not?' he said thickly, his hands stroking over her bare buttocks. 'They're true.'

Emily stiffened when his hands dropped down to the back of her thighs, then came up between them.

'Sebastian, no,' she pleaded, even as her whole body trembled. 'Please stop.'

The anguished note in her voice finally got through to Sebastian. Not an easy thing to do at that precise moment. He really meant it when he said he couldn't get enough of her.

He couldn't.

His success with her last night had really gone to his head. Even this morning, he'd needed the fix of her surrendering to him one more time. And now, here he was, needing it again, despite having surely proved their sexual compatibility by now.

If he ignored her protest and succeeded in seducing her against her will, things might backfire on him. As much as he wanted Emily again—with an addictive passion which superseded anything he'd felt with Lana—he wanted her as his wife even more.

'Fine,' he said through gritted teeth, and yanked the robe back down. 'I would never do anything you didn't want, Emily. But it might be wise if we removed temptation by getting dressed, then getting the hell out of here.'

He hadn't meant to speak in such a harsh tone, but damn it all, he was more frustrated than he could ever remember.

She whirled around, her face flushed, her big blue eyes dilated with desire.

'It's not that I don't want you to make love to me. I do,' she confessed shakily. 'Just…just not out here. And not like that.'

Aaah. So it was romance she was after now. Sebastian took the coffee cup out of her hands and put it on the balcony railing. He could do romance. When he had to.

But first…

Her eyes widened when he undid the robe again, then stripped it from her body. Sebastian feasted his eyes on her voluptuous curves before sweeping her up into his arms and carrying her inside.

One hour later, Emily was sitting silently in the passenger seat of Sebastian's car as they left the hotel, certain that any offer of marriage was now not on Sebastian's agenda. He'd had every opportunity to mention it. But he'd gone quiet after their last lovemaking, a ridiculously tender episode which had left Emily close to tears. She would have rather him ravage her than make love to her in such a gentle fashion, his eyes never leaving hers from the moment he entered her.

What had he been hoping to see?

Whatever, she'd denied him the satisfaction of witnessing her umpteenth capitulation by closing her eyes and coming very quietly. Afterwards, she'd dressed without saying a word, then accompanied him downstairs in a state of almost weary resignation to her fate.

Loving Mark had brought her heartache and bitterness. Loving her father had brought her dismay and disappointment. Loving Sebastian was going to bring her to a depth of despair she could hardly imagine.

Because he would never ever love her back.

'I'm taking the coast road back,' Sebastian explained when he turned down a different road from the way they'd come. 'I want to show you the new Sea Cliff bridge. It's quite spectacular,' he added with a smile, his first for ages. 'You haven't seen it already, have you?'

'Only on the television,' Emily replied, her low spirits immediately lifting.

Even on the TV it had looked truly amazing, a huge serpentine construction which followed the cliffs, but away from the fragile escarpment where rock falls were common. At one point it even snaked out over the ocean itself.

'We'll stop and walk across it,' Sebastian went on. 'There's a pedestrian path for sightseeing.'

'I'd love that,' Emily said sincerely, taken aback but pleased by his suggestion. 'Just as well I wore my jeans and joggers.'

It didn't take very long to reach the bridge, and it was truly amazing. All too quickly, however, they'd driven over it, Emily appreciating that Sebastian wouldn't have seen much at all, having to keep his eyes on the road.

At the northern end of the bridge there was a parking area to one side for people who wanted to walk the bridge. Sebastian turned into it and parked next to a small bus, out of which a group of Japanese tourists were pouring.

'What a pity we don't have a camera,' Emily said

when she saw all the Japanese tourists taking snaps of everything.

'Wait here,' Sebastian said and walked over to a Japanese man who had three cameras hanging round his neck. After a brief conversation and an exchange of money, he came back with a camera.

'Fire away,' he said as he handed it to her. 'It's digital and simple. You just look through there and if you like the shot, press that button.'

'You speak Japanese?' she asked, amazed.

'I had to go to Tokyo on business a couple of years back and thought it best to learn. Damned hard language to master.'

But he would have mastered it, Emily realised ruefully, just as he mastered everything he set his mind to. He'd mastered her last night all right.

'Come on,' he said after she'd snapped a few shots. 'Put that around your neck and let's walk.'

They made it across from one side to the other in about fifteen minutes, though they didn't rush. On the way back, Sebastian stopped at a point where, when you looked over the side, far below you could see the sea crashing on to rocks. Emily took some photos of the spray hitting the base of the concrete pier, then of the ships on the horizon. There were lots of them, huge tankers and cargo vessels. The larger south coast towns were sea ports, which shipped out coal and steel.

'All finished?' Sebastian asked when she finally took the camera away from her eyes.

'Yes. I'll put them up on my computer tonight and…oh!' she gasped.

There, sitting on the railing in front of Sebastian, was an open ring box containing what had to be the biggest diamond ring she'd ever seen.

CHAPTER THIRTEEN

'MY GOD!' Emily said, turning stunned eyes to him. 'Where…where did that come from?'

'I bought it yesterday morning when I went into the city.'

Emily blinked. He'd bought it *yesterday*?

'I would have given it to you over breakfast, but you made me promise not to mention marriage again till we left the hotel. Well, we've left the hotel, Emily,' he said, picking up the box and holding it out to her. 'So I'm asking you again. Will you marry me?'

Shock held Emily speechless for a long moment. She'd been so sure he wasn't going to ask her.

'You…you really are too much, Sebastian,' she heard herself babbling. 'To buy a ring like that before you even proposed.'

'I presumed you'd say yes.'

'It must have cost you a fortune!'

'A quarter of a million.'

Emily's mouth dropped open.

'It's no more than you deserve,' he said. 'You're a very special woman, Emily. Very special indeed. I want you to be my wife more than anything I have wanted in a long time.'

Emily stared at him. Did he really mean that?

She would be foolish to believe everything he said to her. Or to misinterpret what he said. What Sebastian wanted more than anything was for his life to go along as smoothly as before, when she was taking care of his house and Lana was sharing his bed. The only difference now was that she would be doing both jobs. And yes, she would have a new title. That of wife, rather than housekeeper.

'And if I still say no?' she blurted out.

His head jerked back in surprise, his eyes darkening. 'Then this ring will be consigned to the depths of the Pacific Ocean.'

'What? Are you insane?'

'Not at all,' he bit out. 'What would you expect me to do? Return it to the jewellery shop and ask for my money back? Or keep it on the off chance I might propose to another woman in the future? I don't think so, Emily. I don't think so at all. So what is it to be? Your finger or Davy Jones's locker?'

Emily groaned. 'You really are a wicked man. You know I can't let you throw it away.'

'Then you're saying yes?'

'Yes,' she said with a shudder of defeat.

Was she mistaken or did he sigh with relief as he took the ring out of the box and slipped it on her finger?

His tossing the box away startled her, as did his raising her left hand to his lips. A strangely old-fashioned gesture, she thought. But rather sweet.

Afterwards, he put his arm around her shoulders

and started leading her back across the rest of the bridge, talking to her as they walked.

'You won't regret your decision, Emily. What we shared last night was incredible. It proved that we are sexually compatible, which was one of your main objections. As for my being ruthless…I am a tough businessman, but I never act unethically. I am also very loyal by nature. I promise I will be faithful to you. I will stand by you no matter what. I will care about you and commit myself only to you. You have my solemn word.'

Emily was touched by his speech, but glad that he didn't mention love, because she simply would not have believed him.

Who knew? Maybe their marriage did have a chance of happiness.

Whatever, she was committed to the union now and, once committed, Emily aimed to do her best to make it work. She was not a person to be half-hearted about anything she did.

They were nearing Sebastian's car when his cellphone rang. Emily knew it was his, because she recognised the tune.

'I thought you'd turned that off,' she said when he stopped to fish the phone out of his trouser pocket.

'I turned it back on before I left the hotel. Here, take my car key and get in while I answer this call.'

Emily heard him say, 'Yes, John,' before he could possibly have known who it was on the other end. So he'd been expecting this call.

Emily sat in the car, fiddling with her ring and watching Sebastian through the windscreen. The exasperated look on his face was a bit worrying. Clearly, things in Queensland were not going well. After a few minutes, he put the phone away and strode back to the car, his expression frustrated.

'I have to go away,' he said as he climbed in behind the wheel.

'Oh, no. When?'

'This afternoon. John's booking me a flight to Brisbane, then a car to take me to Noosa.'

'Noosa,' she repeated with a sigh. That was even further away. 'When will you be back?'

'Not sure at this stage,' Sebastian said as he gunned the engine and backed out of their parking spot. 'Depends how long it will take to fix the problem. With a bit of luck I might be back tomorrow evening.'

'Oh…' Impossible to keep the disappointment out of her voice.

He slanted her a sharp look before driving off. 'Don't go imagining that I want to go, Emily. I don't. I'd much prefer to stay home with you.'

Then don't go, her heart screamed at him. Let someone else do it. Send John.

For a good minute neither of them said anything further.

It was Sebastian who spoke first. 'Look,' he said. 'I'm a businessman. And a highly successful one. I didn't get that way by being lazy or sloppy. Or letting my lesser lights do my job for me. Besides, I'm the only one who has the immediate clout to fix this problem.'

'And what problem is that, exactly?' she countered, doing her best to replicate his matter-of-fact tone and not get all emotional on him. She knew he would hate that. 'I realise that when I was your housekeeper you didn't have to explain yourself to me. But I think, as your fiancée, I have the right to be confided in a little more.'

She could see that he was taken aback by her stance. But eventually his head nodded.

'You're right,' he said. 'I'm not used to answering to anyone. I've come and gone as I pleased for years. But I can see that has to change. What would you like to know?'

'Just what the problem is. And how you're going to fix it.'

'Right. Well, I'm building these luxury retirement homes in Noosa and we got behind schedule because of some bad weather. Unfortunately, a lot of people bought these villas off the plan and their contract says they can move in next month. I organised for the builders to work seven days a week to catch up, but the foreman has suddenly walked off the job, wanting a bigger bonus. Now the rest of the men have walked, making similar demands. It's a case of blatant blackmail. I should just tell them all to get lost and hire another construction team, but that takes time and won't get these retirees into their villas on time. Lots of businessmen might not care about that, but I do. My word is my bond and I gave my word.'

Emily felt very proud of him at that moment, and slightly more confident that their marriage might just work.

'Then you must go,' she urged. 'But please... hurry back.'

'I fully intend to,' he said, and shot her the sexiest smile.

Her stomach flipped over. 'Will…will you have to leave as soon as we get home?'

'Pretty well.'

'Oh…'

'Does that "oh" mean what I think it means?'

'What do you think it means?'

He smiled. 'Don't worry. I'll do my best to make good time and give us a few minutes alone together.'

'Just a few minutes?'

'Ravishment doesn't take long.'

Heat zoomed into Emily's cheeks.

Sebastian shook his head at her. 'You like it quick sometimes, so don't pretend you don't. That's one thing I never want you to do, Emily. Be less than honest with me. I like the calm, capable woman who runs my house. But I also like the wildly passionate woman you become in my arms. There will be no room for embarrassment or inhibitions in our sex life. Do I make myself clear?'

'Yes,' she said, secretly thrilled by his words.

'Now, is there anything *you'd* like to say to me about our future sex life? Anything you like or don't like?'

Lord, there wasn't anything she didn't like with him. There was one thing, however, which was going to bother her. Big time.

'Would it be all right if I bought a new bed for your room tomorrow? The one you have reeks of Lana's perfume.'

'New bed. New carpet. New everything, if you like. Be my guest.'

'But I can't get all that done in one day!' she protested.

'I suppose not. No worries. We'll bunk down in one of the guest rooms till it's all done.'

'One of the guest rooms,' she repeated, startled.

'You don't expect me to share that dinky little four-poster bed of yours, do you?'

'No…'

'Not that I intend to confine our sex life to beds and bedrooms.'

Emily's head whirled as her bottom squirmed. She really had to get their conversation—and her thoughts—off sex.

'I think I'll go to the hairdressers' tomorrow,' she said abruptly. 'Have my hair cut and lightened.'

He glanced over at her. 'You mean I'll be coming back to a glamorous blonde?'

'I don't know about glamorous…'

'You could be seriously glamorous, if you want to be. You have all the right equipment.'

'I will have to glam myself up before I marry you, Sebastian.'

'I actually like you as you are, Emily. But I know women. Their self esteem seems irrevocably tied in with how they look. When I get back, I'll organise a credit card for you and you can go to town on your wardrobe as well.'

Emily frowned. 'I do have some money of my own, Sebastian. I've hardly spent a cent on myself since I started working for you.'

'I have to confess, I do like it that you're not marrying me for my money. But let's be honest. As my fiancée, and then my wife, you'll be going lots of places with me. The other women there will think me a miser if my wife isn't decked out in the latest designer fashion. So humour me, will you, and let me pay for your clothes, and whatever else you might need.'

Emily sighed. 'I don't think I've thought out what marrying you will fully entail, Sebastian. It sounds complicated, being the wife of a magnate.'

'You'll manage.'

Would she?

Suddenly, Emily wished her mother was alive. She really needed to talk to someone—someone who cared about her and wouldn't just give lip service to her concerns.

It was appalling to think that she had no one to confide in. No girl-friend. No relative. She wasn't close to any of her aunts and uncles, perhaps because none of them lived in Sydney. All her grandparents had passed away, her parents not having been all that young when they'd married and had her, their only child.

Before she'd found out the awful truth, she might have asked her father what he thought of her marrying a rich man who didn't love her. There'd been a time when she'd believed him to be a wonderful man. A warm, caring, compassionate person who'd chosen to become a doctor because he had a vocation to help people.

Her mother had believed the same thing. It was a relief to Emily that her mother had never had her eyes opened to the truth about the man she'd married.

'You've gone all quiet on me,' Sebastian said. 'Are you tired?'

'Positively wrecked,' Emily replied. 'You must be too.'

'I was, till you agreed to marry me. Now I feel I could conquer the world. And hopefully make that idiot foreman get back to work,' he added wryly.

'What will you do? Read him the riot act?'

'I can't afford to get into any protracted arguments or negotiations. I'll just make him an offer he can't refuse.'

Emily stared down at her ring and wondered if that was what that had been. The offer she could not refuse.

'I'll make sure I'm home by tomorrow evening,' Sebastian said. 'And I'll take you out somewhere to celebrate our engagement.'

'Don't be silly. You'll be way too tired. I'll cook us something nice at home.'

Sebastian shook his head. 'I appreciate your consideration, but no. We'll go out. So get yourself a good night's sleep, then hit the shops tomorrow and buy yourself something seriously sexy.'

Emily's blood fizzed with a whoosh of excited anticipation. She was sitting there, making mental plans for the next day, when Sebastian leant over and gently touched her arm.

'Yes?' she said, her head whipping round in his direction.

He smiled softly at her before returning his eyes to the road.

'Now that we're engaged, would you mind telling me what you argued with your father about? You don't have to, but I'm curious. You don't seem the family feuding type.'

Emily sighed. 'Actually, I was just thinking about him a couple of minutes ago.'

'When you went all quiet on me?'

'Yes.'

'What did he do, Emily?'

'He started an affair with a colleague. *Before* Mum died. Dr Barbra Saxby. Blonde and beautiful and young enough to be his daughter. Of course, I wasn't supposed to ever find out. But I'd stayed on at home after the funeral. I wasn't in a fit state to join the workforce. I felt too depressed. Dad pretended he was doing me a favour, but I saw later that it suited him, having me there to cook and clean for him. Anyway, when I was out shopping one day, I saw them having lunch together in a restaurant. You didn't have to look too hard to see that it wasn't a business lunch.'

Emily still couldn't think of that moment without reliving the shock—and the distress—she'd felt on seeing that woman all over her father like a rash. It had only been a few weeks after her mother had passed away, after all.

'What did you do?' Sebastian asked.

'That night I confronted Dad with what I'd seen. Initially, he claimed there'd been nothing between them before Mum died, but I knew he was lying. Eventually, I wheedled the truth out of him. He broke down and said that he'd needed the comfort of a woman. He claimed he still loved Mum and would always love her. But life went on and he couldn't spend the rest of his alone. He said he was going to marry Barbra and that was that.'

'I see,' Sebastian said. 'I can imagine you were very upset.'

'That's putting it mildly. All the neighbourhood must have heard me screaming at him. I totally lost it, I can tell you. That night, I packed my bags and moved out. I stayed at a cheap motel and started looking for work. I still didn't feel like getting back into the hospitality industry. I couldn't face having to be bright and breezy with everyone. When the employment agency suggested the position as your housekeeper, I jumped at it.'

Sebastian nodded. 'Now I know why you seemed so sad at times when you first came to work for me. And why you have trust issues with men. First your boyfriend, and then your father. You know, I tried to find out some more about your background when you had a drink with me occasionally, but you always steered the conversation away from anything personal.'

'Did I? I didn't do it on purpose. It must have been subconscious.'

'No one likes to talk about the skeletons in one's closet.'

'You sound like you have a few.'

'Who, me? No, no. I was just talking in general.'

Emily didn't believe him. There was something he was hiding from her. Something in his past which had hurt him.

'So what about *your* parents?' she asked, feeling she had the right to know something of his upbringing.

'What about them?'

'Are they still alive? They never visit, if they are.'

'They were killed in a car accident when I was eleven.'

'Oh, Sebastian, that's dreadful! You must have been traumatised.'

'It wasn't a pleasant experience. But I got over it.'

Emily stared over at him. How typically male to dismiss such a tragedy with a few understated words.

'My grandmother took me in,' he went on before she asked. 'She was a wonderful woman. You remind me of her, you know?'

'Your *grandmother*? Well, thank you very much!'

He laughed. 'Not in looks. In your calm demeanour.'

'You keep saying how calm I am. I'm not always so calm. I learned a degree of composure when I worked on reception at the Regency. You come across some difficult clients in the hospitality industry, I can tell you. And of course I had to keep a tight rein on my emotions when I was nursing my mother. It wouldn't have helped her if I'd gone around crying all the time. Which was what I wanted to do.'

'It's not such a bad thing. To learn to control one's emotions.'

'I suppose not. I presume your grandmother has passed away?'

'Unfortunately, yes. Just before I made my first million. I would have loved to have bought her the world. Not that she probably would have appreciated it,' Sebastian added with a warm smile in his voice. 'Gran didn't hanker for material things.'

'They're not the be-all and end-all,' Emily said.

'Maybe not. But when you've been as poor as I've been, Emily, you feel differently about money.

People like me go one of two ways. You either fall by the wayside or you're driven to succeed.'

'Well, you certainly succeeded. But there comes a time, Sebastian, when enough is enough. Maybe you should slow down a bit.'

'I intend to. With you. And our children.'

'Our *children*? You mean you want more than one?'

'Absolutely. If I'm going to take the plunge into fatherhood, I wouldn't want to have just one. It's too lonely for the child. Which reminds me. Now that we're getting married, do you think we could dispense with the condoms? Or am I going too quick for you again?'

Emily shook her head at him in disbelief. 'Are you always this decisive?'

'Pretty much so. But maybe I should mention that I've run out of condoms and we don't have the time to stop and buy some more.'

'That's blackmail!'

'No,' he said with a sexy grin. 'That's negotiation. So is it full steam ahead with the baby-making project before I have to jet off into the wide blue yonder?'

'You always make it impossible for me to say no!'

'Come now. You want to say yes. You know you do.'

She closed her eyes, then sighed. 'Very well. Yes…'

CHAPTER FOURTEEN

'Wow!' the hairdresser exclaimed when his job was finished. 'Here. Let me show you the back.' And he held up the mirror so that Emily could see the back of her new hair-do.

'Oh, yes,' she replied happily. 'You've done a wonderful job, Ty. Thank you so much.'

'You know, sweetie, I wasn't too sure when you came in this morning and asked me to cut your hair short, then colour it blonde. But you were right. It looks fabulous on you.'

It did. It really did. And she did have an elegant neck. Truly, she looked ten years younger, and very much in fashion.

Which reminded her of her less than fashionable wardrobe, not to mention Sebastian's request that she buy something seriously sexy for tonight.

'I'm going to hit the shops now,' she said happily as she picked up her handbag and stood up. 'I need some new clothes to go with my new look.'

'And your newly engaged status,' Ty said with a

pointed glance at her ring as they walked over to the desk together.

'Oh. You noticed,' Emily said, genuinely surprised. She'd only been to this hairdresser twice before. Once for a trim a few months back, then last week when she'd been going for that interview.

Of course, hairdressers were observant people. Especially gay ones, which Ty obviously was.

'Hard not to notice a rock like that, sweetie. Looks like you've landed yourself a real prize.'

'He's my boss.'

'The one you were planning on leaving?'

Emily realised she must have chattered away quite a bit at the hairdresser's last week. She did that when she was nervous.

'Yes, that one,' she admitted.

Ty's finely plucked eyebrows arched. 'The mobile phone magnate?'

Emily winced. What *hadn't* she told him?

She nodded as she handed over her credit card.

'Ooh,' Ty said with tightly pursed lips. 'Clever girl.'

'I'm not marrying him for his money, Ty.'

The hairdresser's dark eyes gleamed knowingly. 'Of course not. Now, when I do your hair for your wedding don't forget to mention this salon's name to all and sundry.'

Emily laughed. 'You're a wicked opportunist.'

'Takes one to know one, sweetie. Now, sign here.' And he placed the credit slip on top of the counter.

A wicked opportunist?

Emily thought about that description of herself as she walked from the salon. Was that how the cleaner had viewed her this morning when Emily had revealed she'd become engaged to Sebastian over the weekend?

Julie hadn't said much, but she'd had a look in her eyes not dissimilar to Ty's.

Emily supposed there might be quite a lot of people who thought the same thing. She wouldn't be the first housekeeper to snare her wealthy employer as a husband, the same way some female secretaries did, both having the opportunity to use their close-quarter jobs as a stepping stone to further intimacy.

But anyone who knows me would not think that, she reasoned.

But who of Sebastian's friends and employees really knows me?

None of them.

All they know is my housekeeper image, the one with the mousy hair and clothes and personality to match.

If I suddenly show up on Sebastian's arm, all glammed up, they're sure to think I'm a gold-digger. At the same time, I can't marry Sebastian looking frumpy.

I'm damned if I do, and damned if I don't.

Her cellphone suddenly ringing had Emily's heart leaping and her hands diving into her bag. It had to be Sebastian, letting her know when he'd be coming home. He'd rung her last night once he'd got off the plane, then again this morning, insisting that when she went out today she take her mobile with her.

'Yes?' she said, heart fluttering.

'Where are you?'

It *was* Sebastian.

'Down at Birkenhead Point.'

'Shopping for a new dress?'

'For a whole new wardrobe.'

'In one day? I doubt you'll manage that.'

'You could be right. I've just spent all morning having my hair done.'

'How does it look?'

'I think you'll like it.'

'Did you ring that employment agency and tell them you weren't accepting that job?'

'Yes. They weren't too pleased.'

'They'll get over it.'

'How are things going up there?' she asked.

'I've already persuaded the foreman back on the job, for a price. But I don't want to leave prematurely. I'm going to talk to all the other workers this afternoon and offer them bonuses as well, if they bring this job in on time. I don't want to be running back up here next week, when things go pear-shaped again. Which they might if that idiot foreman opens his big mouth and blabs about his extra bonus.'

Emily's heart sank. 'Does that mean you won't be home tonight?'

'Are you kidding? Wild horses won't keep me away. I just can't guarantee my time of arrival. At the moment I'm booked on a plane which will get me home around eight. But there's one an hour earlier. If I can make that one, I will. But it's doubtful.'

'That's all right, as long as you make it tonight. Do you want me to book somewhere for dinner?'

'Nope. That's my job, one I can easily do from

here. Now, go get yourself that new dress, and if you spot a bed you like, buy that as well. I'll pay you back, of course.'

'I'd rather you be with me when I go bed-buying. You did say I could change everything in that room, remember? I wouldn't want to choose anything you didn't like.'

'Fair enough. I'd better get going.'

'Sebastian…'

'Yes?'

I love you teetered on the tip of her tongue.

'I miss you,' she said instead.

'I miss you too. That's why I'm bending over backwards to settle this today.'

'Ring me if things go wrong and you can't make it.'

'That won't happen. Have a good day now, and don't stint on what you buy.'

She didn't stint. She was downright extravagant, having to make two trips back to the car park with all her parcels. She bought more clothes and accessories in that afternoon than she had in the last five years. Fortunately, she had a healthy limit on her credit card. But she spent right up to that limit, choosing a variety of outfits, ranging from casual to dressy to evening wear. There were no dreary or dull colours in her new wardrobe, either. Everything was vibrant and colourful, in keeping with her new blonde hair.

The traffic was bad by the time Emily headed home, peak hour having well and truly arrived. Despite it not being far from the shopping mall at Birkenhead Point to Hunter's Hill, it was rising six by the time she reached home. The sun was very low in the sky and the shadows from the trees around the house were long against the stone walls.

Emily parked her car outside the garage door, then set about the job of carting her parcels up the stairs to her apartment. Once they were all in her bedroom, she spread everything out on her bed, putting the accessories with each outfit.

The dress she was going to wear tonight was exquisite. Made in turquoise silk, it was a wraparound style with a deep V neckline, three-quarter sleeves and a wide matching belt which was heavily beaded. She'd seen the dress displayed in a boutique window and fell in love with it instantly. Fell in love with the accessories as well, which included turquoise sandals and evening bag—also beaded. Completing the outfit were long crystal and turquoise earrings which fell to her shoulders and made her long neck look even longer.

Emily could not wait to put it all on again. But she thought she'd better have a shower first and freshen up her make-up as well. Who knew? Sebastian might make it home by seven, which was less than an hour away.

By twenty to seven she was totally ready and thrilled to bits with her appearance. Her blonde hair looked sensational against the turquoise.

'Now that's a woman who won't look out of place on Sebastian's arm,' she told her reflection.

Not able to sit and wait patiently in her apartment, Emily decided to go over to the main house and wait for Sebastian there. Maybe she could go up to his bedroom and pass the time, working out what kind of furniture and carpet would best suit. Hopefully, she could persuade Sebastian to take tomorrow off work. Then they could get started on ridding the room of Lana's perfume, not to mention her lingering presence.

Sebastian probably hadn't noticed, but there were still some things of Lana's hanging in his wardrobe. Some cosmetics on the vanity unit as well. Plus a half empty bottle of that dreaded perfume.

Emily hadn't dared throw any of it out before this. But tonight, she would.

Taking her evening purse and set of keys with her, Emily had locked her door and turned to walk down the stairs when she noticed a light shining through Sebastian's bedroom window.

He must have just arrived home, she thought excitedly and hurried down the stairs.

'Sebastian!' she called out on entering the downstairs hall.

No answer.

Maybe he'd jumped into the shower and couldn't hear her.

Emily ran up the stairs, thinking how typical it was of a man not to ring her from the airport and let her know he'd managed to get that earlier flight. Still, perhaps he hadn't wanted to stop, choosing instead to bolt for the taxi rank and jump into the first available taxi.

As she hurried along the upstairs hallway, she couldn't hear any shower running. There again, the walls in this house were extremely solid, unlike modern homes. Hard to hear anything much from room to room.

His bedroom door was slightly ajar. Emily stopped and knocked, calling his name at the same time.

Still no answer.

Emily's chest tightened as she reached out to push the door open. Something was wrong here. Very wrong.

She called Sebastian's name again as she walked in, her stomach contracting the second that hated scent hit her nostrils.

It was too strong. Way too strong.

Lana was lying on the bed, sleeping, wearing nothing but an emerald silk robe. Her riot of red curls were spread out on the pillows, her robe gaping in all the right places.

Clearly, the woman still had keys to Sebastian's home. Also, clearly, she had left her Italian husband and come flying home to Australia, back to her one true love.

Nausea swirled in Emily's stomach, bile rising right up her throat into her mouth. Of all the things she'd imagined happening if she took the risk of becoming involved with Sebastian, this was not one of them. She'd thought—no presumed—Lana was out of their lives for ever.

As though sensing her standing there, Lana woke with a start, then sat up abruptly, her wide green eyes confused as they swept over Emily.

'Who the hell are you?' she demanded to know as she swung her feet over the side of the bed and stood up. 'Oh, don't tell me Sebastian's got himself a new floozy already.'

Emily might have felt sick inside, but no way was she going to show any fear in front of Sebastian's ex-girlfriend.

'Don't you recognise me, Lana?' she said with seeming calm. 'It's Emily.'

'Emily! My goodness, what have you done to yourself? Had an extreme makeover?'

'No. Just had my hair done and bought a few new clothes.'

'Trying to attract Sebastian's attention, no doubt,' Lana sneered, standing up and retying her robe. 'I always knew you were stuck on him. Well you've wasted your time, sweetheart. I'm back and he's still all mine.'

'Not quite,' Emily said and coolly held out her left hand, the diamond sparkling in the lamplight.

Lana stared at her hand, then up at her face. 'Are you telling me you're engaged?'

'Yes.'

'Since when?'

'Since yesterday.'

'My, but you are a fast little worker, aren't you?'

'You've been gone over a month, Lana,' Emily pointed out.

Lana laughed. 'Most of which Seb spent texting me and begging me to come back to him.'

Emily didn't believe that. No way would Sebastian beg anybody for anything.

'In the end he came after me, all the way to Milan.'

'I do know that, Lana,' Emily said coolly. 'He told me. But not to get you back. To have done with you once and for all.'

'Really? I presume then that he didn't tell you that he had sex with me. Less than half an hour before I walked down the aisle. I was wearing my wedding dress at the time, might I add.'

All the blood drained from Emily's face.

'Your fiancé's sexually obsessed with me. Has been ever since the first night we met and I went down on him in the back of a limo. He loves it that I can make him lose control and do things he wouldn't normally do. It drove him crazy, my marrying another man. Which is exactly what I planned. I never intended to stay with that boring, fat old coot. I just wanted to make Seb suffer for not marrying me himself. The way I see it, he only asked you to marry him to punish me. It's a revenge thing. Now that I'm back, he'll drop you like a hot cake. Because I'm the one he really wants. Not you, Miss Ice Cool. You might be able to set a nice dinner table, but I'm the one who lets him screw me on it.'

'In that case, I'll be buying a new dining table as well,' Emily said, determined not to let this creature destroy her. Not to her face, anyway.

'As well as what?' she snapped.

'As well as all the furniture in this room. I don't want any reminders of you hanging around the house.'

Lana laughed. 'Then you'd have to get rid of the whole place. Because I've screwed the master of the house just about everywhere in this place. Even in the garage. I'll bet you'd never let him do you there, Miss Prissy.'

Emily's teeth clenched down hard in her jaw. 'Then you'd be dead wrong, Miss Slut-Face.'

She received some satisfaction from standing up to Lana. But there was no joy for her in this exchange. A great pit was already opening up in her stomach.

'Does Sebastian know you're here?' she asked, not sure what she'd do if this creature said yes.

'No. He does not,' Sebastian snapped.

When Emily whirled to see Sebastian striding into the room, her legs went to jelly. Immediately, Lana ran past her towards him, bursting into crocodile tears at the same time.

'Oh, Seb, I'm so glad you're home,' she sobbed as she threw herself into his arms.

Emily watched, appalled, as Lana snaked her arms up around his neck and pressed her thinly clad body to his.

'I didn't know where else to go,' she cried. 'Alfonso didn't want me. He just married me to hide his homosexuality from his family. He spent our wedding night with his lover.'

What an act, Emily thought disgustedly. And what a story!

If Sebastian had been a violent man, he would have done violence right at that moment. When he glanced over Lana's shoulder at his lovely Emily, who was looking heart-stoppingly gorgeous, he could see the distress in her eyes. And the disgust.

He hadn't overheard much of their conversation. But he suspected Lana must have said something to upset Emily very much.

With less than gentle movements, he disengaged Lana's talons from the back of his neck and forcibly pushed her away. Then he walked over to put his arm firmly around Emily's waist, drawing her to his side.

'I'm sorry, Lana,' he said coldly, 'but your marital problems are not my concern. You're also not welcome here. In case Emily hasn't told you, we're engaged to be married.'

Lana took a long moment to gather herself, tossing her red curls back from her shoulders as she surveyed the two of them together with calculating green eyes.

'Yes, she told me. Couldn't wait to. But you don't love her, Seb. You love me. You know you do.'

'I know I don't,' he said with a dry laugh. 'I never did. It was just a sexual infatuation, and I'm well and truly over it. And over you.'

'Really? Well, you were still infatuated last week,' she snapped. '*Very* infatuated. Oh, yes, I told little Miss Prissy about what you did.'

'I'm sure you couldn't wait,' he bit out, hating the way Emily stiffened against him. 'Just as I can't wait to get you out of my house.'

Whipping his mobile out of his trouser pocket, Sebastian flipped it open and ordered a taxi. It didn't take him long to get what he wanted. The taxi company knew he was a very good client.

'There will be a taxi at the kerb outside the gates in ten minutes,' he told a furious-faced Lana. 'Don't keep it waiting.'

'You can't do this to me!' she screamed. 'I'll sue you, you bastard. I'll take you to court for palimony.'

'Do that and you'll lose, *Countess*. The moment you married, you lost all chance of getting a cent out of me. Now, get dressed. Your ten minutes is already ticking away. Come, Emily, the smell in this room is too much for the nose.'

Sebastian steered her from the room, but he could feel the underlying resistance in her body.

'Don't let her ruin things for us, Emily,' he said as he led her along the hallway.

'You had sex with her,' Emily replied, her tone flat and disbelieving. 'In her wedding dress.'

'Look, I didn't go through with it. I stopped once I realised what I was doing. That was why I drank too much on the flight home. Because I was so disgusted with myself for letting that tramp almost seduce me. Trust me when I tell you that I don't love her or want her any more. I'm so over Lana, it isn't funny. You're the one I want, Emily. You have to believe me.'

Emily stopped at the top of the stairs and raised hurt eyes to his.

'No, Sebastian,' she said, her voice hollow and hurt. 'I *don't* have to believe you.' And, loosening her arm from his grip, she ran down the stairs ahead of him.

Sebastian chased after her, full-on panic twisting at his guts. 'What are you going to do?' he called after her.

She didn't reply, just ran faster.

He caught her outside the back door, grabbing her arm and spinning her back to face him. 'You can't run away from me like this. We have to talk this out.'

She shook her head, her face pale but her eyes determined. 'There's nothing to talk about. I can't marry you, Sebastian. Or live in this house with you.'

'But you love this house!'

'I don't any more.'

'Why not? Damn it all, Emily, what did Lana say to you?'

'It doesn't matter.'

'But it does matter. Tell me.'

'Very well. She said you did it everywhere in this house. Even in the garage.'

Sebastian grimaced. Oh, hell.

'I'll buy us a new house,' he said straight away.

She shook her head, her expression sad. 'Oh, Sebastian. You can't buy your way out of this problem. The thing is I...I...'

'You what?'

She shook her head in an anguished fashion. 'I find I can't marry without love after all. It's just not me. I'm sorry, Sebastian. I really am, but I've made up my mind and this time you won't change it. I'll be gone as soon as I can pack all my things. Don't worry about severance pay. I'll waive that in lieu of working out my notice.'

'Don't you dare give me that bloody ring back!' Sebastian snapped when she started easing it off her finger.

'All right,' she returned in that quiet, calm voice which he usually loved but which was driving him mad right now. 'I won't.'

Sebastian frowned, then gaped when she walked over and tossed the ring into the pool. As a gesture went, it was as dramatic as it was awfully final. He watched as she continued to walk away from him with her head held high.

The male ego part of him wanted to race after her and drag her back into his arms.

But the more logical part knew that any caveman technique would not work. Not this time.

So he whirled round and strode back inside to have one final confrontation with Lana before she left. He reached the bottom of the stairs just as she was coming down, bags in hand.

'You knew the Count was gay when you married him, didn't you?' he threw at her.

'Of course,' she snapped.

'He paid you to marry him.'

'My, my, you and Sherlock Holmes would make a good pair. But not you and Miss Prissy. And you know why not, Sebastian? Because she's in love with you.'

'*What?* She told you that, did she?'

'Not in so many words. But I've always known she was in love with you. Women sense these things about other women. That's why I never could stand her.'

'You're wrong,' he said, thinking that if Emily loved him she wouldn't be leaving him.

Lana laughed. 'What's the problem with her loving you, Sebastian? Not that I don't already know. You don't want a woman's love, do you? Just her body. And, in Emily's case, her ability to run a smooth household. The little fool is going to be miserable, married to you. And you, you cold-blooded bastard, once you get bored with your bland, boring, goody-two-shoes bride, you're going to come looking for me again. And you know what, lover? I won't knock you back. But next time, I'll come at a price.'

'Whores always come at a price, Lana. But I have some news for you. I don't know if Emily loves me or not, but I know *I* love *her*, more than I ever thought possible. Emily is no man's fool. Neither is she bland or boring. She's a warm, intelligent, sexy woman. Oh, yes, *very* sexy, in a way someone like you could never hope to be. Now, get your sorry arse out of here!'

'You're the one who's going to be sorry,' she threatened, her face going bright red.

'Give it a rest, will you?' Sebastian said scornfully as he swept open the front door. 'Go back to Milan, where you can be what you've always been. A vain, shallow poseur.'

Lana huffed and puffed, then stormed out.

Sebastian banged the door shut after her, then turned to walk thoughtfully down to the kitchen.

Could it be possible that Emily loved him?

He hardly dared believe it. For what was there to love about him?

Lana was right. Till recently, he had been a cold-blooded bastard.

Still, he had to find out. Had to make Emily look him in the eyes and tell him that she didn't love him.

CHAPTER FIFTEEN

WHEN the knock came on her door, Emily groaned. She'd been packing as fast as she could, knowing full well that Sebastian would not simply let her leave.

The two suitcases which she'd brought with her eighteen months ago were stuffed full and all the clothes she'd bought today were back in their plastic bags. Another five to ten minutes and she'd have been safely out of here.

Steeling herself for more Sebastian-style arguments, Emily walked to the door and opened it.

'Please don't start again,' she said straight away. 'I'm going shortly and that's final.'

'Do you love me?'

The unexpected question sent all the breath rushing from her lungs.

'Lana said you did,' he went on, his eyes searching hers.

Emily knew that confessing her love for him would be the kiss of death. She'd almost admitted it earlier, stopping herself just in time.

'What would *she* know?' Emily threw back at him.

'That's no answer, Emily. I want to hear you tell me that you don't love me. Because I love you.'

Shock at this even more unexpected statement was swiftly followed by fury.

The crack of her hand slapping his face with all her might echoed through the night air.

Sebastian swore as he lurched back on the small landing, his hand lifting to his reddened cheek, his eyes wide and disbelieving.

'To tell a woman that you love her when you don't is beneath contempt,' Emily cried, tears flooding her eyes. 'Get out!' she yelled, pushing him wildly in the middle of his chest. 'Get out of my sight!'

He grabbed her hands and shook her. 'I'm not lying, Emily. I *do* love you.'

'I don't believe you,' she sobbed. 'I'll never believe you. You're just saying it to get your way.'

'No,' he said, shaking his head. 'I'm not. If you think about it, it's not something I would say if I didn't mean it.'

Emily groaned in despair. Because she knew he would.

'You're upset, Emily, and not thinking straight. Look, Lana's gone. Why don't you come with me over to the house and I'll pour you a brandy? You need to calm down. You're overwrought.'

First lies and now kindness. Next thing he'd start kissing her and she wouldn't know which way was up.

Oh, no, she wasn't falling for that any more!

'I don't want to go over to the house and have a brandy,' she choked out, her shoulders shaking under his grip whilst hot tears cascaded down her face. 'I want to get out of here, away from you.'

Sebastian saw the truth in her face. Heard the truth in her voice. Lana was right. She did love him. For why else would she be like this?

'And I want you to get your hands off me!' she raged on, even as she wept.

Sebastian grimaced as he struggled to do the right thing. His first instinct was to pull her into his arms and show her how much he loved her. But he could see that might backfire on him big time.

'All right,' he muttered, lifting his hands from her shoulders. 'All right. But I don't think you should go anywhere tonight, Emily. You're not in a fit state to drive.'

'Don't you dare tell me what I can and cannot do. I'm an adult woman and I know exactly what I'm capable of. And I know what you're capable of, Sebastian Armstrong! You had sex with her, in her wedding dress!'

Sebastian winced. If only he could go back in time, he'd never have gone to Milan last week. But his ego had driven him on.

Lana had been the first female to break up with him and he simply hadn't been able to handle it. Not because he'd loved her. But because he'd thought of her as his. His pride had been stung by her leaving him for another man.

Emily wasn't leaving him for another man. She was just leaving him. Period.

He had to find a way to handle this better or he was going to lose her. Not just for now, but for forever.

'Where will you go?' he asked quietly.

'That's none of your business.'

Sebastian tried not to panic, reminding himself that she would take her mobile phone with her, no matter where she went. Contacting people was pretty easy these days. If the worst came to the worst, he could hire a private detective to find her.

'This is not the end of us, Emily.'

She dashed the tears from her eyes and gave him a determined look. 'Oh, yes, it is, Sebastian. Now, if you'd please get out of my way, I have a car to pack.'

Sebastian decided offering to help her was not going to work, either. Damn it, but he didn't know what to do. He'd never felt this helpless before. To simply walk away seemed weak and wimpish. But what else could he do?

'I'll be in touch,' he said, before turning and walking slowly back down the stairs, his spirits sinking with each step. His caveman instinct kept warning him that he was making a mistake, letting her go like this. But his sensitive new-age guy side— the one he'd discovered since becoming involved with Emily—told him to be patient.

Good things come to those who wait.

Or so they said.

At the same time, nice guys often did finish last.

If you love someone, you let them go…and they'll come back to you.

He'd read that somewhere.

Sounded like a whole load of bulldust in Sebastian's

opinion. But what did he know? He'd never been in love before.

It was sheer hell, this love business.

When he heard Emily's car go down the driveway, it felt as if someone was inside his chest, ripping his heart out. She'd gone. She'd really gone. Lord knew where. She'd said she had no friends.

Suddenly, the house was deathly quiet and depressingly empty.

It was Sebastian who reached for the brandy.

'I'll get her back,' he vowed as he downed the first swallow. 'If not tomorrow, then the next day. Or the next.'

His voice sounded sure. But down deep inside, Sebastian was not convinced.

As she'd said, he could not buy her. Or persuade her with words of love. Because she didn't believe him.

Seducing her a second time wasn't a viable option, either.

Which left what?

For the first time in years, Sebastian was stumped.

CHAPTER SIXTEEN

DR DANIEL BAYLISS was sitting in his lounge room reading, when the front doorbell rang.

With a puzzled glance at his watch, he rose, then went to answer it.

The sight of his estranged daughter standing on his doorstep filled Daniel with instant joy, despite her slightly apprehensive expression. He'd dreamt of this day but never thought it would actually happen.

'Emily!' he exclaimed. 'How lovely to see you. Come in. Come in.'

'Oh, Daddy,' she cried, her face suddenly crumpling.

Daniel's heart lurched. His daughter hadn't called him Daddy since she was about ten years old.

He did what any father would do. He gathered her into his arms and just hugged her, tears filling his own eyes. Now he knew how the father of the prodigal son had felt. Only this time it was more the case of the prodigal father.

Had Emily forgiven him at last for what he'd done?

He sure hoped so.

But he suspected it wasn't forgiveness which had brought his daughter home to him. It was something else.

'Come inside,' he said gently at last and led her down to the kitchen, sitting her at the large country-style table whilst he popped on the kettle, then took the box of tissues which he kept on the counter and placed them next to her.

He didn't say anything. Or ask anything. He just stood there and waited till Emily was ready to talk.

'You're looking well,' she said at last.

'You are too.' Better than she'd ever looked.

She laughed, then sobbed, her eyes filling anew. He moved forward and held the tissue box out to her. She snatched several out and shook her head, clearly annoyed with herself for crying again.

'Where's Barbra?' she asked after she'd blown her nose and gathered herself.

'In Africa, working for the United Nations.'

Emily frowned. 'You didn't marry her?'

'No. I realised after you left that I didn't love her. Whether you believe me or not, your mother was the only woman I have ever really loved.'

'Then why were you unfaithful to her?'

Daniel shook his head. 'A lot of men are unfaithful to wives they love, Emily. Sometimes it's difficult to explain why. Sex to a man is not always an expression of love. Sometimes it caters for an entirely different need. With some men, the need is just sexual. Or perhaps the craving for a new experience. Some excitement to spice up their mundane lives. With me, I think it was the need to know I was still alive. And, of course, my ego was flattered by Barbra's attentions. I'm sorry that you found out I wasn't the hero you always imagined me to be, Emily. But the awful truth is that most men aren't heroes. They're just human beings, with all the faults and flaws that go with being a male.'

'You're right there,' she said with the kind of bitterness which only came from a personal and very recent hurt.

Daniel realised things had to be very bad indeed to send his daughter running home to him. When she'd left eighteen months ago she'd said she would never talk to him again as long as she lived.

And he'd believed her.

Emily was a deceptive character, her seemingly calm, compassionate personality hiding a heart that could be as wildly emotional as it could be incredibly stubborn. A typical Scorpio, once wronged, she found it very hard to forgive.

'Why don't you tell me about him?' he asked gently.

Her eyes flashed up to his.

'Come now,' he said. 'This is why you came home, isn't it? To have a loving shoulder to cry on. And I do love you, Emily. I'm your father. I've also been known to give a few words of wisdom in my day. Doctoring isn't always about prescribing pills, you know. The best medicine is often a sympathetic ear and some sensible suggestions.'

'As long as you don't tell me I've been a fool.'

'Why? Have you been?'

She nodded. 'Yes. A big fool.'

'Then I don't need to tell you that, do I? Now, let

me get us both a nice cup of tea, and then you can tell me all about what you've been up to this past eighteen months.'

Emily told him everything.

It wasn't easy, especially when it came to relating what had happened during the last few days. But she didn't leave anything out. What was the point in confiding, if you left things out?

He didn't interrupt. Or ask stupid questions. He just let her talk. And talk. Then talk some more.

Finally, she related the argument she'd had with Sebastian tonight, plus her dramatic exit.

'I should never have agreed to marry him in the first place,' she said wretchedly. 'But I was weak. At first, I just wanted to go to bed with him. And then... then I wanted to stay there.'

Daniel sighed. 'Sexual desire can be a very powerful drive, Emily.'

'That's why I had to get away,' she cried. 'If I'd stayed, he might have tried to get me back into bed. And I probably would have gone. I just can't think straight when I'm around him.'

'You love him.'

'Maybe I don't. Maybe it's just what you felt for Barbra.'

'You don't believe that, Emily. And neither do I. I know you. You love this man. And he loves you, if I'm not badly mistaken.'

Emily stared at her father across the kitchen table. 'How can you say that?'

'Emily, no man proposes marriage to their housekeeper just to stop her from leaving, no matter how good she is at her job.'

Emily shook her head. 'You don't understand. Sebastian does things differently from most men. He doesn't follow conventional standards. Trust me when I say he doesn't love me. What he loves is a peaceful, well run home, with no hassles. I created that for him. That's why he proposed. To keep the status quo. If he got a convenient bed-partner thrown into the bargain, then so much the better.'

'Maybe that was true, to begin with,' her father conceded. 'But something changed along the line, probably down in that hotel in Wollongong. Because that didn't sound like a very peaceful episode you had with him earlier tonight. Hell, girl, you called him a liar, screamed at him and slapped his face. Yet he still wants you. Trust *me*. That's love.'

Emily opened her mouth, then closed it again. 'You really think so?'

'I really think so,' her father replied firmly. 'So yes, Emily, you have been a fool. But not in the way you think. You started being a fool the moment you walked away without doing what your Sebastian asked you to do. Calm down and talk things over.'

'But he…he had sex with that disgusting woman! Less than a week ago!'

'So what.'

'*So what?*'

'Yes, so what. Clearly, he was disgusted with himself afterwards. Tell me, daughter, did he stand by you when that woman showed up?'

'Yes…'

'Did he look at her like he wanted to screw her right then and there?'

'No…'

'Did he show her the door in no uncertain terms?'

'Yes, but…'

'But nothing. The man deserves a medal for exemplary conduct under difficult conditions. And what did you do? You threw his ring into a swimming pool.'

'Well, I…I…'

'Look, do you or do you not love this man?'

'I've just spent the last hour telling you that I do!'

'Good. Now, I have one other thing to clear up in your female mind. You said he made love to you in the garage yesterday, is that right?'

Emily flushed at the memory of their hot encounter against his car. 'Yes. And he made love to *her* in the garage too!'

'No, he didn't. He had sex with her in the garage. You, he made love to. How old did you say Sebastian was?'

'Forty.'

'Forty,' her father repeated drily. 'For heaven's sake, Emily, a man of his age and wealth will have had any number of women. I doubt this Lana is the first female he's had in a garage. Or on a stupid dining table. One of the reasons you fell in love with him in the first place is because he's an experienced man of the world. I know you, Emily. You like successful men. You like it that they know what meal to order and what wine to drink. *And* how to make love properly. Even when you were a teenager your boyfriends were always several years older than you. They all dressed well and drove flashy cars.'

Emily had to agree. 'Yes, they did, didn't they?'

'You will enjoy being the wife of a billionaire. Especially one who loves you.'

'You really think he does?'

'I do. But what I think doesn't matter. What do *you* think?'

'I think I would be very foolish to believe that without further evidence. But I also think I should go back and find out for myself.'

'What a sensible girl.'

'Besides, something else has just occurred to me.'

'What?'

'When we did it in the garage yesterday, we… um…didn't use any protection.'

Her father frowned. 'You mean you might be pregnant?'

'It's possible.'

'Then you very definitely need to go back and talk to him.'

'What time is it?'

'Only just after ten-thirty. Hunter's Hill is no more than a twenty-minute drive at this time of night. Why don't you go back before you can find another reason why you shouldn't?'

Emily grimaced. 'The moment I show up, he's going to think he's won.'

'Somehow I doubt that. You have no idea how formidable you can be, Emily, when you really lose your temper.'

She sighed, then rose to her feet. 'Maybe he won't

want me any more. I did hit him. Once. Then pushed him. And he hates that kind of thing.'

'He'll still want you. I'd put my money on it. Now, off you go.'

She smiled. 'Thank you, Dad. I do love you too, you know. I always have.'

'You've no idea how relieved I am to hear that, Emily,' he said with a catch in his voice. 'I've missed you terribly.'

She drew back and looked deep into his eyes, only then realising how much their estrangement had hurt him. She'd been trying to punish him, of course. But enough was enough.

'It was wrong of me to cut you out of my life like that,' she said with true regret.

'I was the one who was wrong. I can't tell you how glad I am that your mother never knew. She…she didn't, did she?'

'No.'

'Thank God.'

'Now, get along with you. And listen to what the man has to say this time. Really listen and don't judge.'

'I will, Dad. Look, I probably won't be back tonight,' she added quickly. 'But I'll call you tomorrow. I promise.'

CHAPTER SEVENTEEN

'MUSTN'T call her mobile number yet,' Sebastian muttered into his brandy balloon as the grandfather clock in the hallway chimed eleven. 'Must be patient.'

Damn, but that was a noisy clock when there was no one else in the house.

'You know what they say about people who drink alone.'

Sebastian shot to his feet at the sound of Emily's voice, the brandy swirling in the bottom of the glass as he spun round.

She was standing in the double doorway which led out into the hallway, something in her eyes preventing him from hoping this was going to be an instantly happy reunion.

'I didn't hear you drive up,' he said, sitting back down in the armchair again with a sigh.

'The clock was chiming.'

'Aah…'

'I've calmed down.'

She looked *too* calm in his opinion. But very beautiful. He loved her new hair. And that gorgeous blue dress. What he would not give to have taken her to dinner tonight and had a lovely romantic evening. Instead, he'd had to contend with Lana showing up and his life being turned upside down.

'I've come back to talk,' she said. 'Like you suggested.'

All of a sudden, he no longer wanted to talk to her. Which was perverse. Maybe it was all the brandy he'd drunk. Or maybe it was that wariness in her eyes.

Whatever, he just wanted to go back into his cave.

'I think I've said all I have to say, Emily,' he told her in a weary voice, then took another sip of brandy. 'I can't make you believe that I love you.'

'Just tell me when? *When* did you decide you loved me?'

'When?'

'Yes, when?'

Women! Why did they have to scrutinise and analyse everything? Why couldn't she just accept his word for it? It would be so much easier.

'Tonight.'

'When tonight? When you found you needed a reason to stop me from leaving?'

Sebastian shot her a frustrated look. 'You really do have trust issues where men are concerned, don't you? It was when I walked into my bedroom and saw the distress in your eyes. I took one look at that bitch, Lana, and I wanted to kill her with my bare hands. Which is so not me it isn't funny. I despise violence of any kind. But when a man loves a woman, his protective instinct becomes very fierce. Or so I've gathered.'

'What do you mean, so you've gathered?'

Sebastian shrugged. 'I thought falling in love wasn't something I was capable of. I've never fallen in love before.'

'If you didn't love Lana, then why did you run after her and have sex with her?'

'My stupid male ego ran after her. And my stupid male body had sex with her. For a few seconds, Emily. That's all. Once I realised what I was doing, and what kind of creature I was doing it with, I stopped. Afterwards, I couldn't get away from her fast enough, or back to Australia fast enough. That's why I caught an earlier flight. Because all I wanted was to get home to you. When I read your resignation letter, Emily, I felt a million times worse than when Lana left me. Her, I could do without. But not you, Emily. I discovered I could not do without you.'

No one could doubt the bleakness in his eyes or the sincerity of his words. Maybe her father was right. Maybe he did love her after all.

'*Why* did you think you weren't capable of falling in love?' Emily asked.

He looked hard at her, his eyes grim. 'You really want to know?'

'Yes, of course.' Why did he think she'd come back, if not to understand him?

'Your father was unfaithful to your mother,' he said. 'My father *murdered* my mother.'

'*What?*' Emily exclaimed, feeling both shocked and bewildered. 'I thought you said your parents died in a car accident.'

'It was put down as a car accident. But it was murder. I was in the car. I *know* what happened.'

Emily shook her head in absolute horror.

'They were arguing at the time,' Sebastian went on, his voice tight with contained emotion. 'They always argued when they didn't have any money to buy pot. When drug addicts are off the weed, they have an anger management problem. Usually, their anger was directed at me. This time, however, I was out of reach, huddled in the back seat of the car. Anyway, Mum said something to Dad about his being a loser and a dole bludger and he went berserk. Called her every name in the book. Told her she was a useless f— mother who couldn't even look after one miserable kid. Which was true. I used to go to school without any lunch and dressed in dirty clothes.'

Emily grimaced, nausea swirling in her stomach. What kind of mother treated her child like that?

Sebastian's eyes reflected the effort it was taking for him to tell her the truth. 'Finally, Dad said he'd show her who the loser in this family was and he drove the car straight at a telegraph pole. Mum was killed outright. Dad died in hospital a few days later. I got out without a scratch.'

Oh, no, you didn't, Emily thought, her heart contracting as she stared into his suddenly dead eyes. You were left with lots of scratches. Inside.

But it explained so much about this man she loved. His need to succeed. His love of nice things. Even his asking her to marry him—a woman he believed was calm and capable. Nothing like his own neglectful and abusive mother.

'And then you went to live with your grand-mother,' she said gently.

'What? Yes. Yes, that's right.'

'Oh, Sebastian, I'm so sorry.'

'For what?'

'For everything. No child should have to go through something like that.'

'No,' he agreed. 'And no child of mine will. Not that I'll have children now.'

'What do you mean?'

'I have no intention of having children outside of marriage. And the only woman I've ever loved won't marry me. You threw my ring in the pool.'

'What if I'm already pregnant?'

He blinked at her. 'How? Oh, you mean that episode in the garage yesterday. You'd have to be very unlucky to conceive on that one occasion.'

'Or lucky,' she said. 'Depending on how you look at it.'

His eyes narrowed, his fingers tightening around the brandy balloon. 'And how would you look at it, Emily?'

She crossed the room to kneel down on the carpet by his feet, resting her hands and face against his knees. 'I would love to have your child, Sebastian,' she said softly. 'I *do* believe you love me. And I really want to marry you.'

Sebastian's hand shook as he put down his brandy, then tipped her chin up with his fingertips. 'You really mean that? You're not just saying it because you might be pregnant?'

'I would never just say something like that, Sebastian. I love you very much. I've loved you for quite some time.'

His eyes shimmered as they searched hers. 'How long is quite some time?'

'I realised my true feelings after Lana left you. But I didn't think I had a chance with you, so I decided to leave.'

'Why didn't you just say yes straight away when I proposed?'

'Because I wanted you to love me, not just marry me.'

'Then why did you throw my ring in the pool tonight after I *told* you I loved you?'

'Because I'm a fool.'

Sebastian groaned as he reached down and lifted her up into his lap. He didn't kiss her, just held her tight, his lips in her hair.

'You made me almost despair tonight,' he confessed huskily.

Emily was struggling not to weep. 'I'm sorry,' she choked out.

'Don't ever leave me again.'

'I won't.'

'I'll sell this house if it makes you unhappy.'

Emily pulled back and shook her head. 'No. You were right, I love this house. We'll just redo the master bedroom. Oh, and replace the dining table.'

'The dining table! What's wrong with the dining table?'

Emily bit her bottom lip. 'Um...Lana said you had sex with her on it.'

'I what? That's a bald-faced lie!'

'You didn't?'

'Never!' Sebastian denied heatedly.

Emily smiled up at him. 'I'm so glad. I really like that table. Now, there's something I have to go and get,' she said as she scrambled off his lap. 'Something I left behind.'

'What?'

'Stay here,' she commanded. 'Don't move. I won't be more than ten seconds.'

She was gone a full minute. Sebastian was about to get up and follow her when he heard a noise behind him. He turned and she was standing there, naked and dripping wet.

'My God, Emily,' he gasped, lurching to his feet.

'I had to get my ring,' she explained as she came forward. 'I knew you'd have left it in the pool.'

He smiled as he pulled her shivering body into his arms. 'Well, it wasn't much good to me without you.'

His hands moved up and down her back, his lower body hard up against hers, his instant arousal pressing into the soft swell of her stomach.

'I think it's time we continued with our baby-making project,' he said, scooping her up into his arms and carrying her, not towards the stairs but out to the pool. 'How's the water?' he asked as he lowered her to her feet, then began stripping.

'Lovely and warm, once you're in.'

They jumped in together at the deep end, kissing under the water before they surfaced.

'What do you think would have happened if you'd let me join you in here last Friday night?' Sebastian asked as she wound her arms around his neck and her legs around his hips.

'I don't know,' Emily replied. 'What do *you* think would have happened?'

'This,' he growled.

Emily gasped as Sebastian entered her.

'Then this,' he added, cupping her buttocks with his hands and beginning to move her back and forth against him.

Her lips parted on a sigh, her eyes growing heavy with pleasure.

'Tell me you love me,' he commanded.

'I love you,' she said and smiled at him.

He smiled back. 'You were so right, my darling. Sex *with* love is much better than without. We're going to be so happy, you and I. And we're going to be the best parents in the whole wide world.'

They married beside the pool two months later, their first child—a daughter—arriving seven months after the happy event. They called her Amanda, which meant 'worthy to be loved'.

Emily's father never remarried. He became a close friend of Sebastian's, a devoted grandfather and an even better doctor.

* * * * *

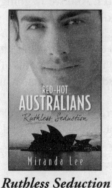 

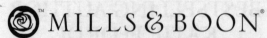